BOOKS BY SUZA KATES

The Savannah Coven Series
Whisper of a Witch
Conviction of a Witch
Binding of a Witch
Haunting of a Witch
Possession of a Witch
Deception of a Witch
Suffering of a Witch
Boys' Night Out (E-novella)
Vengeance of a Witch
Sacrifice of a Witch

The Ssisters' Grimoire Trilogy
The Sisters' Grimoire (Novella)
Winter Fae

The She Series
She Who is Hidden

Single Titles
Hallowed Eve
The Penance Stone

WINTER FAE

THE SISTERS' GRIMOIRE TRILOGY

SUZA KATES

ICASM PRESS
SAVANNAH

Published by Icasm Publishing LLC
5710 Ogeechee Rd. Suite 200 #278, Savannah, GA 31405
www.icasmpress.com

Library of Congress Cataloging-in-Publication Data

Kates, Suza
Winter Fae / Suza Kates
        p. cm.

ISBN-13:978-1-942318-13-2
ISBN-13:978-1-942318-14-9 (ebook)
I. Title

Printed and bound in the United States of America

10 9 8 7 6 5 4 3 2 1

For Pop and Marlee-
Who knew in-laws could be such a blessing?

1

Tate Whiteburn set down her mug and glanced through the coffee-shop window. The skies above Bar Harbor, Maine grew meaner by the minute, with clouds roiling and bubbling like an angry witch's cauldron.

Word was a nor'easter would make landfall by night, adding the harsh sting of rain to the cold bite of December, so she should probably pack up and head home soon.

For three hours she'd been sitting at the high top table, coffee sipping and time slipping, focusing on her laptop.

She was mildly disappointed to be done with this particular project. As a history buff, she'd enjoyed the textbook on societal norms of medieval communities. And as an editor, she appreciated the author's clarity and mastery of grammar.

Words, she thought, even badly arranged words, were something she could relate to. Their flow and usage came easily to her. The rules made sense. The results were controllable.

And she took comfort in the normality of her work, as it was the only thing in her life that remained predictable.

A squeal outside the window drew her attention. People on the streets dashed to the shelter of cars, casting wary eyes up as lightning bolted and thunder drummed through the island town.

Their main concerns likely involved nothing more complicated than staying dry, picking up a child from hockey practice or dance class, deciding what to have for dinner. Just carrying on with their perfectly normal lives. Dealing with perfectly normal worries.

Oh, how she envied them.

Tearing her eyes from the broody sky, she looked back to her laptop and read the last few paragraphs again. Satisfied, she hit save and stretched her arms high.

Now she was ready to get back home. And back to her mother.

Tate was uneasy leaving her for any length of time, even though Sami and Fiona were both there at the house. So she'd texted her sisters every half hour like clockwork.

Until Sami wrote back in all caps, threatening offensive acts involving Tate's cell phone if she didn't give it a rest.

Despite the reassurance that everything was fine, the worry persisted, and even her third steaming cup of hot Italian Roast did little for the cold sensation lodged in her chest. It sat there like a jagged chunk of ice, refusing to melt.

She'd first felt it as soon as she'd left home. An ominous premonition.

A sense that something was going to happen.

When the chill spread, she rubbed the bumps on her arms until her skin heated and turned red. When that didn't warm her, she reached into her purse, seeking comfort in the dagger she carried.

She ran her fingers over the sheath, envisioning the blade it protected, an enchanted mixture of iron and gold. One of three weapons her mother had forged years ago, before her . . . disappearance.

For twenty years, Tate and her family had believed her mother dead. That she'd fallen from a cliff and been carried out to sea.

For twenty years, they'd believed the worst.

Then two weeks ago, everything had changed. Their mother was alive and had been right underneath them the entire time. Literally. A labyrinth of tunnels spread beneath their property, and it was there she'd been held captive, taken by an enemy none of them ever knew existed.

An enemy who'd come to kill three little girls in their beds.

Hellana's plan had been simple. Destroy the children, destroy their magick. All to prevent the husband she hated from making use of their abilities, their unique gifts.

The power of bloodlines.

Tate shook her head to dispel the memory and closed her laptop with a *whump*. Behind her the barista used the milk frother, filling the room with its hiss and gurgle. A trio of girls laughed and chattered nearby.

But nothing blocked the haunting echo of his words. *I will call upon you again.* Hellana had been defeated, but her husband was still out there.

Emuirdane, an Iele Fae prince who wanted—needed—something from the Whiteburn sisters. Something he was willing to kill for.

Lifting her hand, careful to turn away from the other diners, Tate conjured a small white flame and watched it dance in her palm. Power sang through her veins, and the frozen knot in her chest finally relaxed.

She had only two weapons in her arsenal. Her newly-learned witchcraft, and the blade in her bag.

With a sudden, urgent need to beat the storm, she gathered the computer and her pile of notes, pulled on her ivory wool coat, and pushed through the glass door to exit onto Cottage Street.

Outside the air held the scent of ocean and impending rain. She paused to draw one long, calming breath. And as if in answer, large drops pelted the top of her head.

With no umbrella, she had no choice but to dash for her car parked one block over.

But a sudden wind blasted through her, cold and sharp enough to pierce bone. A torrent of rain fell from above, and Tate jolted to a halt. *Something is wrong.*

She cringed when a hot line of electricity arced down in front of her. The jagged line left no mark, but the cement where it struck began to pulse.

Then the movement spread, growing up and into the air until it writhed like a thousand invisible worms. Behind it, a woman pushing a bright red baby stroller crossed the sidewalk, her face visible, yet strangely distorted.

Tate had seen this happen before, a distortion of the atmosphere, a blending of realities. So she knew what was coming. She knew *who* was coming.

Dread rolled down her back like ripples over a winter pond.

For one fleeting and foolish moment, she wanted to run. But logic kicked in and held her in place, because there was no running, no hiding. Not from his kind.

Emuirdane was of the Farworlds. He was magickal, powerful, narcissistic, sadistic.

And he was coming for her.

The spatter of raindrops quickened, as if in warning, but with no other option she stood her ground, air rattling in and out of her tightening lungs. He emerged from the invisible doorway and pierced her with obsidian eyes.

Tate's breath stuck like a barb in her throat.

"Hello, Tate. We meet again." Emuirdane nodded in his regal way and gave a slight bow, a gesture due more to formality than respect. But his slick veneer would never fool her again.

Panic fisted inside her chest, squeezing and grinding until her vision burst with dark blotches like a Rorschach test. Her mind swirled with denials.

This was happening too fast. He'd come back too soon.

Raven-black hair fell to his shoulders, framing features that could have been carved from moonstone, the skin so pale, almost luminescent. Tate was startled all over again by his unnatural perfection. His beauty was compelling. Alluring.

Deceptive.

As he edged closer, Tate caught a whiff of ozone, as if he'd ridden here on that streak of lightning. The magic inside her sparked and hissed, sensing a threat.

She took an instinctive step back and cleared her throat, pushing back against the suffocating anxiety. "Emuirdane," she said, her greeting as stiff and frigid as the pavement beneath her feet. "Why are you here?"

Laughter, brief and deep, rolled from his throat, the sound more menacing than thunder. "Ah, Tate." He smacked his mouth as if savoring the aftertaste of her name. "Straight to business with no time wasted on pretty or polite words. Exactly as I expected."

He circled her, forcing her to turn to keep him in sight. "And precisely why I sought you out instead of your sisters. You, the eldest. The pragmatist."

Delight danced in his black eyes, and his lips—far too red against his pale skin—curved with pleasure, with approval. Endorsement from a snake.

He stepped closer and stroked a finger along her jaw. "It is time to begin, and I have chosen you to perform the first task."

Tate closed her coat tighter, as if she could keep both rain and his intentions at bay. "What sort of task? You know we aren't ready, not after only two weeks of training."

"Oh, two weeks is a very long time, a very long wait . . . for some." His eyes flashed with unease and grew distant. Then they snapped back to her face. "And you have been given this grace period as a time of peace to enjoy your reunion with your mother. Time," he added, tilting his head, "that *I* have allowed you."

He smoothed his hands down his charcoal-gray overcoat. Paired with dark pants, the modern outfit was a change from the doublet he'd worn the last time Tate had seen him. The snug jacket with pointed shoulders had shown just how out of place he was here.

Not here in Maine. But *here*. In the mortal realm.

His clothes may have changed, but he still wore the elaborate silver pin on his left lapel, and a matching ring on his right hand. Brilliant green stones glinted in both, and in their depths, the oily swirl of Emuirdane's magick churned.

Tamping down on her own rising power, Tate maintained an impassive tone. She needed to appear in control, collected, and unafraid. "You said you wanted us to master our powers, but we just discovered them. I don't know what you want from us, but if we aren't strong enough, we won't be any good to you."

"Now, now." He waggled a finger at her. "You are too wise to bargain and too cautious to lie. *Especially* to me." His eyes tightened at the corners. "I know how swiftly and surely you've come into your magick. With your mother's guidance, your knowledge and confidence have grown, as well as your strengths."

Tate brushed at the rain running down her face and into her eyes, blinding her while panic returned like a vise around her ribs. "Just give us another week."

Emuirdane whipped his hand out to grip her chin. "I can wait no longer. Time grows ever more precious, and I must demand my due."

A man hurried past them but paid them no mind. It was as if he didn't see them, as if they weren't even there. A glamour, Tate realized. A favored trick of the Fae.

Unseen by others, Emuirdane closed in, crowding her, looming over her. He bared his teeth, revealing long, sharp incisors. "Do you refuse me, Tate Whiteburn? Do you renege on the deal?"

"How can I renege on a deal I never made?" She twisted to wrench free, but he held tight, the cold, bony tips of his fingers digging into her jawbone.

He leaned in, his face darkening. "I saved your mother's life when she was but an infant. If I had not intervened, you and your sisters wouldn't be here at all. You. Would. Not. Exist." The shadows beneath his eyes spread while the hollows of his cheeks lengthened, literally deepening as his fury emerged. "So whether you agreed or not, you are indebted. *To me.*"

Tate's heart was in her throat, but she was the only person standing between him and her family. "You're twisting things. There are rules—"

Thunder clapped like a gunshot, as if summoned by his rage.

And that block of ice was back in her chest.

"But I am Iele," he said. "The rules in my land are slightly more . . . flexible. If you deny me now, I will be within my rights to take payment of another form. But be warned, I expect nothing less than a life exchanged for the life I saved."

"A life ex—"

He slashed his hand through the air, silencing her. "Sweet Fiona will do nicely, I think." He growled low, his hulking frame blocking out the angry skies. "In fact, I could leave you now and go to her. I could spirit her away to my world before you could take three steps."

His dark eyes closed like a man on the verge of ecstasy. "Mmm. I wonder. Will she taste as sweet as she looks?"

"No." Tate gripped his wrist to loosen his hold. But like his power, his strength was unearthly.

He ran his tongue around his lips, the red tip flickering obscenely. "First I'll have her in my bed chamber." With his other hand, he grabbed Tate's hair at the base of her skull and ripped her head back. "Then again, in my dungeons."

Lines of pain streaked through her scalp, but Tate pulled against his grip to meet his night-black eyes. She bared her teeth. "You won't touch my sister."

Emuirdane forced her face to the side and lowered to the exposed skin of her neck. Tate tensed, afraid he would sink his fangs in and drink. But he only pressed his lips to her fluttering pulse.

"Oh, I will touch her in ways your human mind can't conceive. And once I'm finished, I'll give what's left of her to my soldiers. She is small—and mortal—but she'll provide hours of entertainment. Perhaps even days."

His tongue flicked against her skin. "If she is strong enough."

"Stop this!" Still clutching his wrist, Tate released her magick and shot a stream of white fire into his arm.

His clothes burned for a moment before he puckered his crimson lips and blew, dousing her flames with ease. "Oh, yes," he murmured, the lusty croon in his voice making her gorge rise. "I love it when they try to fight back."

He gently kissed her lips and released her. Then he patted her cheek, and grinned.

As if he hadn't just threatened to have her sister gang-raped to death.

She slammed both hands into his chest but he barely moved. "Just tell me what you want!"

"Long ago, your grandfather's fate was foretold, his life linked with mine. Prophecy predicted a union, you see. A human marriage, a blending of two bloodlines."

"I've heard all of this before." Still quaking with rage and fear, Tate glared.

But Emuirdane was unfazed, using a finger to caress the silver brooch at his breast. "Once, I believed your mother was the one I needed, a child born of this union. But I was wrong. She was only the vessel, meant to pass on the strength of Romani and Welsh power."

He dropped to a harsh whisper. "These powers are magnified in you and yours, the sisters three. It is the Daughters of Nadia who were always meant to serve me."

He lowered his head to glower at her from beneath his brows. "Bring me what I desire, and you need never concern yourself with me again."

That was all Tate wanted. "Fine." She brushed her hair from her face, the black strands now fully drenched. "Tell me what to do, so

I can get started. So I can end this."

"I cannot tell, for only you can see." With a smile that made her nape prickle, Emuirdane reached inside his dark coat. "You and your sisters must find the questions. As well as the answers."

This time when he took hold of her, his hand on hers was firm but painless. "Are you ready to begin your quest, Tate? Do you have the strength? The cunning?"

Winds whipped and howled around them, but she narrowed her eyes against the sting. "I'll be whatever I have to be. To save my family."

Emuirdane pulled his hand from his pocket and closed his eyes. "So be it." On a low moan, he pressed an object into her palm— flat, round, heavy. "Take this. It is your *heolig*."

"My what?" She looked down to see what he'd given her, but everything started to spin and blur. The bricks of the buildings, Emuirdane's sickening smile, and the sullen gray sky all grew fuzzy and indistinct.

Colors bled into one another and dizziness swamped Tate. A slow, hard pull began in her gut, as the earth spun like a centrifuge, with her at its center. Her equilibrium tilted, the pull in her stomach growing longer, tighter, until she feared she'd be sick.

She pressed a hand to her belly and gave a brief cry when the earth disappeared from beneath her. She dropped suddenly, but just as quickly was caught inside a void, a bubble of calm absent all sound or light. She floated in the warm, silent vacuum as seconds stretched.

Then she fell like a stone until the ground rushed up to her again. She impacted hard and crumpled to her knees.

When she looked around, Cottage Street was gone. She was no longer standing on the sidewalk in the pouring rain. No longer with Emuirdane.

She was all alone and kneeling in the snow, lost in a world of shadow.

2

Tate blinked several times, and the shadows became shapes. Tall and menacing, they crowded around her. Cringing into herself—from both fear and cold—she sucked in breaths of the freezing air, gulping them in until her vision cleared, and her mind accepted.

For a moment, she'd sworn an army surrounded her, but the soldiers were only forest evergreens, standing proudly, trimmed in white powder. Snow was falling here instead of rain, and the dreary afternoon had been replaced with crisp, cold night.

With her eyes focused, she studied the landscape. The green-needled trees covered gently rising hills, all blanketed in the pristine snow. Moonlight lay like a gentle lover, casting everything in a pale and exotic blue.

Wherever she was, all was silent. No wind blew, no animal stirred. The only movement came from overhead as stars glittered in a ceiling of midnight.

Where was this place? How did she get here? She might have convinced herself that none of this was real, that it was all a dream. Or even a Fae glamour, a spell so strong it turned suggestion into reality. At least for mere mortals like her.

The last was plausible, because Emuirdane had done this. He'd sent her here.

But her clothes were still soaked from the previous rain, and the frigid weather felt real enough. Her toes were numb, her face and fingers raw, and cold crept past the wet fabric to prick her flesh with thin, sharp fingers.

The object Emuirdane had given her was heavy in her hand, so she uncurled her fingers and studied the strange disc. Ivory in color, smooth like polished granite. She rubbed her thumb over its surface, and gasped when particles glittered in the wake of her touch.

He had called the disc a heolig before pressing it into her palm. And not only did it sparkle with power, the stone radiated warmth.

But what was she supposed to do with it?

Clutching the disc to her chest, she scanned the area again, hoping for a clue. Or a beacon of fire, she thought with a grimace, while uncontrollable shivers racked her body. Every direction she looked held the same trees, the same unspoiled snowy rises.

One touch, and the heolig had brought her here. She could feel its power flowing, pressing for release. The relic in her hands pulsed with magick . . .

So magick had to be the only way out. The way back home.

With shaking hands, she inspected the disc. She skimmed a finger across one side, but the surface was flat and smooth, no bumps or ridges, no marks of any kind.

After another pass to be sure, she flipped the disc over. The sensitive pads of her fingers immediately bumped across grooves. Holding the stone piece up, she angled it under the moonlight for a better look.

There were several indentations—long, thin, and winding. They intersected in the center where they connected to a small depression.

Tate brushed her thumb over the slight divot. She pressed down.

A deep chime echoed from within the forest, a hollow ring, like the strike of a large brass gong. Sound waves shook the trees, shuddering streams of white frosting from their limbs.

Then the percussion rolled into Tate, thrumming through her body, all the way down to her marrow. But even as she quaked, intuition responded.

She'd touched the heolig. She'd triggered the call. The summoning.

Her magick rose and hummed beneath her skin. A chill raced over the nape of her neck, raising tiny hairs along its path.

She didn't understand the disc's purpose, or the meaning behind the chime. All she knew is that she had to follow the sound and locate the source.

But what would she find? The mysterious item Emuirdane wanted? Could she finish this now, all by herself? Fulfill the contract and be done with him forever?

Surely, it wouldn't be that easy. But he had spoken of a quest only seconds before Tate had been propelled to the strange land. To a forest worthy of any winter faerie tale.

But her family had starred in this particular story for far too long.

She could at least be thankful they were safe at home, because she worked better alone, without the distraction of others and how they might be affected by whatever problem she faced. When she was the only one at risk, it was easier to focus, to muscle through and get the task done.

She'd learned early in life that love was a vulnerability, and that seclusion could serve as a type of armor. Though she'd missed her family—and others—in the years she'd been gone, her separation had dulled the constant fear of loss. Over time, she'd gotten used to the loneliness, and somewhere along the way estrangement became her norm.

Solitude became self-preservation.

Until her mother's return. And that particular love was something she'd needed for so long, she simply couldn't run away from it. She couldn't suffer that loss a second time.

But now, just as her mother had returned, she was at risk again.

Her mother, her sisters, her entire family were in danger, because of Emuirdane's selfishness and greed. His desire for whatever mysterious object waited at the end of Tate's unwanted *quest.*

Which meant completing this search was the only way to save them all.

I can do this. She clamped her aching fingers around the disc, felt its enchantment throb against her palm. *I will do this.*

Ignoring the frozen sensation climbing to her ankles, she dragged her feet through the deep drifts, disturbing the once-perfect scene. She headed deeper into the trees, where their boughs grew thick and blocked out the moon.

Soon darkness encroached from all sides, with nothing but forest in every direction. She slowed her steps and spun in a circle, suddenly disoriented and unsure where to go.

As if to guide her, the chime sounded again, its knell stronger, the bell-like peal louder than before.

She angled toward the vibration, rushing headlong toward it before she lost her way again. But as she ran, the white pines and majestic wintergreens became fewer and fewer, their imposing trunks intermingling with others.

The trees taking over now were still tall, still reaching to the sky. But where the evergreens had been robust, covered with healthy green needles, these new trees were lanky and thin, their slick, shiny bark the color of soot.

After she'd run another few minutes, the woods had changed entirely. Gone were the scrubby green needles topped with snow, replaced by what seemed like acres of the pitch-black trees. Their spindly branches made Tate think of spiders' legs, clicking and rubbing against each other.

There was a breeze blowing here, but the air it carried smelled wrong, heavy and thick, scented with ash. She was still trapped in an enchanted forest, but one ruled by a dark and menacing force.

She continued to make her way forward, but when she spied an open path and made a move toward it, the bizarre trees gave a collective groan and began to move. They bent over the path, as if assaulted by a strong wind, and laced their thin limbs together to form a barrier.

With the path blocked, Tate came to a halt. She glanced both ways, searching for another entry. But the blockade stretched endlessly in both directions.

She had to get through this section of the woods. The source of the chime was on the other side.

A cry from above shattered the stillness, and she jerked her head. A raven stared down at her, its feet locked around a bare black branch. The bird cawed at her, fluttering its wings and thrusting its head forward.

The creature's meaning was clear. *Stay away.*

Tilting its head and fixing her with one beady eye, the raven screeched at her, beak open wide, then gave another fierce flap to punctuate its message. *Turn back.*

Anxiety fisted in Tate's gut. Why had the world around her changed? Had she done something wrong? Furrowing her brows, she looked down at the disc.

Snowflakes stuck to her cheeks, her eyelids, and frost had surely bitten the tips of her toes. But nothing would stop her. She refused to give up.

She stomped her frozen feet to circulate some blood and called up to the bird, "I'm supposed to be here." She tried again. "I have this!" She held up the heolig, hoping it would buy her safe passage.

Instead the raven lifted its face to the sky and screamed more shrilly. Three more ebony birds darted to the tree, landing on the branches to join the defense. The four of them shrieked at her and stabbed their pointed beaks again and again.

Tate covered her ears to block out the piercing cries. This didn't make any sense. Why send her here only to block her? Was this a test?

Or were opposing forces operating in this strange world? And if so, Tate looked at the disc, whose side was she on? The righteous or the wicked?

Considering she was here on Emuirdane's order, she decided not to think too hard about that last part. The gong resonated again, this time the sound a demanding punch, angry and insistent. No single chime, either. It rang out three in quick succession.

Was she running out of time? What would happen if she failed? Would she be trapped here forever?

She shoved the heolig in pocket and lifted both palms to the birds and trees. She called her fire.

"I don't want to hurt you." She let white flames rise and dance, both beautiful and menacing. "But I must pass!"

The trees blocking her way emitted a loud groan, the eerie sound sad, scared, and resentful all at once.

She held her ground and arced her power higher, closer, not to burn the limbs, but to ensure they felt her heat.

Another moan of outrage and fear, then the branches began to tremble, scratching and creaking as they disengaged from each other. The ravens erupted from the quaking trees, their incensed cries echoing behind them as they escaped.

One by one, limbs unlocked, and the trunks separated to reveal the pathway.

Tate stared down the narrow, shadowy trail, wondering—and half afraid of—what she'd find at the other end. The crooked line of the trail was dark and imposing, so she tossed a ball of fire up into the air, creating a witchlight to drive back shadows and show her the way.

The gong struck again, urging her on. The peal had softened, to an encouraging yet insistent tone. Tate's knuckles ached from clutching the disc, but she held tight and entered the corridor of trees.

The passage ahead was long, and she couldn't help glancing back and forth. Spider leg trees enshrouded her, and if they closed in again, she'd be crushed by their spindly embrace.

The farther she walked, the lower the temperature dropped, until each breath she took scraped at her lungs. She reached again for the heolig, more for its warmth now than anything else.

At last, a small point of light flickered up ahead. An exit. With the end in sight, she picked up her pace and sprinted the final stretch. The witchlight held its position and flew along with her.

She burst from the menacing tunnel of darkness and ran an extra few yards before she stopped to catch her breath. Once again, the surroundings had changed, back to a land of white.

Snowflakes were falling, thick and constant. She stretched out her arm and couldn't see her hand, having made it through the tunnel only to end up snowblind.

Her lips were like ice, her body a never-ending shiver. Frustration was the only warmth inside of her, and it whipped now like an angry fire. She threw out her arms and yelled, "What now?"

But, of course, no one answered.

Her witchlight was still active, so she raised one hand to guide the flames back and forth, side to side, and front to back. Each attempt was met with more tumbling flakes.

The ball of fire danced near an area that appeared to be denser, reflecting more light. Tate moved closer to the veil of falling snow. She reached out, tentatively. Her hand went through, and was immersed in warmth.

Holding the heolig out before her like a tiny shield, she stepped through the white curtain as one would step through a waterfall. She entered a large ring of evergreens, their clean, pine scent filling the air. Air that seemed humid and balmy compared to where she'd been.

Tate almost sobbed with relief, though it was still cold enough for snow to accumulate on the trees that encircled the clearing like guardians. Despite the light dusting, green, glistening grass covered the ground, and across the bright swatch of color loomed a huge stone mound.

The monolith was at least twelve feet tall and half as wide. Granite, like the disc, but deep gray instead of ivory. The profiles of a man and a woman were carved into the stone, staring inward at each other. Their heads appeared to be human but were attached to the curving bodies of two giant serpents, their long tails joining to form the shape of a heart.

Inside that heart was a Celtic cross.

Soothed by the calmer atmosphere, she stepped closer for a better look. Here was her goal, what she'd been meant to find. The relief had been chiseled by hand, of that she was sure. And old wasn't quite the right word to describe the work of art. This, she thought with a shaky, reverent sigh, was *ancient.*

As she trailed her hand over the sculpture, small brown birds started flittering to the ground. Dozens of the small creatures alighted on the pure green grass, settling near the base of the monument, near her feet.

Sparrows. Twittering and chirping and hopping. They seemed to be excited by her presence, and she could only hope they'd be more welcoming than the last birds she'd encountered.

Turning her attention to the stone again, she caressed the cross in the center of the heart. The sparrows grew agitated, converging into a dense mass around her.

Tate halted and gave a weary sigh. Surely these sweet, tiny birds wouldn't stand against her.

Then she noticed a round shape in its center, slightly indented. Without question, without a single doubt, she knew the relic Emuirdane had given her would be a perfect fit.

So she touched it.

And discovered the sparrows weren't so sweet after all.

Several sprung up and arrowed straight at her face. One swooped close enough to graze her cheek with its wing. She ducked a second time, nerves jangling with fear, when a booming gong rolled through the clearing. The loud noise startled her, nearly making her drop the disc.

She was right on top of the source. The chime had sounded from deep within the gray stone.

But instead of obeying like the trees and ravens, the sparrows grew bolder, one flapping near her ear while another landed on her wrist and pecked at her hand. She shook away the bird, but not before crimson blood pooled on her chilled flesh.

The small birds dive-bombed and swarmed at her, while still more gathered in the trees, trilling mindlessly with their high-pitched cries. She would swear they shrieked *Don't! Don't! Don't!*

Birds, trees—they were of nature. Her magick was of nature.

As a tiny seed of doubt sprouted, she paused.

But then she recalled the terrible power Emuirdane wielded. She pictured her uncle and grandfather trapped in an endless sleep, her mother imprisoned in glass.

The need to protect those she loved rose up like a black wave to drown the nagging uncertainty. *I have to do this. I'm the only one who can.*

She raised the heolig, and slammed the disc into the hole.

Light streamed from the point of contact, and the sting of magick coursed up her arm. Even as her fear renewed, Tate pressed harder, holding stone against stone.

The luminance took on a pale purple hue, spreading out over the wall and blushing the snow in lavender. She blinked against the brightness as the birds went crazy, diving and screeching.

Intense power flooded her system, so sizzling and severe it drove her to the brink of pain. A scream began to build in her throat, but she clamped her jaws together and forced herself to stare into the light.

Writing appeared all around the cross, strange signs and characters she didn't recognize. But as she stared, mesmerized, they burned into her memory.

The monument abruptly went dark and dizziness overtook her, the same disoriented sensation from before on the sidewalk. Gray granite, white snow, and evergreen trees whirred past her, blending into streaming ribbons of color.

Tate didn't fight, but let herself go, welcoming the change she knew was coming. She floated for several seconds, waiting to settle down and feel her feet beneath her again.

But instead of snow or asphalt, a solid warmth enfolded her, followed by a touch on her cheek and a gentle shake of her shoulders. "Tate," someone said. "Tate, wake up." The voice above her was male, his tone persistent, and . . . familiar.

Her head was still woozy as if trying to catch up with her constantly-relocating body, but she fluttered her eyes open and stared up into her rescuer's face.

Her body clutched, her heart stumbled.

Because the eyes she met weren't simply blue. They were the-sea-in-summer blue.

They were Tate's-first-love blue.

She might have escaped the enchanted forest, but she definitely wasn't out of the woods.

Yes, she knew those eyes. Just as she knew the arms that held her.

All she could think was, *Oh, no* as she clung to him like a frightened child and whispered, "Jack?"

3

The man Tate had done her best to avoid for the last seven years was staring straight at her.

Shock was a drug in her veins. Her ears filled with the rush of her blood, and her head seemed to be floating above her body.

Worse, he wasn't just looking at her but had her tucked in his lap, one arm cradling her and the other cupping her cheek. Against her chilled flesh, the heat of his skin seemed unreasonably hot, almost searing.

She didn't jump up and run, but she did edge her face away until he dropped his hand, unable to do much more than gape up at him. "What are you doing here?"

Brow wrinkled in concern, blonde hair dripping with rain, he shook his head. "I think the better question is, what are *you* doing here?"

Her stomach rolled and her mind searched for a way out, a way to prevent this conversation. The one she'd evaded for so long, by evading Jack. Her voice shook when she said, "I guess you're wondering why I'm back in Bar Harbor."

"Actually," he lifted one tawny brow, "I'm wondering why you're passed out on the sidewalk."

"What?" That wasn't the response she'd anticipated, but she latched on to the escape route he'd provided and glanced around. Sure enough, the cheery coffee-shop logo was on the window behind Jack. And once again, she was stuck in the falling rain.

This must be her day for inclement weather. "So." She blinked water from her eyes. "I'm back."

"Back from where?" His expression of concern shifted subtly to confusion.

"Back . . . back," she stuttered, searching for a way to recover from the slip-up. "I'm back awake?"

She let a limp smile slide over her lips. "I'm a little fuzzy on what happened." Boy, was that an understatement. And after everything she'd just experienced, was it any wonder her head reeled and her thoughts scattered?

The time-shift had muddled her senses. And being so close to Jack was only making things worse. She needed distance to clear the fog from her mind, the roar from her ears.

She tried to sit up, and Jack tried to help her. But his hand slid down and grabbed her hip, his fingers branding her backside.

Tate went utterly still.

Physical awareness snapped into her system. Locked in place by the sudden intimacy, she allowed herself a slow perusal of the man he had become, cradled against him, firmly yet gently, the hard length of his thighs pressed against the back of hers.

A navy thermal shirt molded to his chest beneath the jacket, and the first hint of golden stubble shaded his jawline. She could see that time—in its completely sexist way—had only enhanced his features, giving testament of a life well worn to the planes and angles of his face.

Her fingers itched to trace the sculpted mouth, just as she used to, as well as the shallow line that she knew would dimple when he smiled.

Jack had always had a beautiful smile.

Her skin tingled but not from the cold. Her lips parted slightly all on their own. And as the heat of his body flowed into hers, the shock of seeing him began to curl and tighten, pooling in her belly to become an altogether different sensation.

She couldn't look away from those deep blue eyes, and with gazes locked they stared at each other, breathing in sync through several pounding heartbeats. Jack simply continued to hold her.

And she continued to let him.

She gripped his brown jacket with both hands, fingers curling reflexively as she sucked in a breath, licked her lips, and—

Wait a minute.

She jerked upright. *Where is the disc?*

The bag with her laptop was still strapped on her shoulder but her hands were empty. Flustered, she patted at her coat and smacked her palms all over her torso.

"What is it? What's the matter?" Jack's arms tightened around her as if she was fracturing and he could hold her together.

With the discovery of the round, hard lump in her pocket, she exhaled slowly. "I just . . ." She couldn't look at him again. "I thought I'd dropped something."

There was no time to elaborate and, thankfully, Jack didn't have time to ask, because the door of the coffee shop swung open to release the trio of chattering girls Tate had seen earlier. They barreled out with a surge of noise and a flurry of legs.

One of them almost tripped over Tate and Jack before she stuttered to a stop. The girls' stares made Tate acutely aware of the picture she and Jack made, and heat flooded her cheeks.

She took the opportunity to tap his elbow in a signal for release. "I can get up now. I feel fine." She leaned to one side, trying to ease from his lap.

Jack tightened his grip. "I'll take you home."

"There's no need," she said. "It's not that far and—"

"Forget it, Tate." His voice held a don't-bother-to-argue edge that she remembered well. "I'm not letting you drive right now." He lifted a hand to shield her face when the rain's tempo increased. "If something happened to you . . ."

An emotion she couldn't name shadowed his face, and he

clenched his jaw. "Your grandfather and Uncle Brit would never forgive me if you passed out again while behind the wheel. If you were near the cliffs and . . ."

"No. You're right." She spoke quickly before he added anything more. She could tell he was trying not to mention her mother, a woman he still believed to be dead after she'd fallen from those very cliffs.

Her instinct was to blurt out the truth, to break the good news. After everything she'd shared with Jack, after all the times he'd been there for her . . . he was the one person she wanted to tell.

But even though her mother wouldn't stay cloistered in the house forever, and the fact that she was alive would come out eventually, the decision to herald that announcement was hers. Not Tate's.

"Do you think you can stand?" Jack asked, pulling her from her thoughts.

"Oh. Sure." Tate nodded, but before she understood what was about to happen, he picked her up and set her on her feet in one smooth move. Her head went woozy from the sudden change, so she stumbled right back into his arms.

Her face landed in the crook of his neck, against his bare skin, and . . . *Oh.* Tate went limp. Because now she could smell him, the barely-there scent of clean, crisp soap mixed with the lingering smell of . . . sawdust.

Hmmm. Jack. He smelled like Jack.

Nostalgia stirred, latching onto sweet but distant memories, before pulling them up to the surface. Along with Tate's sigh of pleasure.

A knuckle eased under her chin to lift her face. "Are you going to pass out again?" The brusque tone made her eyes pop wide, and she realized she'd let them drift to a dreamy, half-closed state.

"No," she bit out, stepping an arm's length away. "No. I'm not." She struggled to regain some control, not to mention her pride.

Jack was still the only man who'd overloaded and overwhelmed her senses.

Apparently, he still did.

Then she took a better look at his face, noticed the glower, and wished she could slip away one more time. But this was a reality she couldn't run away from, an atonement that was long overdue.

Apprehension clutched in her gut, and she eased back another step. She'd made a quick recovery and was standing on her own feet.

And that seemed to be all that was needed for Jack to let his true feelings show.

Anger was in the set of his jaw, muscles clenching beneath the stubble. Accusation narrowed his eyes and burned within the blue.

Here was the man Tate had been afraid to come home to. The one she'd loved. And then left behind.

Based on his clenched fists, he still despised her for it.

Unable to face him, Tate whirled away, intending to put some space between them, but her legs felt like frozen lumps. She managed only a few hobbled steps before Jack took her shoulders to turn her around. "My truck's this way."

He pulled his head in the opposite direction, keeping his grip on her as they trudged through the downpour to a red Jeep Wrangler parked just across the street. Tate could tell by the scrapes and dents this was his work truck, used to harvest and haul blocks of wood he used for his art.

Jack jerked open the passenger door and went around. He slipped off his wet jacket and tossed it in the back before getting behind the wheel.

Still self-conscious, Tate climbed silently inside. But as soon as he cranked the engine to blast heat from the vents, she released a soft moan and leaned in, giving thanks to the gods of automotive ingenuity.

Ignoring her now, Jack pulled from the curb with a jerk, but soon he slowed and drove with caution. In weather like this, the island's slick roads could easily turn to ice.

Despite the soothing warmth, Tate's pulse tapped steadily. She lowered her lashes to covertly study him again, cataloguing how he'd changed, or how he hadn't.

He was still rangy, but had fleshed out nicely, more proof of his muscular build revealed by the pushed-up sleeves of his shirt. His hair remained the tawny color of wheat, his skin slightly tan, but that could be credited to days in the sun, as he'd always been one for the outdoors.

She frowned at how wet his faded jeans were from where he'd stopped in the rain to check on her. And had then stayed with her.

Helping an unconscious person on the ground was a basic consideration, and one most people wouldn't think twice about. But Tate's deep-seated shame flared to life anyway because, however basic, it was a kindness she didn't deserve. At least, not from Jack.

She turned her attention back to her window, listening to the static hush inside the car and the constant patter of rain. They followed the roads away from town and started along the winding route into the woods, toward her home.

They wove through the woods, along the cliffs, and back into the shelter of trees again. Clouds the color of iron churned over the Atlantic, ominous and surly. Like the man beside her.

The closer they drew to her home, the more anxious she became. She felt a desperate need to break the heavy silence, to broach the subject floating between them. Like a naval mine, their past drifted precariously, waiting for one wrong touch, one wrong word, to set it off.

They turned onto the road to her house, and she sensed him sending her sidelong glances. Watching, analyzing, but never saying a word.

When at last the truck turned into the drive, lightning

pitchforked across the blackening sky and Tate jumped in her seat.

The last time lightning had struck near her house, it had unearthed an old chest. And a horde of family secrets.

Secrets, she now understood, that had been in play for years, affecting her and her sisters—their lives and emotions—in ways she'd never suspected. But she couldn't tell Jack about any of that, and she wouldn't use it to excuse how she'd treated him.

Whether planned or not, this was a chance to reach out and tell him how sorry she was.

Though she owed him so much more than a simple apology, and words could never undo the damage she'd done. They couldn't repair the young and fragile trust Jack had once given her, the promise she'd abandoned, or the friendship she'd destroyed.

With this in mind, it took every bit of her fortitude to face Jack directly, to look him in the eyes. Her mouth went dry. She pressed a hand to her rolling stomach.

One of them had to make a move. One of them had to say *something*.

Jack had no idea what to say.

After all the times he'd pictured this moment, the many ways he'd imagined what he'd do, what he'd tell her—here, finally, was his opportunity. And all the questions he'd planned to ask—the answers he would *demand*—just flew from his head as if snatched up by the howling winds.

His heart blocked his throat, it seemed, leaving him no choice but to sit there, simmering, waiting for her to take the lead.

There was no way she could justify what she'd done, but he still wanted a reason. He needed one. Because if it was even halfway reasonable, moderately forgivable, then the ugly scar she'd left him with might finally start to fade.

On the drive here, he'd recovered some of the insult, some of the scorn he knew he should show her. But before that . . . God help him.

When he'd seen Tate lying on the ground, unconscious and so eerily pale, he'd forgotten to be furious with her. He'd forgotten she was a traitor.

Instead, he'd been jolted by a rush of old feelings—concern, tenderness. And that old bastard heartache, springing out like a sly predator, as strong and vicious as the day she'd gone. The day she'd deserted him.

The animosity he'd nursed for so long fled. Without a second thought he'd dropped to his knees and scooped her into his arms. Her lips blue, her skin so cold and wet. The sheer terror had staggered him.

Then she'd looked up, the brown eyes he knew so well brimming with fear and confusion.

And his heart had woken from a seven-year sleep.

She still enthralled him, the effect instant, potent, and undeniable. The revelation left him rough around the edges, and more than a little resentful.

How could he still feel that way? How could he care so much for a woman who had shown him such disregard?

Even now, he couldn't believe they were sitting side by side in his truck, windows misted from damp clothes and the heat of mingling breaths.

Just like that time after the homecoming game, when they'd taken shelter in another vehicle, parked in another section of the forest—and had steamed the windows in an entirely different way.

He shook his head to dispel the memory, just as Tate finally spoke.

"Thank you for helping me today. And for the ride."

Jack hiked his shoulder, an unconcerned gesture, as though he could brush her off like a bothersome fly. "I wouldn't leave anyone lying in the streets that way."

He didn't say "Even you," but he could hear the implication hanging in the air.

The hitch in Tate's breathing told him she'd heard it too, and a strange expression flashed across her face. Guilt? Rejection? It was there and gone so quickly he couldn't say, and she immediately sat up straight, her features glossing over with a protective shield. "Still," she said, "I'm grateful."

She paused a moment, but he could see she wanted to add something more. He watched her, noting every wring of her hands and fidget of her legs. She was jumpy, edgy and anxious.

The knowledge didn't give Jack near the pleasure he'd once thought it would. He waited quietly, and slipped on his own of mask of indifference.

She tucked her hair behind her ears, a nervous gesture she apparently hadn't outgrown. The glossy black was cut shorter these days, to just above her shoulders.

But her eyes, well, they were exactly the same. Deep, dark, and haunted, with a touch of the fragility she'd always done her best to disguise. She still tried to conceal it, as she'd done back then, by holding her chin at a defiant angle.

As if she were always guarding the gate.

"I know this isn't the ideal time or place." She spoke so quickly, she caught him off guard. "But I think there are things that need to be said."

He studied the dashboard, asking himself what good this would do him. He had no business sitting here with her, holding out for some long-overdue explanation. Besides, he thought, listening to the vents blow heat, he couldn't trust a single word that fell from her lips.

Jack worked with blades every day of his life, and despite the pretty picture she made he knew Tate Whiteburn held a keen, sharp edge. She was the one, after all, to teach him his greatest lesson.

That the deepest, the most painful cuts, were the ones you never saw coming.

She sighed and said, "I'm not sure where to start—"

"You're not?" The question lashed out of him, packed with sudden rage. He could feel the leading edge of his fury pushing and shoving for further release. The sarcasm came naturally to his tongue. "You've only had seven years to think about it, Tate."

First she flinched. But then her mouth pressed into a firm line, and she notched up her chin.

In exactly the way he loved.

"Yes, I have. Seven years, and all that time without a word from me. Not a single message or phone call. Not a gesture of apology." The breath she drew was ragged. "You have every right to be upset. But hear me out, Jack. I really feel that—"

"No. Oh, no. It's too late for that." He held a hand up. "I don't want to hear about your feelings. How *you feel*," he emphasized, "holds no interest for me."

He angled toward her, pinned her in place with his heated glare. "At this point, I only care about one thing. I only want to know. One. Thing."

He let the anticipation, the ripe brutal tension, fill the air, and then he lowered his voice to a growl. "*Why?*"

She rubbed her palms, glancing down at them as if seeking guidance. But they must not have answered, because she shook her head. "It's not a simple answer." Her eyes were watery when she looked back to him. "I wish I could explain. I honestly do. But there are certain things I can't tell you. Things you wouldn't understand."

"Things I wouldn't understand," he repeated, his voice empty. "Right." He made a disgusted sound deep in his throat. "That's some apology, Tate. If that's what it's even supposed to be."

The leather of the seat squeaked when she edged just a bit

closer, reached out her hand as if she might touch him. Then she thought better of it and dropped her arm. "I know this is coming far too late, and I should have talked to you before, but I'm here now. I'm trying."

Jack couldn't stop the harsh, sarcastic bark of laughter. "You're here because I practically stumbled over you while you were in trouble. Let's be honest, Tate. If I hadn't found you out there today, we wouldn't be having this conversation. Probably never would."

Fury bonded with resentment and pain, and all the other emotions that had prowled inside of him for seven years. Together, they rose and beat from the inside out. The cab of his truck suddenly felt like a cage.

He had to get out of there, away from her. Before all of it broke loose and raged free.

"Never mind." He gripped the steering wheel, squeezed until the vinyl bit into his flesh. "Forget about it, Tate. Just stop. I don't need anything from you."

"I understand." Her voice was a weak breeze. "I just wanted to say . . . I'm sorry."

"And now you have." With a yank of his hand, he put the truck in reverse. He jerked his chin toward the house. "You'd better get inside. Before things get ugly."

Jack spoke of the storm, gathering darkness and violence as it rushed toward land. But his eyes—filled with another kind of warning—stayed steady on hers.

She opened her mouth as if to speak, her body stiff. Changing her mind, she gave a small nod instead and turned away. Without another word, she slid out and shut the door behind her with a soft click.

Jack watched her walk along the flagstone path then thumped the steering wheel, cursing himself, and her. He forced himself to keep his eyes on her, to drink her in, as she climbed the porch steps of the sprawling white Victorian.

When she reached the front door, she stopped and turned toward him. Even with the distance Jack felt the pain. Tate was still a dangerous blade, and she'd sliced through him after all.

Her clean cut opened a bittersweet wound of loss and regret, two things Jack had experienced too much of. So with tires spinning on sodden gravel, he finally ripped his eyes away and roared out of the driveway.

Starting now, he would take his cues from Tate, keeping his focus forward and on the road ahead.

He thrust the stick into drive and peeled over asphalt. And starting now, right *fucking* now, he swore he'd never look back again.

4

With the door closed, Tate rested her forehead against the heavy oak. Her wet clothing dripped a steady stream on original parquet floors of gold- and cherry-toned wood, while outside the wind gusted and raindrops struck the house like bullets.

She'd clean the water up soon, but just now she needed to take a moment. A few minutes to breathe, to blank out the animosity and scorn she'd seen in Jack's eyes

Eyes that had once been so bright, so kind. And filled with love for her.

But what had she expected? She couldn't blame him for not wanting to listen. Her apology had not only been feeble, but far too late.

Seven years ago, she'd created a rift, and over time, it had grown into a chasm. Now mending the deep, jagged break between her and Jack would require much more than one impromptu and awkward conversation.

Chance had brought them face-to-face, and Tate could no longer deny the truth she'd skirted around all this time. The real reason she'd feared seeing him again.

She'd always pretended she was doing him a favor by staying away, by not reminding him of who they'd been together, and what she'd ruined. The truth was, she was the one who didn't want to remember.

And now she did. She remembered too much, because one look

at Jack had brought down the walls she'd built for herself. The ones she'd believed so tall and sturdy.

One look. And they'd shattered like sheets of frost.

That sense of foreboding was finally gone from her chest, but only because a wretched emptiness had moved in to take its place. A vacancy throbbed inside her now, more physically uncomfortable than her wet clothes and frigid skin.

Those problems, at least, she could do something about. She lifted her head from the door, bolstered by the idea of a hot shower, a change of clothes, and a hearty meal.

Then, once she'd regained her balance, she'd tell her family about Emuirdane, the vision, and the message she'd seen in the forest.

The shining symbols from the great stone pulsed like neon in the front of her mind, enticing her to solve whatever riddle they contained. Unfortunately, a headache was growing in the center of her forehead, right where the images blinked. So bright. So insistent.

She pressed two fingers to the epicenter and silently chanted. *Hot shower. Dry clothes. Food.* In that order.

But when she turned from the door, she found her sister Sami leaning against the wall. With her riot of mahogany curls unbound and an apple in her hand, Sami eased her generous mouth into a mischievous grin.

"Well, well, well." She hooked a finger through a loop on her corduroy pants and strolled casually toward Tate. "Who was that I saw dropping you off? Surely it wasn't . . . it couldn't have been," she faked a gasp, "Jack Helmsford."

"Not now, Sami." Tate kept her hand on her face and bore a sharp right, blocking her sister out, and climbed the wooden stairs to the second floor. She'd had enough drama of the evil faerie and ex-boyfriend varieties and was certainly in no mood to add Sami to the list.

Plus, her headache was threading out with thick, crawling

vines of pain. "I'm wet and cold. I'm going to shower." Every word was short and pointed, and to further punctuate her bad temper, she stomped her way up the steps and into the bathroom before shutting the door with a satisfying *whump*!

Fifteen minutes later, Tate strolled downstairs. Her hair was still wet but now smelled like strawberries from the fruity shampoo she'd used. An attempt to have a slice of summer on what had turned out to be a cruel winter day.

Female voices drifted from down the corridor, a beacon promising warmth and security. Tate felt suddenly lighter as she made her way back to the kitchen.

The sprawling room had changed little over the years with walls painted a soothing sage-green and the glass-faced cabinets still a classic ivory, as well as the bricks of the arched fireplace. An orange blaze danced within to combat the chill, meeting the storm with rebellious flame, quelling nature's violence with human comfort.

In the center of the large room stood a long wooden table. Multiple scratches and gouges told of its age, as well as its status as a cherished antique. Several lengths of dough sat on the surface, fully risen and ready to bake. It looked like Fiona had been busy.

Her youngest sister stood with their mother over a simmering pot of what smelled like vegetable-beef stew, and Tate took a moment to enjoy the scene. After her tumultuous day, the embrace of home and hearth was a much-needed balm to her spirit.

But it hadn't always been this way.

For years, Tate had stayed away from home. There'd been too many reminders of her mother here, pictures and mementos— memories in every room, each one causing more agony than joy.

And now she knew why. The stabs of pain hadn't been simple recollection. She'd actually been sensing her mother's presence.

She'd always chalked it up to grief, a period of mourning that would never end. Not while she was surrounded by the people and places that reminded her of what she'd lost.

But now, she thought as affection bloomed, now they reminded her of what she'd found.

Emotion filled her so unexpectedly her eyes burned and her throat closed. Having her mother back in their lives could still be a jolt, a staggering punch of happiness.

It was an odd combination, the old sorrow and the new joy. They always seemed to get tangled up like an endless ribbon, neither able to exist without the other.

Tate sniffed, watching the two cooks of the family so deep in discussion, and was smiling softly when Fiona, the youngest, and most tender of them all, noticed her in the doorway.

"There you are. Feeling better?" Fiona was the only Whiteburn woman with brilliant green eyes, and they shone now beneath a cap of short, black hair. "Sami said you were drenched. How'd that happen?"

Tate wore her red flannel robe, its huge pockets large enough to keep the heolig out of sight until she was ready to share. She slipped her hand in and rubbed the disc. Should she stall long enough for them all to enjoy supper together?

Or spoil the cozy ambience with the unpleasant truth?

She was saved from having to decide when Uncle Brit came in the door from the side yard. Just home from his law office, he wore a trench coat over a gray business suit, his black hair sleek and shining from the rain.

He immediately caught her eye. "Hey, Tate."

"Hey." She grinned, grateful for the interruption.

"I just passed Jack."

The grin dropped. "Oh."

Brit ducked into the mudroom to hang his wet coat. "Was he here?"

Sami, slumped at the table, crossed her arms on top of the wood. "Oh, yeah. He was here." She pretended to study her nails but made no attempt to hide her sly smile.

Fiona came over and picked up the trays of dough. "Don't keep us in suspense, Tate. The last we heard, you were going to the coffee shop. Then Jack brings you home and you're soaked through." She took the trays to the oven, slid them in, and closed the door. Then she popped up straight and sent Tate an expectant look.

The same look everyone else in the room was giving her.

Sami tapped her fingers on the table. "There's got to be a story there."

Tate exhaled. It looked like she'd be spoiling the mood after all. "Fine." She let her arms rise and slap back down to her sides. "You want to know? I'll tell you. I was passed out in front of The Most Excellent Bean. That's how I got wet."

"What?" Fiona jerked away from the counter.

"You passed out?" Her mother dropped the spoon into the pot to clank against the side. "Are you okay?"

"Yes. Yes," Tate said, batting her hands in the air firmly in a "sit down" manner when Sami rose from the table. "I had an experience. Then Jack found me and brought me home. End of story."

Right, she thought. As if they'd let her get away with that.

"What do you mean you had an experience?" For once, Sami didn't latch on to the mention of Jack, but her brown eyes narrowed with suspicion. "Was it Emuirdane?"

Tate nodded, her hand still in her pocket. "Yes."

Brit furrowed his brows used his serious lawyer voice. "Start from the beginning."

"Tell us everything." Her mother stood with one fist to her stomach.

Tate tried to seem nonchalant. "It's a long story, and everyone should be here. Let's talk when Granddad gets here. Or maybe after dinner."

"Let's talk now." Her mother's expression was stern, her back straight as a sword.

Tate blinked in surprise. Her mother still hesitated at times, unsure what her role was and whether or not she should insert herself into the lives of three grown women. Her three little girls who had truly grown up in the blink of an eye.

But at the mention of the Iele, her maternal protective instincts rose to the forefront. "What did Emuirdane say?" she demanded. "What did he want?"

"Emuirdane?" Granddad plodded into the kitchen, his cane hanging from the crook of his elbow by the handle, a fierce-faced silver falcon. "Damnation. Every time I take a nap I miss something."

In truth, their grandfather missed very little. He was, however, adept at hiding things. His cane, for example. Its slim wooden length seemed innocuous, but in truth concealed a lethal weapon, a long, thin sword. One her grandfather—currently sporting some serious bed-head—wielded with astonishing dexterity.

He and her uncle Brit had not only hidden their fighting abilities, but had kept their magick a secret. They'd also cast a spell on Tate and her sisters to repress their powers, hoping Emuirdane would find them useless and leave them alone.

That plan, clearly, had failed, and though they might be forced to deal with the Iele prince, at least they would do so as a family. Whole and complete. And they would have never found their mother without their magick.

And they might never have learned of their abilities, if not for a surprise visit from a golden woman, a messenger from the goddess *Dea Matrona*. For reasons unknown to Tate and her sisters, the ancient deity had taken up their cause.

But they had only three days, the messenger had said, just three days to harness their gifts and find a key. The key to their magick, their happiness, and their lives.

The key, they'd soon discovered, was their mother.

"Um, Tate?" Sami took a step closer, slipped her hands in her pockets. "Sorry about giving you a hard time before. I thought you were just upset about Jack."

"No. It's okay. I was upset because of him too." Defeated, exhausted, Tate went to the table and dropped into a chair near the fire. She needed the warmth on her face. "I've had a very rough day, too much coffee, frozen panties, and," she whimpered, "I got pecked by a sparrow."

"You're safe now." Her mother's voice was calming and her face full of understanding as she walked over and put her arms around her. "Just sit here and take all the time you need."

Sami scrunched up her nose and angled her head toward Tate. "You had frozen panties?"

With a groan, Tate pressed her palm to her forehead.

"I'm just saying." Sami held up her hands. "It sounds uncomfortable."

Tate couldn't stop the laugh. "Well, I may have exaggerated. But . . ." She pulled the stone disc from her pocket and set it on the table. "It all started with this."

In the comfy kitchen, with her family around her, and the scent of baking bread filling the air, Tate told her story. She recounted her meeting with Emuirdane, the snowy forest, the great stone with its strange carvings, and how she'd woken on the sidewalk.

She did not mention waking up in Jack's lap.

As she talked, the heolig passed from hand to hand for inspection by all. When the stone disc made it to her grandfather, he traced a finger over its surface. "You said he called it a heolig?"

Tate nodded and accepted a bowl of stew from her mother.

"The name is from my native Welsh. Heolig." With his accent, Granddad pronounced it *hell-ick*. "Path or pathway. Though I'm not sure how that applies here." He scratched his cheek and slid the disc over to Tate.

"Maybe the symbols will tell us," Tate said. "I have a feeling I won't stop seeing them until I get them out of my head. Write them down."

"I'll get something." Sami jumped up and rushed from the room.

Granddad thumped a hand on his knee. "You should never have had to go through that, Tate." He glanced to Fiona and Brit, and finally Nadia, his daughter. "None of you should have. This is my bargain struck. I'll call on Emuirdane. And by God, he will take his payment from me and only me."

"No, you can't!" Tate reached for him, her splayed fingers landing on the table, just shy of his arm. Fear bared its claws and ripped into her gut. "You didn't hear Emuirdane's threats today. The things he said he would do if we didn't bring him what he wants."

She tried not to look at Fiona as she pictured what the Iele talked of doing to her sister. "I despise Emuirdane." She hoped he wasn't listening now. "But he was right about one thing. Fiona, and Sami, and I carry the power. Even you said we were stronger than both Mom and Grandmother ever were."

"Yes, but—"

"This is for us to do, Granddad." Fiona put her delicate hand over his gnarled one. "This is our part, and you know we would never let you sacrifice yourself."

"But I should let you?"

"They won't, Dad." Tate's mother put her hand to her chest. "Oh, I hate knowing and feeling the truth of this, but it was always meant to be the girls. My heart breaks a little to acknowledge that, but who are we to question Fate?"

"Or a goddess," Sami said, walking up with a yellow legal pad in her hand. She dropped the paper in front of Tate, but not before a look of determination passed between the two of them and then Fiona.

A silent agreement that this was their fight, that they would stand together. The sisters three.

Their bond, their sisterhood, gave Tate a surge of strength, so she turned her attention to the pad and scratched out the symbols she'd seen in the vision. When the final sign was drawn on the pad, she put the pen down and passed the paper to her grandfather.

With the barest glance, he said, "This is *Hen Gymraeg*. Old Welsh. Hmm . . . used from the mid-eighth century to the twelfth."

"Can you read it?" Sami asked.

Granddad chuckled. "Not quite. But I believe there is a section in Nadia's book." He glanced to his daughter.

She nodded. "Yes, there's a portion dedicated to the old languages, both Welsh and Romani." Her eyes grew misty as she glanced to her daughters. "But it's their book now. The sisters' grimoire."

"We can use the grimoire to translate this message?" Fiona asked.

Sami set her spoon in her bowl. "Tonight? Could we get an answer tonight?"

Granddad's silver brows winged up as he considered. "If the lexicon is complete, then I don't see why not."

With her belly full and her skin warmed, Tate glanced to Sami and Fiona. "Then what are we waiting for?"

5

After their mother had been kidnapped, the attic had been locked up and abandoned, left to become a dust- and spider-ridden storage room. The number of spiders had never been verified, but to Tate's mind, they'd seemed countless, with huge glowing eyes and long hairy legs, just right for grabbing up little girls.

A smile kicked up one side of her mouth as she studied her uncle Brit, the one who'd greatly exaggerated the menacing arachnid presence. Again, just part of the smokescreen he and Granddad had perpetrated to keep her and her sisters from being too curious. To keep them from finding their magick.

But after the golden messenger's visit, the truth came out, and the attic was reborn, transformed into an airy space with a lemony-clean smell. The same sweet scent Tate recalled from her early childhood, when her grandmother had still been alive, and her mother still present.

Now the spacious room served its intended purpose again, a mystical headquarters where tables, crystals, and various brass oddities all gleamed from the care they now received. On the far end sat an ornate desk of heavy dark wood, situated between high shelves that held rows of leather-bound books.

A collection of magickal rocks and crystals rested inside a glass display case, nestled atop rich, red velvet. Bloodstone, obsidian, cat's eye—multiple stones glistened and shone. All except the three belonging to Tate, Sami, and Fiona. Those they kept in their rooms.

"I wonder if we should update Kat," Tate said, thinking of the candle-slash-occult storeowner, and new friend, who'd guided them in their selection of athames, personal stones, and other tools they would need for witchcraft.

"I'll call her tomorrow," Fiona said, "to let her know Emuirdane's been active again."

Tate gave her sister a grim smile. "Good. Because I don't trust him to play by the rules, even those laid down by his own kind."

"You think he'd go after Kat?" Sami asked, stopping in her tracks and taking up a fighting stance.

"I think he'll do anything to manipulate us if it means getting what he wants."

"Damn his faerie ass." Sami curled her upper lip. "I'm so ready to get this done." With a sharp pivot, she turned and headed to the long table where their grandfather was already leaning over a huge tome, its pages spread and supported by an antique bookstand.

The grimoire had been passed down by their mother's side of the family for generations, largely full of Romanian spells, folklore, and general magickal knowledge. Then their mother had seen fit to add Celtic legends as well, as she was the first of mixed bloodlines.

"On second thought," Fiona said, "I'll call Kat tonight." Then she followed Sami to where she stood looking over Granddad's shoulder. His head was bent, already comparing the symbols Tate had written down to the lexicon of *Hen Gymraeg*, the old Welsh language.

Brit had moved to the far end of the room where he perused bookshelves, while their mother was in the corner by herself. She pulled the chain of a stained-glass lamp, and violet-hued dragonflies against a verdant garden backdrop were set aglow.

Tate had intended to join Sami and Fiona, but decided to let her sisters take over this task instead. She'd done more than her fair share today. That, and she was still working on her "control-freak-qualities" as Sami so lovingly phrased it.

So instead, she crossed to stand with her mother where the lamplight spilled over an old hutch. Tate marveled over the bright colors of the stained glass. "Grandma's lamp." She traced the outline of yellow jasmine, so brilliant in detail she could almost smell it. "The colors are still so beautiful after all this time."

Her mother nodded. "We have a penchant for passing things down in this family."

Tate chuffed. "That's an understatement."

They shared a smile before her mother's expression turned serious. "Whatever this message reads, whatever it tells us, I know you and your sisters are ready for it. But . . ."

Tate touched her arm, concerned. "Mom, what is it?"

"It's just that . . . I would carry this burden for you if I could. I would do it in a heartbeat."

"I know that." Tate glanced to Sami and Fiona. "We all do. But you've already paid such a high price, and this time the battle falls to us."

Her mother sighed. "Yes." Then, "Let's go over the defenses one more time."

"Mom." Tate laughed. "I can recite them in my sleep."

"Well, humor me. One more time."

"All right." Tate gazed at the hutch. The aged wooden cabinetry housed a mortar and pestle, various spell books, and other implements used for casting. The shelves were slowly filling up with bottles of herbs.

She pointed out four of them—two yellow flagons, a small pink container, and a corked green bottle. "A mixture of marigold, rose, and hazel into sallet oil. Dab onto your pulse points as you would perfume," she quoted her mother verbatim and winked at her, "to ward off the secret people. The Fae."

"Good." Her mother nodded. "And?"

"We can use our fire, telekinesis, and our daggers, but only in a true battle. The iron we probably won't need, since it's a defense against the traditional Fae, but the gold is for Emuirdane. I mean, for Iele."

"And you'll attack only if your life is threatened." Her mother pointed her finger. "Never needlessly provoke the Fae."

A chill crab-legged down Tate's spine. *Especially when you can't beat them.* Like today, when Emuirdane had blown away her fire like the tiniest of birthday candles. Before he laughed at her.

But she wouldn't tell her mother that part.

"Though their power is boundless, the Fae most love a battle of wits. Be careful what you agree to if you see him again. Make no promises."

"Mom." Tate took her mother's hands in her own. "We know all this. We've been over the rules a hundred times. We may not be as experienced as we'd like, but whatever the message says, we have to act on it."

She locked eyes with her mother. "We don't have a choice. Emuirdane has run out of patience."

Her mother squeezed her hands. "I'm sorry. I don't mean to frighten you. I just . . ."

"Feel like you have rocks in your stomach?" Tate chuckled. "So do I." She shrugged her shoulders and worked up what she hoped was an encouraging smile. "Maybe those symbols will tell us what we need to know. We could have an answer tonight and be rid of Emuirdane by tomorrow."

"I hope so, sweetheart." Her mother gave another squeeze, then she let go. She reached up. She tucked Tate's hair behind her ears.

And just like that, lost memories flashed. Tate's first day of school. At the doctor's office for chicken pox. When she'd broken the handprint ashtray she'd made for Granddad.

Each time, her mother had soothed her hurt and dried her tears. And she'd tucked her hair behind her ears.

Just as Tate still did to this day. For comfort.

Overcome, she grabbed her mother in a hug. "I love you. So much. I just want to make sure you know that."

Rubbing her back, her mother made soothing sounds. "I do. And I love you too." Her voice rasped with the threat of tears.

They stood there for a few more seconds and held on to each other, each giving and receiving a measure of solace.

Their sentimental moment was interrupted when Granddad slapped his hands to the table. "I don't believe it." He whipped his head back and forth until his eyes fell on Nadia and Tate, and then Brit. "Come over here, all of you. You need to see this."

This time, Tate's mother was the one to wink. "I'm not that worried. I know my girls." She stroked Tate's cheek. "And you've got this."

Tate hiked a brow. "You've been watching MTV again, haven't you?"

"What can I say?" Her mother shrugged. "It's riveting."

Laughing now, Tate wiped her eyes and walked with her to see why Granddad was so worked up. Sami and Fiona stood quietly beside him, their expressions inscrutable.

"What does it say?" Tate asked when she drew near.

Granddad held the yellow paper in his hands like a herald about to deliver the day's news. "I'll read it again." His blue eyes were wide and focused.

Tate felt her mother slide in close and rest a hand on her shoulder as they listened to Granddad deliver the translation. His deep voice rolled with lyrical cadence straight from the green hills of Wales.

Trust the heolig from the heart
Poison waters to recede
Daughters of Nadia must find a way
Jeweled Ceffyl to be freed

Tate was processing it all when Fiona spoke. "The daughters of Nadia. That's what it says." She pressed her hands together as if to pray. "How can this be? Both Tate and Granddad agreed that this," she gestured to the disc lying on the table, "this heolig must be centuries old."

"Some sort of prophecy?" their mother whispered.

"But Emuirdane never mentioned it," Tate said, turning to her. "In fact, he thought *you* were the one he needed. He didn't even know about us when he came to Granddad. We hadn't been born yet, and he didn't find out about the role we would play until much later."

"But someone knew." Granddad cleared his throat. "Whatever ancient powers created this heolig, they knew." He shuffled his feet and handed the paper to Sami. "Perhaps the same powers that created the Jeweled Ceffyl."

"You know what it is?" Brit asked, brows knit together. "I don't remember your mentioning it."

"It's an old Welsh myth." Granddad pressed a knuckle to his mouth. "Back in the days, when Idwal Foel of Gwyndedd razed the lands. The story goes that a young child was locked outside a castle keep, nowhere to run or hide, and vulnerable to Foel's approaching army. The legend holds that the child prayed long and hard to the gods, until they finally answered. A jeweled figurine appeared in her hands, allowing her one wish that she could use to save herself."

Granddad sucked in a breath. "One wish. One desire." His eyes flicked around, meeting those of his gathered family. "It's what Emuirdane wants. To be granted his one desire."

Sami flung her hands out. "He already has power and magick. He's Fae, even royal Fae, for pity's sake. What could he possibly want that he doesn't have?"

"I don't know." Granddad blew out a breath. "But the notion

terrifies me."

"That's not our concern." Tate crossed her arms. "I'm sorry," she added when Granddad gave her a questioning look. "But I have to think about this family first. I can't worry myself with Emuirdane's greed. If we are fated to find this Jeweled Ceffyl, then we will. What happens in his land is his problem."

"Right." Sami met Tate's eyes. "We'll do our job, which is to fulfill the contract, and that's it." She turned to their grandfather. "But just so we'll know what we're looking for, what exactly does a ceffyl look like?"

"Hm? Oh." Granddad ran a hand through his silver hair. "It's a horse, a silver statuette covered in gemstones. Hence the name."

"I'm more worried about the poison waters." Fiona edged closer to their mother. "Because I think I know where they are."

"Where?" Brit asked, watching Fiona closely now, just as Tate was.

"Remember the lake we passed?" Fiona asked her sisters, before sending an apologetic gaze to their mother. "There was one in the caverns."

Now Tate understood Fiona's reluctance. She was afraid of upsetting their mother by mentioning the horrid place where she'd been held prisoner.

"You saw a lake?" their mother asked. Then she patted Fiona's arm. "It's fine, sweetheart. I'm free now and, honestly, I have very few memories of that place. I was essentially asleep the whole time."

Fiona put her head on their mother's shoulder just as Sami snapped her fingers. "You're right, Fee. All three of us reacted to that lake. We all sensed its danger."

Certainty rose up in Tate. "Fee is right. We have to go back." Down into the tunnels beneath their property. "There must be a source of power below. It's why Hellana and Mom were pulled there when their spells and magick collided."

She looked to her grandfather. "Maybe it's what drew you and Grandma here. Why you bought the land in the first place."

Granddad got a faraway look in his eyes, as if trying to recall. "Could be."

"Let's go, then." Sami started to move when their mother held up a halting hand.

"Don't even think about it," their mother said. "You are not going down there at night. Especially during a storm." Lightning flashed outside the round window to back up her argument.

Tate was as eager as Sami to be done with goddesses, faeries, and even jeweled horses, but one look at Fiona's white face and she took up her mother's stance. "We'll go tomorrow, during daylight hours."

Sami grunted and rolled her eyes. "Okay. I know when I'm outvoted." Then she cocked a grin and touched her hair. "Besides, the rain makes my curls hella frizzy."

Granddad's mouth went thin and flat, and he shook his head at Sami. But at least Fiona and their mother laughed, lightening the somber mood that had crawled in around them.

Sami lifted a careless shoulder. "Since we've solved the riddle and discovered we're not only witches but pre-ordained to find a cute little horse for a big bad faerie, I'm going back downstairs to get extra sustenance for tomorrow's adventure."

"How can you still be hungry?" Brit asked, falling in with Sami as they headed for the door and down the narrow stairwell.

Their mother kissed Fiona's cheek. "I think I'll have more of that delicious herb bread baked by my talented daughter. See you downstairs."

After she'd gone, Tate asked her grandfather, "Do you mind if I take a look?" She reached for the paper Sami had dropped on the table.

"Of course not." Granddad stepped aside. "The message was meant for you and your sisters." He frowned. "Odd though, the way it rhymed in English. As if it was meant to be translated all along."

He tilted his head and looked to Tate. "Then again, I guess it was."

Fiona crowded closer to look over the lines of the message again. "Do you think that's all this means, Tate? That the Ceffyl's somewhere in the lake?"

"Maybe. Why not?"

"Because if it's that simple, why were we chosen? Why does Emuirdane keep saying we're the only ones who can find what he wants? That our magick is what makes us *the ones*?"

Tate only shook her head. She had no answers for her sister. "I guess we'll find out."

But those rocks in her stomach had begun to churn.

6

Emuirdane stood atop the castle pinnacle, hands clasped behind his back and chin up as he leaned into the bracing wind. The high point of the tallest tower was his favorite place to spend time alone and survey the vast lands over which he reigned.

Situated on a rise, Castle Draviski stood in a position of power and dominance, an imposing fortress constructed to lord over the sprawling valley. Much as the king who lived within her halls lorded over the citizens below.

Emuirdane inhaled the frosty air. The citizens, the lands, and the entire kingdom belonged to him, in truth if not yet in name.

He was the son of the king with too few heirs, and that king, even now, lay elsewhere in the castle, a skeletal figure barely clinging to life. A monarch past his prime, whose only spots of color were the crimson droplets spewed by his ruined lungs.

Gold dust. That was the culprit. His father's illness was a result of death in disguise, an innocuous-looking bottle of his favorite bog whiskey, rigged to expulse a cloud of aurum powder with a simple twist of the lid.

Terrorism, act of war, or political intrigue? Despite rigorous interrogation, none of the castle guard could say how the whiskey had gotten through inspection, or past the poison tasters who lived to die on a daily basis.

The bottle must have still been sealed, or so the council proffered, and never opened by any hands other than the king's.

But how could such a travesty occur? Such a breach in security? Who should be punished? Executed?

The first days after his father's attack had been a panicked frenzy, as none of the servants, guards, or members of the royal court held any answers. The chaos had only quieted after Emuirdane stepped in, assuring them the perpetrator would be found. He would see to it himself.

No one questioned his right to do so.

And no one mentioned his absence on the day his father was poisoned, nor dared voice suspicion that his safe distance was due to anything other than coincidence. Why would they? The burst of golden powder had affected only the king, and the maids who'd cleaned the king's chambers afterwards had but mild cases of contact poisoning.

If Emuirdane had been in the castle, he would have likely escaped unharmed.

But he'd made sure to be far away. Nowhere near the solar with its thin coat of golden dust.

Despite the fact he would benefit from the king's demise, he felt confident that none who roamed the castle halls would question the heir apparent, the sly and handsome prince who would soon rule them with a fist not as bloody and brutal as his father's, but surely as deadly. A fist one would never feel grasping and squeezing until it was too late.

A fist crowned with a silver ring, and a green stone seething with power.

Emuirdane lifted his face to the chill wind and placed his hands on the balustrade. He looked at the gemstone on his finger and sensed the snap of magick as it looked back.

His mother had given him the ring along with a breastpin, both valuable and mystical heirlooms.

He was like her, his shrewd mother, and with her long-deceased, he prided himself on the graceful viciousness he'd inherited from her. Elegance and cunning were rare traits in these harsh, savage lands. Far too many in this place relied on their baser instincts—a swinging mace or raw magick. *Unrefined* magick.

Allowing his pit-black eyes to drift, he fixated on the far end of the valley where the distant, jagged peaks of Mount Mohorat pierced the sky like sharp, iron swords. The high crests were gloomy and bare, with no blade of grass or crystal of ice brave enough to make its home there.

Though menacing, the mountains sat still and dark. No balefires burned with imminent threat. No war drums echoed through the deadly passes. All was placid, and all was quiet.

For now.

"My Lord." A kingsguard stood behind him, as per protocol, awaiting acknowledgment and permission to speak.

Emuirdane turned slightly and tipped his head.

"The seer has news."

Excitement stirred within him, but Emuirdane's face remained neutral. "Go on."

As he listened to the guard's report, a vellgar screeched in the sky, tightened its wings to its body, and dove for the kill. He watched the bird of prey as he absorbed every detail of the soothsayer's vision.

The old woman, Ruxandra, was the strongest psychic in the entire realm, and her enhanced sight was vital to his cause. She kept an eye—so to speak—on the three who held his fate within their mortal hands.

He was capable of observing the Whiteburn sisters, but the chore grew tedious, and he'd decided to let the old woman monitor them instead. Because soon she would be the only who could.

Incredibly gifted and older than fire, Ruxandra could know their movements and their words at any time. But more importantly, in any place.

When the kingsguard finished his report, Emuirdane gave

another slight nod, this time of dismissal. Then he waited for the other's footsteps to fade before turning to go inside the tower himself.

Candlelight glistened on the curving, stone stairwell, lighting the way for his descent to a lower level. He exited into a wide corridor, the surroundings instantly more opulent and adorned in finery.

Sconces lined the walls, bedecked with shining crystals, and a sumptuous carpet ran the length of the hall. Its plush fibers, the color of blood, silenced the clap of his boots.

The castle itself was massive, and this particular wing consisted of many chambers. Only two, however, were occupied. The largest quarters belonged to him, and on the end distant from his, in the most lavish of rooms, is where he kept his wife.

Halting outside a large vaulted door that narrowed to a point on top, he knocked lightly with his knuckles. "Hellana?" He did not wait for an answer but pushed inside.

Several years after their union, he had outfitted these quarters especially for her, directing the staff to use as many shades of blue and green as were found in the seas near VeiLani. His wife's mother hailed from the coastal kingdom, and he'd hoped the gesture would be taken in truce.

All these years later, he still longed for marital accord, but at least he'd learned how better to deal with his mate.

He scanned the room, searching for a glimpse of pale skin or the shimmer of a gossamer gown. Hellana dressed as her mother's people did, bare midriff and gauzy skirts, as if she lived in that warm ocean clime instead of Emuirdane's frigid mountains.

He didn't see her right away, but she was here somewhere. Of that he was certain. Several strides of his long legs carried him through a wide doorway and into the adjoining sitting room. There he saw the heavy chain, its dark links camouflaged by the onyx marble tiles shot through with gray.

A lustful smile eased across his lips when he caught sight of her lithe form. She stood on the balcony looking toward the North. He was so pleased to have her back, his dear Hellana. Though human years were such a small slice of time, he'd missed her utterly in the two decades she'd been gone.

But now she was bound to him again, both legally and physically. His blacksmiths had forged the chain she wore, its links made almost entirely of volsug.

Second only to gold, volsug was one of the most feared metals in the realm, able to subdue an Iele's magic, sucking them dry, making them as weak as a human.

Carefully avoiding the chain, he stepped into the very female room. Settees of silver and aquamarine were drowning beneath sequined pillows, and thin, filmy curtains of azure-blue floated in the same hearty breeze he'd enjoyed above on the pinnacle.

For a moment he watched his wife, wondering if she contemplated leaping over the side. But the chains harnessed her in such a way that even if she jumped, she would be safely caught not far below the stone terrace.

Her chains had been measured and secured with specific requirements. Hellana was confined to safety, unable to reach any weapon. Powerless to do harm to any servant or guard, her husband, or herself.

Now that he had her, she was never leaving him again.

Even through death.

He approached quietly, though he knew she was aware of his presence. "Good news, my love," he said amiably. "Nadia's daughters have made progress. The seer tells me they have deciphered the heolig's message."

Hellana did not respond, but her fingers clenched in the folds of her gown, the deep blue shade of her beloved sea, the same color as her eyes as well as her hair. She gave him her profile, pert nose lifted in arrogance. "They will fail yet. They are too weak."

Emuirdane's smile slipped, but for only a heartbeat. "Not so weak. If they managed to defeat a VeiLanian princess such as yourself."

Her voice lashed at him. "With your help, you traitorous bastard."

This coming from the wife who had run away, stolen his breastpin with its stores of magick, and attempted to murder the three girls who would ensure her husband's triumph.

Emuirdane bristled. Yet she called *him* traitor?

Rubbing both palms down his finely-crafted doublet, he loosed a breath and preserved his patience. "I have not come to quarrel." His tone, though elegant with qualities of his royal upbringing, now held the sharp edge of a blade.

Hellana whipped around, eyes blazing like blue flames, no longer the tranquil waters of her maternal heritage. "Then why are you here?"

He could tell by the rapid rise and fall of her breasts that she already knew the answer.

So instead of wasting words to fall on spiteful ears, Emuirdane simply turned around, re-entered her bedroom, and strode to a chifforobe in the far corner. A place Hellana's chains did not allow her to reach.

He opened a drawer and retrieved an enchanted blanket, one that would protect him from the magick-leeching properties of her restraints. Then he stepped to a crank embedded in the wall.

With one hand, he turned the handle in a clockwise manner, secretly delighted by the sound of coiling metal. The sound made by the spool concealed within the wall, grinding slowly, reeling in Hellana's chains.

The huge metal strand tightened, before beginning a slow crawl along cerulean carpets, across gray-veined tiles, and finally over the silky sheen of Hellana's bed. The length of chain then vanished into a hole in the wall, right where a headboard should have been.

A screech of fury bounced within the living quarters, soon followed by his furious wife. Her hands gripped and tugged the chain, though she knew from experience the resistance was futile.

"You putrid son of a Babadesh whore!"

Emuirdane put a hand to his heart. "You wound me, love. Why must you always fight?"

"Because you sicken me." She stomped her pale, bare foot and spat in his direction. "I may be your prisoner again, and those human weaklings may pursue your precious Ceffyl, but they will not survive. They will fail."

Laughter poured from her pink lips, the sound as sharp and brittle as glass. "And we both know what will happen when they do."

Jaws clenched, Emuirdane didn't deign to respond. He breathed deeply and turned the crank.

"One day I will be free." Hellana dropped her head and glared from under pinched brows. "I swear this, *husband*." The title dripped with disdain. "One day I will have my vengeance."

Eyes like a sea of fire narrowed into slits. "Vengeance on you." She tossed back her glorious mane. "And on my baseborn father."

Ignoring her curses and threats, Emuirdane rotated the handle until a large ring clinked against the stone wall. The metal loop held two smaller chains connected to the manacles on her wrists.

Pulled against her will onto the bed, Hellana sat with her knees packed tightly beneath her and her face averted. Still huffing, she refused to look at him, to watch as he disrobed.

Emuirdane carefully peeled away the leather baldric from across his chest before easing out of his costly raiment. He took his time, enjoying the slide of clothing over his skin.

He became aroused and grew instantly hard, his canines lengthening to sharp, piercing points. Fae used their fangs for all manner of enjoyment, but he preferred his for a certain kind of biting.

A particular brand of tasting.

Once naked, he picked up the blanket and tossed it over his wife. Cautiously keeping the charmed material between his hands and any portion of her chains, he grabbed her ankles and pulled her legs out behind her.

With a delicate touch, he smoothed the blanket up her legs and over her body, taking the filmy layers of her dress along with it.

Hellana tried to kick out at him, but he expected this last useless attempt. Using his magick, he pinned her feet to the silk sheets, then ran his hands over her skin, tracing the curves of her lovely calves.

"I am so happy you've returned to me." He kissed behind her knee. "My beautiful wife." Settling himself between her legs, Emuirdane lifted her hips. "I love you."

"I abhor you!"

He rubbed his nose in her hair, so long and gleaming, like a deep blue waterfall. "You are so beautiful."

Her voice broke. "You disgust me."

"But you are mine." Despite her thrashing, her growled wishes for his death and disfigurement, Emuirdane entered his wife. "And soon the Ceffyl will be as well."

Hellana pressed her face to a pale blue pillow. She screamed her rage.

Unaffected, he continued to move inside her. "Soon, my darling, I will have you both. Yes, soon . . ." He moaned with pleasure. "I will have it all."

7

Jack punched the pillow and pressed his face against it, shutting his eyes in yet another attempt to fall asleep. The soft patter of rain should have soothed him into slumber, but after a night of short, fitful bouts, he couldn't find it in himself to be optimistic.

He rolled over on his back and rubbed the heels of his hands against his bleary eyes. The first gray light of dawn was creeping into his bedroom so, with a sigh that sounded more like a groan, he gave up on getting any more rest, threw back the covers, and stood.

With a glance through the window, he assessed the state of his yard. Limbs hung at broken angles, a teal patio chair lay overturned in the wet grass, and remnant autumn leaves speckled the ground like confetti. The nor'easter had wreaked havoc on Bar Harbor, leaving plenty of damage and debris behind.

But the storm ripping through town all night wasn't what had kept Jack awake. No, that he blamed on the woman who'd blown into town. The woman who'd laid waste to his peace of mind, just as the gale-force winds had the island.

Worse than any natural disaster, hurricane Tate had rolled over him without warning, leaving her own brand of destruction in her wake.

Jack gnashed his teeth and heaved another sigh, because he, of all people, should have known better. After the initial worry for her had passed, he'd told himself he could spend the short drive to her house in her presence without any ill effects.

But a flash of her face had been too much, and five minutes with her had been far too long. Seeing her again had been like walking straight into the tempest, and he'd wrestled with the consequences all night long.

Jack shook his head and surveyed the chaos outside. Dismayed by the mess and disgusted with himself, he staggered to the kitchen to start his morning pot of coffee, two hours earlier than usual. Then he opted for a hot shower while the java brewed.

Lifting his face to the steady stream, he let the pounding heat wash away his fatigue and any lingering thoughts of Tate. Determined to keep her out of his head, he performed a mental rundown of the day's to-do list. He was almost grateful for the clutter he would have to clean up outside, physical labor to burn off some frustration left over from last night's encounter.

Once he had the yard in respectable shape, he'd turn his attention to his current work-in-progress. The piece he was making involved intricate chip carving, detailed work that required concentration and a steady hand.

Losing himself in creation would serve as a worthwhile distraction and, as it had so often in the past, his art would bring him a kind of solace, tranquility, and deliverance from whatever troubles plagued his mind.

As he toweled off, he pictured the unfinished sculpture on his worktable, a custom order for a repeat client. Rarely did he let anyone guide his creations, but for Mrs. Ames he'd always make an exception. She'd been his first big sale and his best PR, helping launch his career and land his first gallery show.

She was also seventy-eight years old and a sweetheart to boot. If she asked for it, Jack would do his best to carve her the moon.

But before he laid hands on the clock plate she'd requested, he had to forget about Tate. He could feel the tension in his back and arms, like coiled steel cables. Far too tight for the precise detailing of his current project.

And he refused to let her affect another single day of his life or influence another piece of his art.

Not like she had before.

After veering to the coffee pot for a cup of morning addiction, Jack took the back staircase that led up from the kitchen to the open loft above his garage. The messier sawing and chopping that often occurred at the start of a project took place out back in his workshop. That's where he kept the heavy machinery, like the lathe and workbench.

But here, he thought as he opened the door, is where the real magic happened. The open loft and bevy of windows allowed an expansive view of Frenchman Bay and its never-ending blue. The sun was little more than a glimmering line on the horizon, but even the dark waters were a spectacular sight.

He hadn't owned this house when Tate had left him, but the sculpture she'd inspired held a place of honor. Despite the angst he still associated with the piece, he'd never been able to sell it. And there'd been offers—many offers—including one from Mrs. Ames.

The piece had been a turning point for Jack, and the first creation fed solely by emotion.

The first week after Tate had left had been a seven-day blur of beer, take-out food, and ESPN binging. But on the eighth day, something had clicked deep inside. He'd woken up on his couch, with a hangover from hell, and without the aid of caffeine or aspirin he'd gone straight to the spare bedroom that had then served as his workshop and studio in one.

He'd picked the ugliest, most scarred piece of wood he could find, plopped it onto the table, and gone to work. Hours he'd sat hunched over the scrap piece, boring and scraping until the center was carved out, not coming up for air, water, or food until he'd had no choice but to sweep up the pile of shavings and sawdust at his feet.

The piece had taken him days, and now every time he studied it he was amazed by the fluidity of the lines, the design that had appeared once knots and knobs had been sanded down.

The beauty found beneath blemishes.

Thin, sinuous extensions curved up from the outer edge and back toward the center, so fine and fragile it was a wonder none had snapped under his grief-laded hands. Of those who'd seen the completed work, some said they saw tree limbs or arms, even tentacles, while other more esoteric minds envisioned a wounded spirit, reaching for something it couldn't have.

That's what Jack saw. That's what he'd been.

So after days of cutting, carving, and sanding, he'd given the piece a dark, tragic stain, applied varnish, and burnished until it gleamed like polished onyx.

Then he'd named it. *Hollow*.

Short, simple, and reflective of how he'd felt during those awful days, when he'd been so full of anguish and loss he'd feared the ache would swallow him whole.

And though the emptiness creeping up on him now was a mere echo of that pain, he couldn't deny that the ache was there. The sense of loss was back.

And Tate had caused them both.

The rising sun revealed the ocean's deep blue, but the scene gave Jack no peace today. He turned his back on the sculpture, his fingers tensing on the handle of his mug. *Damn it, Tate.*

Was he ever going to shake this feeling and be rid of the nagging betrayal? Would he ever be truly, completely, one-hundred-percent over the woman who'd deserted him?

No, he admitted with a silent snarl. Not until he understood why she'd left the way she had. They'd been young then, both dreaming of *more* and *different*, as twenty-somethings were wont to do. But none of that explained her behavior.

Leaving him without a word had been cruel and cold, not at all like the Tate he'd known. And this was the crux of his problem. He needed to understand what had happened to the girl he'd loved, the friend he'd cherished.

What could have made her treat him so callously?

He shoved aside the questions he'd asked himself for so long. They always ricocheted inside his troubled mind, but he never received a response.

Too many years he'd spent in the dark when it came to the demise of their relationship. He was done wondering. It was time for answers.

He marched out of the studio, slapping the light off as he passed. There was no way he'd be getting any work done, not today or any other. Not until he'd settled things with Tate. Once and for all.

He didn't dare touch the delicate clock face, not with anger and rigidity riding up his back in vengeful waves. He needed to relax, to be able to focus, and he could do neither until he found clarity.

And only she could give him that.

He was no longer the confused and dejected boy who'd wallowed in grief. After he'd accepted that she was gone, he'd picked up the scattered shards and put himself back together. The breaks had healed, and he was a stronger man for it.

But it was clear to him now that he'd never put it behind him, that he'd never be free, until he heard what she had to say. Until she told him *why*.

Down in the kitchen again, he stared out the picture window above the sink, wondering how long he should wait. It was still too early for a surprise visit, so he'd kill some time by cleaning up the yard, burning off some of the resentment rising in his chest while he was at it.

He could wait a couple more hours, but no longer. Then he was going back to the Whiteburn house, and back to Tate.

Leaning against the counter, he fleshed out his new plan, realizing the promise he'd made last night was about to be broken.

Because he would look back. He would see her again.

And this time he wasn't leaving until he had what he needed.

8

The rain had only ceased a half-hour before, leaving droplets on the trees that shone like tiny diamonds. The woods were preternaturally silent as Tate and her family strode through, as if even the winds and winter creatures understood the gravity of the task at hand.

This was the first time they'd returned to the forest behind their home since the night a blue-ink beetle had guided the three sisters, leading them to the network of tunnels and caverns that spread beneath their property. The night they'd discovered an underground world, full of threats and mystical sights.

The night they'd found their mother alive, trapped in a cursed glass box of Hellana's making. Where she'd been for the last twenty years.

Tate glanced aside, recalling her mother's serene yet motionless face as she'd slept under magick's spell, and wished for the tenth time she'd been able to convince her to stay behind. She shouldn't have to go back down there, to the bowels of darkness where she'd been imprisoned for so long.

Tate walked next to her mother, wanting to be at her side. Sami and Fiona were in front of them with Brit even farther ahead, taking point. Granddad brought up the rear, claiming he didn't want to slow them down.

But Tate had seen his sly scrutiny of the terrain, his cane-sword combo clutched in his hand as he searched for any sign of danger.

Her kind and elderly grandfather had transformed once again into the warrior persona he usually kept hidden.

In fact, her entire family had changed, their dynamic and roles completely redefined when she and her sisters had learned of their true heritage. There were no more secrets between them, no more protective omissions. But the acceptance of power had come with a hefty price.

They were all bound to Emuirdane now, little more than servants to a creature whose greed and corruption were boundless.

Their peaceful home was no longer a safe haven, but rather like a snow globe that had been shattered and resealed. Tate could feel ever-watching eyes on her and her family, entities who peeked through the cracks of their fractured existence.

And now, too often, they slipped inside.

Tate cast her cautious eyes from shadow to shadow, channeling the fire of her magick and holding it in her palms. Ready to be unleashed.

No one spoke, turning the vast forest into a grand and silent temple of nature. The only sound to reach Tate's ears was the low rasp of waves, rolling in to smash against the base of the cliffs.

She breathed in the fresh scent of rain-washed earth, trying to embrace the stillness, the unity of her family, the sense of reverence. But suspicion prickled at her nape, a sense of foreboding that had her stopping to turn back in the direction of their house.

Had she heard something? A voice? Or had her imagination played a trick on her troubled mind?

"Tate?" Her mother paused alongside her as she too looked through the trees. A master of herbs and spellweaving, she wore an assortment of small pouches suspended from her belt. They had no idea what they would find in the caves below but had come prepared with all manner of weapons.

Her hand drew up to palm a sachet at her waist as she strained to listen. "What is it?"

Shaking her head, Tate rubbed her arms through the thick sweater she wore. The wool protected her from the elements but couldn't fend off the chill spreading inside her. Neither could the flowing heat of her power. "Nothing, I guess. Just nerves."

The sun made a valiant attempt to filter through the clouds and the lacework of bare branches above, but only thin shafts reached the sodden collection of leaves on the ground. With soft steps, their group pushed onward, moving without conversation until they broke free of the trees.

The harsh blue of the Atlantic spread before them as Brit and Sami edged closer to the deadly precipice. To reach the tunnel entrance, they would have to wind down the pass cutting across the face of the cliffs, exposed to forceful winds and a fifty-foot drop to the jagged rocks and grasping sea.

Tate had to raise her voice over the tide and fearful breeze. "Granddad, maybe you should—"

"I'm coming with you," he interrupted, the blue of his eyes as sharp and strong as the sword he carried.

Mouth flat and grim, Tate looked to her mother.

"And so am I," she said, anticipating Tate's request before she could form the words.

With a huff of acceptance, Tate began the descent. They were forced to move in single-file, so she slipped in after Fiona but ahead of her mother.

At the bottom, the path leveled out to a small platform, previously disguised by an illusion of bedrock. Now they peered into a gaping hole.

"Hellana's magick is gone," Fiona said, "so the camouflage must have gone with her."

"We should conceal the entrance when we're done today," Brit said, leading them all inside. "We don't want curious kids or travelers poking around down here. Underground tunnels are dangerous enough, but this place is . . ." He trailed off, looking to the piles of rocks on the ground.

Stacked into pyramids and positioned at intervals on either side of the corridor, the eerie mounds were clearly the work of a mystic.

"Those light up," Sami said. "At least, they used to. Hellana must have been powering them too."

Fiona lifted her hands, palms toward the stones. "Let's see if they'll work for us."

Their mother stepped forward. "Wait. Let me do it. You three need to conserve your power." She looked down the black-as-night tunnel. "We don't know what we'll find in the lake or what will be required of you."

"Right," Sami chimed in. "And those scuttle-bug things may still be down here."

At her mention of the creatures, Granddad unsheathed his sword just as Brit pulled a bolt from the quiver on his back and notched it in his crossbow. Ancient and lethal, the metal bow had been passed down through Tate's grandfather's side of the family, just as the grimoire had been handed down on her mother's.

Tate's instinct was to reach for her magick, but her mom was right. She needed to save her power for whatever lay ahead, so instead she lifted the dagger from the sheath on her hip. The marbled pattern of gold and iron shone in the greenish-blue light when her mother ignited the stones' enchantment.

One by one they sparked to life, like magickal dominoes rolling down the winding shaft, illuminating the way.

Tate stepped up to block Brit when he would have taken the lead again. "Let us," she said, before lowering her voice so it wouldn't carry. "I want Mom between you and Granddad."

Brit's eyes shifted to his sister, and though he seemed to struggle with the idea of leaving his nieces vulnerable, he tipped his head in agreement. "Keep your eyes open." He fell back to guard from the center.

Tate and her sisters moved forward as a unit, daggers drawn as they followed the muted blue glow deeper into the earth and away from the last wisps of daylight.

A sense of déjà vu shivered over Tate's skin as the narrow corridor curved and descended before finally opening up to a vast cavern. Here was the pool they'd come to find, and the glimmering waterfall that fed its blue depths.

Points of light shimmered within the falling stream, sending wavering reflections of light to the stone walls and ceiling. More of the glowing rocks from before lay on the bottom of the pond, lending their blue incandescence to the water.

Tate, Sami, and Fiona lined up near—but not too near—the edge of the underground pond. The round pool glistened like an aquamarine, as beautiful and mesmerizing as the gemstone it resembled.

On their last visit, they'd carefully skirted around the strange body of water. Even then, they'd perceived its danger, pulled by the mesmerizing beauty, yet sensing the death hidden beneath.

If these truly were the poison waters, Tate was grateful for whatever instinct had made them cautious.

Sami and Fiona both studied the cavern and, like her, Tate was sure her sisters were listening as well. Waiting to hear the telltale skitter that would warn of a creeping monster's approach.

"I think the bugs went with Hellana," Sami said, proving that her thoughts had taken the same track as Tate's.

"Good." Fiona loosed a breath, an echo of her fear shaking out along with the air. "I say we move quickly and get this over with." She reached into the pocket of her green raincoat and retrieved the heolig.

There was no argument that magick came most easily to Fee, so she'd been the one nominated to carry the disc into the tunnels. If the heolig were to react to the thick, noxious power still smudging the subterranean environment, Fiona would be most likely to pick up on it.

But with no such response, she eased closer to Tate, and Sami closed in from the other side. With her sisters flanking her, Tate felt her power surge. They were definitely in the right place, facing the "poison waters" mentioned in the message.

Now they just had to figure out the next step.

Fiona handed the disc to Tate. "Emuirdane gave it to you, so maybe you should be the one to use it."

Grasping the heolig with both hands, Tate held it out in front of her. Other than coming here with the disc, they didn't know what else to do. Seconds passed with no change, no hint of stirring magick.

Sami's face reflected her frustration. "Maybe chant the message?"

Tate nodded. "Why not?" Still holding the disc before her, she spoke the words Granddad had deciphered the night before, her sisters voice blending and rising with hers. "Trust the heolig from the heart. Poison waters to recede."

As one they drew a breath and continued in unison. "Daughters of Nadia find a way. The Jeweled Ceffyl will be freed."

With their combined voices bouncing off the cavern walls, they stood stock-still and waited. Tate was afraid to speak or retract the disc, afraid to break any spell they may have sent out into the universe.

Granddad held no such fear. "Well?" he called out. "Feel anything?"

"No," Sami grumbled, shaking her head.

Fiona sighed. "So much for that."

Frowning at the heolig, Tate bent her elbows to pull the disc back to her, surprised when she felt resistance. "Hey," she whispered, almost afraid to raise her voice. She tugged harder and brought the disc in an inch.

But as soon as she relaxed, it thrust forward like a magnet to its mate. Power flowed up from the water to dance around her, tiny stabs of energy all over her skin like strong static.

Another force was at work here.

"Something's happening," she said. "The heolig is being pulled. It's attracted to . . ." She stuttered when she realized. "To the pond."

"What?" Sami snapped, grabbing the disc, trying to help Tate hold it. "Are you sure?" Her brown eyes dropped to the toxic fluid. "Because if it falls in there, we won't be getting it back."

Tate glanced down to the beautiful yet lethal pool, imagining it would bring a slow and painful death, far worse than drowning. She gripped the heolig so hard her fingers burned, but the pull grew stronger, wrenching her joints when she tried to fight it. "I can't hold on."

"Tate, let go." Her mother ran up and latched on to her waist as if she feared her daughter would be pulled into the water along with the disc. "Let it go!"

Her mother's terrified shout was a catalyst, and she spread her fingers, releasing the heolig. The stone disc shot straight out, hovered for a few seconds, and then slipped into the pond without a sound.

A tremor rolled through the stony ground beneath them. "Back up." Arms flung out to grab both of her sisters, Tate stumbled away from the pond's edge.

But as suddenly as the quaking began, it subsided. Ripples formed on the pond, in the exact spot the heolig had fallen.

"What's happening?" Brit asked. He and Granddad moved up to stand with them, staring at the ripples as they grew to small waves.

Before anyone could reply, the water in the pond split down the middle, parting perfectly and evenly. The two sides built to great swells, rising higher and higher as they pressed against opposite sides of the basin.

"Poison waters to recede." Fiona's green eyes fluttered, her mouth slack as she took in the incredible sight.

Crowded together, the six of them leaned forward, slowly, and with great care. Even with the water's retreat, no one wanted to fall into the crater it left behind.

The liquid center had cleared, revealing bedrock beneath.

No, not only rock. Something else was down there. Something stirred.

Different than the beige and gray stone, dark wisps slithered and spread, like snakes made of mist.

"Are my old eyes playing tricks on me?" Granddad asked as he rubbed the orbs in question.

"No," Tate answered, but she could offer nothing further. No encouragement or assurance. She didn't know what to make of the strange swirls but hoped they stayed at the bottom of the pool. Far, far away.

Dark blues and shadow grays grew more distinctive, and soon other shades emerged, coalescing to paint a picture. Long, thick strokes of color materialized, forming hedge-lined pathways and a black silhouette looming in the background that looked like—

"Is that a castle?" Sami demanded, her voice high and thin, stretched by panic. Or confusion. Maybe both.

Tate's breath rushed from her body, leaving her feeling light inside, as if she'd separated from herself. "What are we looking at?"

"Not what, darling girl." A baritone voice cut through the cave. "But *where*."

Tate whirled to find Emuirdane leaning against a wall. With no apparent concern for the dirty environment, he wore his usual finery, pants and doublet in green so deep they appeared almost black.

"Where?" Tate repeated, the word rasping from her lips of its own accord.

The Iele smirked at her as if she were dense.

"A Farworld." It was Granddad who answered before he shoved Tate, Fiona, and Sami away from the open pit. The one that held a Farworld at the bottom.

And possibly an even greater threat than the waters before.

Granddad clenched his jaws and fists, then stepped up to meet Emuirdane. "No more. This ends now." But instead of lifting his sword, Granddad let it fall, the shiny length clattering against the dirty rocks. "You will take your debt now. From me, and no one else."

"Dad, no." Brit moved to stand with his father.

Tate's mother was right behind him. "I'll go," she said, wringing her hands. "Send me to find the Ceffyl."

Now it was Tate's turn to protest. "That's not going to happen."

Emuirdane simply lifted his hand, all the while keeping his obsidian eyes on her mother. "Nadia, Nadia." He shook his head. "You know your daughters were born for this quest. You gave birth to them for this very purpose."

"The hell with that." Sami lifted her dagger. "We weren't *born* to be your servants."

Tate shoved her own dagger back into its sheath and lifted her hands as she circled around, positioning herself to Emuirdane's left. "Talk to me. My mother and grandfather have nothing to do with this. Not anymore."

Emuirdane looked to her and laughed, his eyes twinkling with wicked delight. "Oh, you needn't worry. I won't touch any of you." He angled his head to the blurry portal. "You must go of your own free will."

The terror she hadn't acknowledged snapped inside her chest to release a soft flood of relief. She relaxed, eased by the knowledge that he couldn't force them to enter that foreign world.

"But," he smiled again, revealing his fangs, "I think you'll want to." He lifted a single white hand and snapped his fingers. "Bring him!"

Movement and scuffling noises drew her attention to the entrance. Two men entered the cavern. Dressed like ancient warriors but in all black, they had huge swords fastened to their backs.

But the fearsome blades weren't what held Tate rapt, unable to move or even speak.

Between them, the brutish warriors held a man, his eyes wild and blood trickling down the side of his face.

Jack.

The center of Tate's chest hardened, petrifying her from the inside out with a new and vicious fear. The awful dread pushed out into her veins, crawling throughout until her entire body seemed made of stone.

Jack saw her then. "Tate!" He began thrashing for release.

Breath catching, she ripped her eyes from Jack to glare at Emuirdane. Another draw of air and her voice lashed out. "What have you done?"

The dark prince blinked like a satisfied cat and held out a hand as if the explanation were obvious. "I've merely provided incentive." He clicked his tongue. "Since you mortals are ever predictable. Tediously so."

"Jack is not part of our family. You can't involve him." Finding her strength at last, she rushed forward, intent on getting to Jack, but Emuirdane moved like mist and gripped her arm to jerk her against him.

Lowering his fangs too close to her neck for comfort, Emuirdane growled in Tate's ear. "Haven't you learned yet, girl? I will do whatever I must to have the Ceffyl. Now you go, and you find it," he tightened his grip on her arm until pain shot up to her shoulder, "and you bring it to me."

She glanced across the cavern to meet's Jack's gaze. The soldiers had subdued him, but fury still tightened his features. He narrowed his eyes at Emuirdane, who was still holding her against him

Her mother and granddad tried to run to her, but Emuirdane flung out his other hand. Tate could still hear their worried voices, but they banged their fists against the air, as if blocked by an invisible barrier.

Sami, Fiona, and Brit advanced on Jack and the two men who held him, but a sphere of green rose up to surround the soldiers and their captive. Flashes of energy arced outward, darting toward her family if any drew too near.

Tate screamed at Emuirdane, venting her frustration. "Leave Jack out of this! You have no right!"

In an instant, the Fae's countenance darkened, the shadows of his true nature playing across his face, rolling just beneath his pale flesh. "I've had enough of your demands."

Tate shuddered, horrified by the shifting beneath his features. His evil was like a plague, slowly eating away at anything he touched.

Whichever way she turned, whatever choice she made, the people she cared about were in jeopardy. She could refuse to go, and he would hurt her or, more likely, someone she loved.

But what horrors awaited her in the Farworld? A land with creatures and peril she was completely unprepared for?

And her sisters? Would they be forced into the unknown along with her?

Tate fought against the tears that threatened, tears of fury and fear. She was so tired of being at this bastard's mercy.

She turned her head and met Emuirdane's empty eyes. "Don't hurt anyone. I'll go to the Farworld."

"Oh, I know you will." Emuirdane thrust her away so that she stumbled and fell. Then he raised his hand and motioned with a quick flick of his fingers.

His soldiers dragged Jack closer to the pond.

Tate saw what was coming, and her stomach twisted. "Don't!"

The men ignored her plea and drove Jack forward, teetering him above the pit.

Above the entrance to the Farworld.

Then they shoved him over the edge.

A scream lodged in Tate's throat as she watched him disappear, then a burst of pale light erupted from the basin.

"Jack!" Scrambling to her feet, she lurched toward the crater, the eerie blue water still parted like curtains. She didn't pause. She didn't consider her actions.

She jumped in after him.

9

At first, Jack had felt himself falling, arms thrown out to catch himself, prepared to strike against the bottom of the pit. But instead of the cavern floor, a blur of dark shapes rushed up to meet him. He waved his arms wildly as the distance below seemed to stretch on endlessly.

And then—he was upright. He was walking into those many colors, his footsteps crunching on a path of white flagstones covered in a layer of frost.

Disorientation rushed his head, so he shook himself and closed his eyes, willing all the things he felt and saw to make sense. He was no longer underground but beneath a wide sky, the deep blue holding a tint of purple. A huge bright moon hovered, outlined by a lustrous silver ring.

The garden around him rustled gently, even when the wind died down. Everything in the vicinity seemed *off* somehow. Not quite normal.

Neatly trimmed hedges formed walls on both sides, their glossy green leaves shaped like stars. He moved closer to touch them, mesmerized by the fat berries he believed to be red, as he had only the moonlight to see by.

But he jerked his hand when a sharp point pricked his finger.

The leaf had moved. He bent his head forward to study the pentagonal leaves, telling himself he was seeing things, that he was hallucinating. To test his theory, he reached out again, carefully.

And when he drew near, the leaf folded in on itself, thrusting its five tiny tips toward him like swords.

Jack stumbled away from the hedge but avoided backing into the one on the opposite side of the path.

He rubbed his eyes. Was he dreaming? Had the blow to his head knocked him out, allowing his subconscious to run free and unchecked?

No, he decided, lifting his hand. Because he'd never known a dream this vivid, where the cold tightened his skin and reddened the tips of his fingers.

Uneasiness surged inside as he studied his surroundings. A light snow fell from the purple-blue sky, a large portion blocked out by the structure towering over the area. He was looking up at a castle. A *real* castle.

He had to repeat that to himself several times before it sank in, as there was no castle near Bar Harbor.

He turned full circle then, and froze when he faced a massive shadow—though blacker than any shadow he'd ever seen—writhing and rolling like liquid.

As he stared, enthralled, Tate walked out of the inky shape. Her frightened eyes settled on him instantly. "Jack!"

She ran to him and he opened his arms. She slipped into his embrace so easily, so smoothly, in a move they had perfected. Once upon a time.

Her body melded with his for a split-second before she leaned back, assessing him for injuries as he did the same for her. With a gentle touch, she cupped his face, searching for the source of blood on his temple.

"Just a shallow cut," he said when her fingers came away red and she gasped. "Head wounds bleed more, even superficial ones."

The breath she released sounded as if it had been pent up tight. "Are you sure?"

Then her eyes met his, held, and something sparked between

them. He couldn't tear his gaze from hers, even as the ground dropped from beneath him again, as he began to fall.

In a way that could be much more treacherous.

Tate's big brown eyes had always done this to him, and he knew he should step back, solidify his barriers. Because he couldn't afford to let her in again, not like he had before.

Tate was the one who withdrew first, dropping her hands to his arms and allowing space to come between them. "I'm so sorry, Jack. You should never have been involved in this."

He took his hands from her waist, though the need to defend her burned in his gut when he remembered the cave and the black-haired man who'd wrenched her arm. "Who were those men, Tate?" His fingers curled into fists. "Did they hurt you?"

"No, no. I'm fine." She eased away, catching his hand and turning her head back to the pulsing black mass. "But we have to get you back."

"Back." He shook his head. "Back from where, exactly?"

A screech shot through the cold air, resonating high above their heads. They both paused to look up, and another jolt hit Jack like a Taser to his chest.

The creature's wingspan stretched wide, far too large to resemble any animal he'd ever seen. Or even heard of, for that matter.

Before he could move or draw a breath, the beast tucked those awful, pointed wings against its sleek body and dove. Its shriek pierced the sky again as it skimmed downward, eventually disappearing behind a distant stand of monstrous trees.

Screw barriers, Jack told himself, and gripped Tate's hand tighter. "What is this place?"

"Nowhere we want to be," she said, tugging him toward the billowing darkness she'd just stepped out of. The one he must have come through as well.

Then she stopped and crouched.

He did the same. Though what could be worse than the winged

beast that had just soared past? "What's the matter?"

"I thought I saw movement on the ramparts." Her terminology reminded him of her historical expertise. The castle was too far for anyone on the high walls to hear them, but he and Tate likely stood out against the white stone and dusting of snow.

Jack scanned the area. They needed to take cover, move closer to the dark walls of shrubbery. But those fierce plants held a threat of their own.

A faint sound, like water sizzling in a pan, carried to him as Sami appeared. The black substance expulsed her, like liquid that wasn't wet. Fiona was mere seconds behind her.

Jack and Tate stood to greet them, and Fiona rushed to him. "You're bleeding," she said.

He gave her a reassuring smile. "I'm fine, really. Just got sucker-punched by . . . well, something that wasn't a fist."

Again the dark shadow rippled, and Tate's uncle emerged.

"Brit. Why are *you* here?" Tate started forward but stopped to jerk her head toward Jack. "Never mind," she said. "We have to send him back."

Brit held up his hands as if to block her. "I don't know how this thing works, Tate." He tossed a frown to the inky blob, its rounded edges undulating, not holding any particular shape. "I don't think we should risk sending him through alone."

As if the strange mass understood their words, the darkness began to shrink in upon itself.

"Wait." Tate let go of Jack's hand and threw herself forward, arms outstretched.

But the form condensed quickly to a small shimmering ball before vanishing altogether with a *pop!*

Tate slid on the frosted stones, skating through nothing but empty air. "No," she rasped, her breath a puff of mist in the freezing weather. She spun back to her uncle. "What about Mom and Granddad?"

"Don't worry, Tate. They're fine," Fiona assured her.

A wave of shock rolled from the top of Jack's head all the way down to his feet. *Did Tate just say "Mom"?* He stepped forward. "Your mother?"

Tate's voice was low, her eyes apologetic. "It's a long story."

I'll bet it is. Jack raked both hands through his hair, wincing when he scraped the open cut. He'd known Tate since childhood, and for all those years he'd believed her mother dead. Had that been a lie? But for what possible purpose?

No. Tate had believed it as well. He was sure of it. He'd been there. He'd seen the grief dogging her every step, and the pain that had caused her to burst into tears at the most unexpected times.

She couldn't have faked such sorrow, and he wouldn't accuse her of that. No matter what else she'd done, he'd never doubt the heartache she'd suffered.

So what was going here? How could her mother be alive?

The blows just seemed to keep coming, and Jack's mind suddenly blanked out. He struggled to absorb it all, trying to understand what any of it meant.

He could feel the tension in the group. The others practically shook with an unspoken urgency, and it was this sense of peril that pulled him back to their quick, low-voiced discussion.

"Emuirdane and his men disappeared as soon as you went through the portal," Fiona said.

Jack didn't know which part to focus on. The fact that Tate's mother was truly alive or the word still echoing in his head. Portal. Had Fiona just said . . . *portal?*

"Nadia is staying back to be with Granddad. I didn't give her a choice." Brit moved in closer. "She was ready to jump in after you, but considering what she's already been through . . ." He lifted a shoulder. "Well, I made a decision."

Tate nodded to him. "Thank you for that."

"Yeah," Sami said. "Mom's already spent too much time trapped in a place she didn't belong." She lifted her face to the looming castle. "Now, apparently, it's our turn."

Tate curled the fingers of one hand and put them to her mouth. Her eyes took on an empty glaze as she stared at nothing in particular.

Jack knew that look—damn it, he still knew her so well—and the distant expression meant her brilliant wheels were spinning.

Finally, she removed her hand and spoke. "We can't go back now, but we already know we won't be stuck in this world forever. Emuirdane said he couldn't come here, and that he expects us to bring him the Ceffyl. So it stands to reason that we must go back to give it to him."

Jack shook his head. "Are you talking about the man you were arguing with in the cave? What is a ceffyl, and why does he want it?"

"I'm sorry, Jack. I promise to explain everything. Soon." She took his hand again, and the gesture turned him inside out.

But he'd heard her promises before.

Dropping her hand, he pressed his mouth into a firm line and put some distance between himself and Tate. He needed to focus on the information he *had* been given and try to process how any of this could possibly be real.

Anything that had to do with his and Tate's unsettled past would wait.

For now.

Tate's eyes flashed with an unrecognizable emotion before she turned away from Jack to face Brit. "Did Emuirdane ever say where we were going? What this place is?"

"No." Brit looked past them to the castle beyond. "And since we don't know if this Farworld is friendly or not, we need to find shelter before we do anything else."

Jack wasn't even going to ask what a Farworld was.

"Shelter sounds good." Sami stomped her feet. "Or I might

freeze to death before we ever start this quest."

"Quest," Jack uttered beneath his breath, deciding to accept whatever they said. Any attempt to apply logic only made his head throb.

Wordlessly, he fell in behind Sami as Brit led them between the hedgerows that turned the stone path into a corridor. At the end they came to a circular area lined with benches of a glittery material, like alabaster but far more pure.

A single tree stood in the very center, its wood as white as the benches but its branches adorned with silver leaves. Thick boughs fluttered in the wind, the shinier bottoms of the leaves tossing back moonlight like mirrors.

High walls of shrubs encircled the area here as well, broken up by the occasional opening. Jack studied the doorways, one far across from where they stood and two on each side, facing each other.

He rotated, observing every detail with an artist's eye. The layout, front to back, side to side, was symmetrical. "This isn't a garden," he said, his stomach dropping. "We're in the center of a labyrinth."

Sami made a growling noise. "Of course we are." She wrapped her arms around her midsection.

"I told you to wear a coat," Fiona said, draping her arms around her sister.

"I prepared for a winter day in Bar Harbor. I never expected to be *this* cold."

"Brit, we have to get out of here." Tate chin-notched to the outer hedge. "It may take a while, but if we keep a hand on the wall as we walk, we should eventually get to the end."

"Don't touch that wall," Jack said when she moved. "Trust me on this."

They all went to the hedge and Jack demonstrated, the tiny leaves reaching for his palm with their sharp needles.

"Okay." Tate raised her brows. "Then I'll hover a hand."

"I'll do it," Brit said. "I have gloves in my pocket."

Tate trailed behind her uncle, then Jack, Sami, and Fiona. Silence descended as they edged around corners and down long aisles until they ended up in another circular area.

This time, there were several trees of white and silver, bordering a small pond that was mysteriously unfrozen in the otherwise frigid landscape. On the far side of open area, a sparkling white pavilion stood out against the green hedges.

"That has to be the way out." Tate had eased back to stand with Jack at some point during the walk.

"I'll go through and scout," Brit told them. "All of you can at least get out of the snow. Just keep hidden."

Jack caught the other man's eye. "I'll go with you."

"No." Sami edged closer to Brit. "You're hurt, Jack. Besides, if something happens, I can always use my—"

"You go with Brit, Sami," Tate said pointedly, breaking in and cutting her sister off. She slid her eyes to Jack. "We need to talk."

Jack didn't know what great secret Sami had been about to reveal, but he was more than ready to dispense with the subterfuge. She'd promised answers, and this may be the only opportunity they would get.

He took her by the elbow and led her to the pavilion. "I think that's a good idea."

As they got closer, he could see a courtyard through the white pillars, one that butted up against a castle wall. A huge set of double doors were there, but they were closed and looked too large to be opened without alerting the inhabitants within

A pathway went in both directions, trailing along the outside of the building, so Sami and Brit decided to split up to search for any place they could take refuge from the elements. Preferably without being discovered.

Fiona quietly retreated to the other end of the pavilion to keep watch, her distance affording Jack and Tate some privacy.

But he kept his voice down when he folded his arms and stared at the woman who'd broken his heart. And still had an overpowering effect on him. "You said you would explain, and now may the best chance we're going to get. What is going on, Tate?"

She tucked her hair behind her ears. "I don't know where to begin."

"Then I'll help," he said. "Does any of this have to do with the complications you mentioned last night? The things you couldn't tell me?"

"Yes."

He furrowed his brow and waited for her to go on.

"My family has a history." She licked her lips. "One I never knew about."

His doubt must have shown on his face, because she touched his bent elbow. "Jack, I swear. My sisters and I only found out about," she flung out her arms, "all of this, a couple of weeks ago, on Fiona's birthday."

"And your mother being alive?"

"A few days later." She pursed her lips. "Jack, this may be hard for you to accept."

After everything he'd witnessed in the past half-hour, he couldn't help but scoff. "Try me."

"I'm a witch." She looked at him, eyes solemn. "I have magick, and so does my family. All of them. But only my sisters and I were ever supposed to come here, to this place."

She didn't wait for his reaction but hurried on to tell of him of even more incredible things.

And in the pavilion's shadow, in the bitter cold, he listened.

He watched her face grow animated as she spoke of goddesses and golden messengers, her mother's rescue and jeweled horses.

Of blood-drenched hounds and evil faeries.

The last part finally broke his composure. "Wait a minute. You're telling me the guy I saw back there was a, how did you put it, a Fae? An eye . . . How did you say it?"

"An Iele. Like the Celtic Fae but more closely associated with Romania."

"And you're here to find the horse statue."

"Essentially, yes."

For the space of several heartbeats he studied her. He saw the truth in her beautiful, if fearful, eyes and was relieved that she was, at last, being honest with him.

But there was still one question he needed her to answer. "What does any of this have to do with why you left me?"

And there it was, finally out in the open.

Tate drew up, going very still as her lips parted. Then, "I was scared, Jack. So scared. And I didn't understand why. I just knew I had to get away from home, because that's where the pain came from."

Jack gathered his courage. He girded his pride. "But I told you I would go with you. I told you I would follow you anywhere."

"I know. I'm sorry." Her bottom lip trembled, her eyes watered.

Jack cursed softly. He didn't know whether he should hold her against him or walk away. He knew what he wanted to do, but that would be unwise.

So he compromised, and took a single step back.

"Did you tell me the truth back then, Tate? When you said you loved me? Or was everything just a lie?"

"No. No, it wasn't a lie. But—"

"Tate," he pressed, refusing to be shut out again. Every time she got nervous she shut him down.

"Wait," she said whipping her head to the side. Then she whispered, "Sami," and darted toward Fiona, but her sister was already rushing to meet her.

"She's being chased," Fiona cried, her voice bouncing off the white stone structure.

"I know," Tate said. "I heard her."

Jack caught up to them both. "I didn't hear anything."

"But we did," Fiona said. "And Sami's in trouble." She raised her hand, and her palm was glowing white.

"Um." Jack ignored whatever was happening there and put his hand on Tate's shoulder. "I'll go. You two hide."

"Jack, no," Tate said. "You don't know what's out there."

"Neither do you."

"And Brit," Fiona cut in. "He may be in trouble too, but we can't hear him."

"Fine." Tate blew out a breath of frustration. "Jack, can you go find Brit?"

"Of course? But what are you planning, Tate?"

Now both of her hands lit up with same white glow as Fiona's. "I'm going to get my sister."

Her expression grew hard and determined in a way that was entirely new to Jack. She'd always been resolute whenever she'd made up her mind about something, but this was more than simple willpower, more than tenacity. A core of strength she'd discovered sometime over the past seven years.

Maybe it was magick?

Whatever the cause, Jack found it insanely attractive.

Damn it.

But he didn't have time to wonder over the change in Tate or the way she still pulled at him. "Be careful. I'll get Brit and we'll meet you back here. We'll lose whoever's chasing Sami in the maze if we have to." With that, he shot down the path to search for Brit.

But he didn't make it as far as the first corner before the other man appeared, sprinting in Jack's direction.

Brit's eyes said everything. He was also being pursued.

Whoever Tate had spotted on those ramparts must have seen her too. And they'd sent out a welcoming party.

Jack half-turned, waiting, and when Brit got closer, he was

panting. "Two guards. Coming fast."

Jack saw the men rounding the corner then, but they were far away. He and Brit had a good lead. "Catch your breath. Sami needs us." He caught the other man's sharp gaze and indicated the castle. "They've known we were here all along."

He glanced back to the guards, alarmed to see how far they'd advanced.

"I told you they were fast," Brit gasped, turning to face the assault. He lifted both of his hands, taking up a stance that told Jack they wouldn't be running away.

The guards skidded to a halt, still at least fifty yards away, and now Jack noticed they carried no weapons.

But then one of the men raised his arm before slashing it sideways through the air. The gesture seemed rather elegant for such an intimidating figure.

"Do you smell that?" Brit asked. "It smells like—"

"Cedar," Jack finished, just as an invisible force slammed into him.

10

A loud clanging sound rattled through Tate's aching head, like chunks of metal in a huge tin can. She awoke and jerked her head, taking inventory of her surroundings.

The first thing she noticed was the bitter cold, as if she'd been sleeping inside a walk-in freezer. The second was the presence of two strange men, glaring at her through a wall of vertical bars.

Not men, she told herself, memories flooding her muddled mind. Not men, but faeries. The distinction made evident by their willowy height and pointed ears. They were unlocking a large metal door, the clanking of keys the noise that had awakened her.

Tate bolted up straight and felt a sharp pull on her hand in the effort. A heavy manacle was clamped tightly around her wrist, a short chain leading from her cuff to another.

She looked up to find that she was shackled to Jack, who sat blinking his eyes groggily, like a person who'd been drugged.

In a sense, he had been. Drugged by magick.

Just like Tate and Fiona, who'd been discovered just outside the labyrinth and assaulted by an invisible spell.

Shaking the heaviness from her head, she studied her environment more closely. Black stone formed the walls, ceiling, and floor, as well as rough-hewn benches positioned all around.

The foreign material was beneath her now, permeating her bones with its arctic chill. Wall-mounted torches burning with bright blue flames cast the dank space in an eerie light.

Darkness and cold. Chains and metal bars. This wasn't just a cell.

Tate cringed. They'd been thrown into a dungeon.

The door burst open then and crashed against the bars. "Wake up," one of the faerie-men barked, his long white hair trailing over his shoulders, stark against the silver armor he wore. Despite his angelic beauty, his eyes were filled with animosity, as hard and dark as two chunks of coal.

The three appeared similar, not simply for the armor they all wore. But also the identical expressions of hate on their faces.

Movement drew Tate's eyes to a bench across the room. Fiona was there, her wrists bound together by a thin wire. While her eyes were wide, Brit and Sami were slumped beside her, cuffed to each other and apparently still knocked out.

Fiona turned and shook Brit's shoulder, trying to rouse him and Sami. But before she succeeded, a second guard, still tall but more husky than White-Hair, rushed over to jerk Brit to his feet.

He came fully awake when the guard's fist plowed into his gut.

"Don't!" Fiona cried, leaping up to defend their uncle. The burly guard shoved her into the wall, her head cracking against the ebony blocks.

Sami was alert now, eyes blinking and swinging wildly around the cell. She tried to raise her hands, but her right arm jerked against the cuff linking her to Brit.

On instinct, and desperate to defend her family, Tate stood, her free hand flashing to her hip. But, of course, her dagger was gone. The iron weapon was poisonous to the Fae. And the very reason they'd brought the blades was the same reason they'd been confiscated.

Next, she tried to call her fire, but the metal around her wrist snapped back, shocking her with a current of what felt like electrified ice. The cuffs had been charmed . . . or, she realized, glancing at the shining threads of silver running throughout the metal, specifically created to subdue magick.

Probably a smart safety measure in a world filled with magickal beings.

She couldn't fight back and, with Jack chained to her side, any move on her part would endanger him anyway. So all she could do was plead for mercy. "Please, stop!" she cried, trying to stave off any more punches. Or at least draw the thug's attention to her instead.

Especially since the brutish guard's fist was poised in the air. He was ready to drive a punch into Sami's face just as he had Brit's stomach.

White-Hair barked a strange word, the tone sharp and quick as if issuing an order. The other guard sneered in response, dropping his hand to his side. But like a bully who'd been thwarted, he gave an unnecessary show of force by jerking on the chain linking Sami's and Brit's manacles.

They both stumbled, and the guard growled at them before shoving Fiona toward the open door. The white-haired leader stepped aside to let them pass and signaled with his hand for Tate and Jack to follow.

A tremor crawled through Tate, but she had no choice but to go where directed. She sent a sidelong glance to Jack, but his expression was shuttered, his eyes forward.

If she didn't know him so well, she wouldn't have noticed the vein pulsing in his temple. But she recognized the sign and the repressed fury it represented.

Tate felt it wise to do the same as Jack, she tamped down on her emotions, doing her best to hide the anxiety that wanted to break loose and take over.

But she would hold on to it. She wouldn't give their captors anything to work with.

At least, more than they already had. Which was everything— she and her family in chains, and a bonus they might not even realize they possessed. Jack. One more person who could be used to coerce Tate into doing whatever they wanted.

So she edged forward and out the door, keeping a tight hold on her own volatile emotions.

Jack's fingers brushed against hers then, the covert touch hidden by the heavy chain and set of cuffs. Was the small gesture meant to caution her? To steady her?

What was going through his mind? Was he scared, confused? Was his pulse thrumming through his veins and into his ears like hers?

Whatever his intent, the fleeting caress managed to wash her with the sense of calm she needed, helping clear the blur of panic from her mind. So she could think.

Because with all other defenses out of play, strategizing was the only protection she had left.

Or was it?

She darted her eyes back as the brute and White-Hair fell in behind her and Jack. Then she focused on Sami and Fiona, both up ahead and trailing the third guard.

She and her sisters could do more than thrust blades and start fires, and they still had one ability at their disposal.

Sami. Fiona. Tate called to them telepathically. *Just do what they say for now. We have to cooperate until we know who we're dealing with and what they intend to do with us.*

Fiona sent back her agreement right away, but Sami took a moment longer. Then finally, *Okay. We cooperate. But if they try to hurt one of us again, I'll be frying someone's pointed ears off.*

It's useless, Sami. The handcuffs block our powers. Tate didn't convey her final thought. That they were defenseless.

Though the three guards were dressed similarly to those from the labyrinth, they also wore leather baldrics that stretched from one shoulder down to the opposite hip. And each held a short but vicious-looking sword.

Trying to divert Sami's temper, she continued the silent

conversation with her sisters. *We have to figure out where we are first. That's the only way we'll know who's taken us captive.*

You mean, who we've invaded? Sami asked. *We were caught in someone's labyrinth, don't forget.*

Tate considered this as they walked down a dimly-lit corridor, illuminated by another of the blue torches. When they came to a set of slick, grimy stairs carved from the same black stone, she paused to make sure of her footing. The huge guard was happy to give her a push.

Tate clenched her jaw but started up, realizing the notion of fried ears held some merit.

She assumed they were being taken to someone in authority, someone who would listen to reason. Maybe she could explain their accidental leap into the labyrinth, use ignorance as a defense, or a last-ditch plea for mercy.

Though for all she knew, they were already being marched to the gallows.

She steered her mind back to the relative safety of logic and calculation and reached out to her sisters again. *We know we aren't in Emuirdane's realm, since he said he couldn't come here himself.*

I've been thinking about the Ceffyl, Fiona sent back. *Both the heolig and the message it gave you were of Welsh origins. Since they are the things that brought us here, we should focus on the Celtic possibilities.*

Tate agreed and would have responded, but they'd reached the top of the stairs. The single guard in front threw open a door. Light blasted into her eyes, and the temperature grew instantly warmer.

Shielding her face with her free hand against the sudden glare, she walked forward into a grand hall. The opulence was worthy of any royal palace, and while the walls were made of the same dark stone as the dungeons, prominent veins of white and silver sparkled throughout the mineral, giving it a lighter hue.

Myriad paintings lined the hallway—landscapes, still-lifes, and portraits, each housed in ornate frames. The décor definitely lent itself to silver and white tones, and lavish sconces lit the way with more of the peculiar blue fire.

Tate didn't want the guard touching her again, so she kept a clipped pace until their group made their way to a set of double doors. At least fifteen feet wide and twice as high, the sheen of silver panels arched to a point at the top.

Two sparkling white statues stood on either side of the doors, feline in essence with maws opened wide. The beasts looked fierce, eyes narrowed in a silent snarl and sharp fangs bared.

Though she dared not touch, Tate examined the animal figures more closely. The sculptures were ice, but showed no sign of melting.

Yet the glacial cold from the basement had lifted from her skin. Some sort of spell? One allowing all who entered the castle to feel comfortable in spite of the cold?

Tate sniffed but smelled only thin, pure air, clean like a winter morning. To test her theory, she huffed out a breath, and the exhaled warmth immediately condensed in the frigid environment.

She cut a look to Jack, still shackled at her side. His jacket was gone, so she rubbed her finger over his exposed forearm and sent him a silent query.

He gave her a quick shrug, seemingly as mystified as she was.

Fiona's voice sounded in her head. *Ice. Silver. Snow. I think I know where we are.*

Me too, Sami answered. *This fits all the faerie tales about the Tuatha de Danann.*

The Sidhe, Tate agreed, wishing she could take Jack's hand in hers as they waited for whatever was about to happen next.

Most legends agreed on one thing—that the Sidhe, the Celtic Fae royalty, reigned over their world in two separate yet equally dominant monarchies. These two empires were also known by other names, such as Seelie and Unseelie or, respectively, as the Summer Court . . . and the Winter Court.

Tate studied a tapestry depicting several Fae with their spiked ears and lithe frames. They wore elaborate robes and stood in an extraordinary garden, where, despite the snowy landscape, white trees with silver leaves bore vibrant red and purple fruit.

The décor was just one more indication that they had indeed entered the Unseelie kingdom. And though the interior was stunning in its beauty, she curled her fingers inward, trying to squelch the magick flaring in response to her fear.

The cuffs she wore zapped her and took care of the problem.

Though her fear persisted.

The Winter Fae were often depicted as evil, versus Summer's good. The consuming darkness that balanced bright Seelie light.

She swallowed against a mouth gone dry, and sent up a silent plea that those tales had been greatly exaggerated.

Then the massive doors opened with a low groan, and no amount of praying could force her lungs to work or her fists to relax.

The chamber before them was vast, with high arched ceilings and towering white columns running along either side. The floors were some sort of white marble, with silver streaks glittering throughout.

Another shove from behind told Tate she'd stopped too long to gawk, so she resumed her trek toward the unfriendly assembly. Countless Fae filled the immense chamber, most in rich, extravagant attire.

Standing apart from the crowd, twelve people waited at the base of a dais. They stood perfectly still, their bodies aligned to create diagonal lines that angled in toward the central platform.

Every one of them watched as Tate and the others were escorted in. Their beautiful and inhuman faces wore expressions ranging from interest and speculation, to concern and unmistakable wrath.

Tate avoided those angry stares, looking instead to the dais, atop which sat a huge frosted throne, and behind it, a pure white tree. A gentle cascade of snow fell from an oval skylight high above, flakes touching down on the ivory leaves like brief, cold kisses.

Then she noticed a female beneath the tree, her back to the gathering. Raven hair fell straight as a razor down her back over a flowing mantle of dove gray.

The regal woman turned, regarding the prisoners with disdain. Without a sound, she glided across the dais and sat upon the icy throne. Her lips were crimson against fair, ethereal skin, and her eyes flashed a pale purple, as cool and enchanting as a January dawn.

They settled on Tate, and panic skittered down her spine. Because the woman regarding them with aloofness held their lives in her cold, white hands. She held the most power of them all.

With a certainty as sharp and bright as the woman's sparkling crown, Tate knew where they were.

And that they were facing the Winter Queen.

"I'm intrigued." The queen's words fell from her berry-red lips like frozen drops. Crisp and precise, they seemed to shatter against the stone pillars. "Five mortals," she settled back into her throne, "in my gardens."

Tate and Jack were now lined up next to Brit, Fiona, and Sami, all in direct sight of the queen. The three guards who'd brought them from the dungeon formed a semi-circle behind them.

A hush settled over the spacious room as the queen sat unmoving, unblinking, her strange violet eyes hard on the humans who had trespassed.

The time had come to plead their case, so Tate stepped slightly forward, her right arm at her side still linked to Jack. "Your Highness," she said, hoping that was the appropriate title.

Voices suddenly rose in the gallery, some in outrage.

The queen jerked upright and flicked a finger. Before Tate knew what was happening, a long, sharp icicle speared into the floor between her feet. Along with the queen's magick came the crisp scent of pine.

"Silence," the cold beauty hissed. Behind her, the tree's white leaves shook as if she were addressing them. As if they feared her anger.

The lethal shard of ice could have been easily directed at Tate's heart instead of the floor. The Winter Queen's version of a warning shot.

Though the spear had missed, arctic cold still pierced her chest. Pure, primal fear.

"Insult me again with unsolicited speech, and I will encase your head in a block of ice." The queen tapped her lethal finger on the armrest of her throne, but no other part of her moved. Not even an eyelid.

Until she spoke again. "You only live now because my curiosity is piqued. I simply cannot fathom the audacity it took for you," here she curled her lip and spat out, "*humans*, to enter my kingdom, my private grounds. All without invitation."

She curled her hand through the air and tilted her head. "Undoubtedly, such an act must be taken as a sign of hostility. No one who belongs here tries to slip inside under the cover of night."

Tate felt an overwhelming need to fidget, to shift her feet, but she was afraid to move. This imperious Fae woman intimidated her in ways Emuirdane never had.

And surely he'd known this could happen. He must be aware of the dangers they would face here. That their coming to this particular Farworld was tantamount to a death sentence.

But then, his life wasn't the one on trial, was it? He must have known their chances were almost none. Yet he'd still forced her and her sisters through the portal.

He'd sent them straight to an unforgiving and all-powerful monarch.

Tate eased closer to Jack, sick to her depths that he was part of this. That Emuirdane had also sent an innocent man to his doom.

A man, she was coming to realize, she cared more about than she'd ever allowed herself to believe.

The queen's unsettling eyes assessed Jack, as if Tate's attention to him had drawn the Fae ruler's as well. Tate held her breath, but the woman's eerie gaze moved on to Brit and her sisters.

Then the queen released a sigh, as if she found them all tedious and beneath her notice. "You." She stabbed a finger at Tate. "Tell me why you dared to enter my labyrinth."

Drawing forth every bit of courage she could muster yet maintaining a subservient mien, Tate said, "We did not intend to be there."

The members of the court tittered, and a few even gasped. Tate would have looked to them in question, but the violent guard stepped forward, drawing his sword with a scraping sound before pressing it to Tate's throat. "You will address the queen with proper respect."

Tate froze, the keen, frigid blade slicing her skin just enough to sting. She sensed Jack's body tensing beside her, heard Fiona's small cry.

Sami's frightened voice whispered in her head. *Tate?*

It's okay. It's okay. Don't do anything, Sami.

From somewhere at her back, the white-haired guard cleared his throat and offered, "Her Majesty must always be referred to as such. Or any equally deferential title."

With a gulp and a gentle nod, to avoid a deeper cut, Tate said, "My apologies, Your Majesty. I meant no offense."

Lips pursed, the queen shook her head. "Foolish mortals." She fluttered her hand at the brute of a guard, and he stepped back, taking his sword with him.

"Now," the queen snapped, "tell me what you mean. If you did not intend to invade my labyrinth," her eyes narrowed, "then why were you there?"

Tread carefully, Tate warned herself. How much could she reveal about why they'd come without enraging the queen even further? Did she know of Emuirdane and the Jeweled Ceffyl?

And even if they meant nothing to the queen, was leniency even a possibility? Could they be pardoned and set free?

Careful, Fiona whispered in her mind, as if she too worried any attempt to save them might finish them instead.

"Your Majesty, we were sent here against our will," Tate said, purposely holding back Emuirdane's name.

Now the queen seemed truly intrigued. "Sent?" She leaned forward, both hands gripping the frost-covered throne. "By whom?"

Tate possessed no particular gifts in the art of deception, and if she tried to lie and was exposed, the arrogant Fae would be insulted and even more furious. "An Iele sent us, Your Majesty." Tate's voice quivered at the admission, but she rushed on. "He holds our grandfather's life in his hands."

That was true. "And," she continued, hoping for at least a small bit of understanding, "he physically forced my friend through the portal, so we would follow."

Above pale purple eyes, onyx brows collided in confusion. "Portal?"

An older Fae man had been hidden in the shadows, but now he hurried to the queen's side. "A *dryys*, your Majesty."

"Ah, of course." She waved again, in that careless way she had. "So few humans come here in such a manner."

Tate wanted to ask what other means there were to travel between worlds, but she stayed mute. And respectful, she hoped. They weren't free yet, even if the queen seemed less intent on punishing them.

"But why would an Iele do this? It is a senseless, pointless act."

Hedging, Tate spoke slowly. "My sisters and I—"

"Sisters?" The queen's back went rigid. Her eyes flashed from Tate to Sami and then Fiona, scrutinizing. "Three sisters?"

Again the court members and crowd began to mumble and whisper, but this time the muted voices made Tate's skin prickle. What did they know? Why the extreme reaction?

And why was the queen studying them all so shrewdly now?

"Pray tell, my dear girl," the queen's violet eyes glowed, "by which name do you address," she breathed deeply and leaned forward, "your mother?"

Tate's tongue tripped over itself. She was afraid to speak but even more terrified to deny the queen an answer. "My mother's name," she focused on the queen, steeled herself, and whispered, "is Nadia Whiteburn."

At this, the monarch leapt to her feet, both hands clasped to her chest. "The sisters three!" The queen made the declaration, waving her arm to encompass the congregation. "The Daughters of Nadia at last have arrived!"

Cheers and laughter rose up to silver rafters high above, and Tate stepped back, closer to her family and Jack.

Crimson lips spread with a jubilant smile, the Winter Queen met her eyes and laughed. "Well, why didn't you say so?"

11

A sharp order from the queen, and the manacles were quickly—but gently—removed from all of their wrists. Then they were whisked away, out a side door, and upstairs to a corridor as wide and ornate as the one they'd followed to the throne room.

Instead of the surly guards, though, they were now led by the queen herself, who'd introduced herself as Faidhia and offered a sparkling new personality to go with her new name.

Tate's head was spinning from the mercurial shift of her status, from a doomed prisoner to exalted guest. And the surprises, it seemed, just kept coming.

She was even more stunned when the queen patted her shoulder and opened a door to a dining room fit for . . . well, royalty. The table was long enough to seat at least forty, with several sparkling chandeliers above, casting off dazzling points of light. Crystal or ice, Tate couldn't be sure, but they surely rivaled the best of Buckingham Palace.

The chairs were a rich peacock blue, and a thick carpet spanned the length of the room, at least sixty feet. The design was mostly white with touches of indigo and, despite all of the other miracles and feats she'd witnessed thus far, Tate could only wonder one thing. How did they keep it so clean?

Servants bustled in and out, arranging an unbelievable luncheon before them. She didn't recognize most of the dishes, but felt comfortable identifying rolls, some type of berries, and three birds that resembled turkeys cooked to a golden gleam.

The queen spread her arms like a game show hostess. "Please, sit and enjoy. I'm sure you're all famished, and it will go a long way to soothe my regret over your imprisonment and," she cast an evil eye to the three guards in the hall, "your *indelicate* treatment."

Tate felt it wise not to mention the icicle-pedicure she'd almost received, looking instead to her sisters and uncle. She received only a shrug from Sami and doubtful looks from Brit and Fiona. They appeared to be as much at a loss for how to proceed as she was.

Then she turned to Jack, and his eyes were calm, giving no hint of whatever emotion might be rumbling beneath.

Without breaking the casual façade, he inclined his head the slightest bit, and Tate took it for the invitation it was. She followed him to the long line of windows and looked out.

Her chest clutched. But not because of the stunning panoramic view. "How did we ever make it out?" She leaned so close her breath fogged the glass.

Outside stretched the queen's labyrinth, aisles upon twisted aisles of the hedge-lined paths they'd navigated the night before. She could see the two silver trees in the center of the maze shining even brighter in the daylight, surrounded by a multitude of perfectly-manicured rows, all dusted in fine white.

"Persistence," Jack said. "That's how we got out. Quick minds and strong wills." He smirked and glanced back to where the queen was pointing out delicacies to Tate's family. "I think we have plenty of those in this room."

"Shhh," Tate whispered but smiled. "Let me get used to the idea of keeping my head on my shoulders before you insult the queen and make her change her mind again."

She laughed lightly, but had to put her hand to her temple when she got dizzy. The enormity of their situation swamped her. She was standing in a faerie castle making jokes about imminent death, a reality that had come far too close for her own peace of mind.

And, she thought, taking in his too-handsome grin, she was doing all of it with Jack.

Her mood plummeted. She caught his gaze and held it. "I'll get you out of here. I promise."

His jaw tightened. "How about we *all* get out?"

She gave a little bob of her head, overcome with the need to apologize, again, for dragging him into this supernatural disaster. But Sami called her name.

With a slight grin for Jack, Tate rounded the end of the table to stand with her sister.

Sami looked excited and wary all at once. "The queen has gone to so much trouble."

"Please, call me Faidhia," the queen insisted.

But can we eat this? Sami asked in Tate's head.

Ah. So that's why her sister was so stymied. Sami was always hungry, but it seemed she was remembering some of the stories they'd read about Fae food.

"Your Majesty." Tate addressed the queen, hoping the use of her title would soften the next words and their probable offensiveness. "This banquet looks wonderful, and you are so very generous. However, we've been warned that mortals shouldn't consume Fae food or they would never be able to eat in their own world again. That human food would then turn to ash in their mouths."

"Thereby trapping them in Faerie," Fiona added, "the only place they could survive."

Faidhia tsked, her lips pursed into a tight red ball. "No, no. You are perfectly safe. Be my guests." She gestured to the table.

When they all turned to stare at the feast but still didn't move, the queen said, "In your stories, have you not also read that we, the Fae, are incapable of telling a falsehood?"

"Yes," Tate replied. One of the legends she'd banked on being true.

The queen nodded, but then her brows lifted. "Oh, but I see.

You did say you've been dealing with an Iele." Her lovely features settled into a look of pure repugnance. "I'm afraid *they*," scorn dripped from the word, "do not have such restrictions and are able to lie outright." More tsking. "Such a disgrace to our kind."

How can we be sure? Fiona communicated to Tate and Sami, all the while giving the queen her sweetest smile. *A liar can proclaim to be honest. How did that old story go? The one with the two talking doors?*

I don't remember, Sami replied, *but we don't know if we'll be going home anytime soon, and if we don't eat, we'll starve.*

The cautionary tales about Fae food were in other books, not the Grimoire, Fiona communicated.

And the Grimoire said unequivocally that Fae could not lie. Sami she dipped her head to the queen, playing the part of diplomat. "Thank you, Your Majesty."

She moved to the table and pulled out a chair, still silently communicating with Tate and Fiona. *I'm going to put my faith in our family's legacy. Mom and Grandmother gave us the information we would need if we ever had to deal with faeries. They wrote it in the Grimoire, because they were sure. I'm going trust in that. In them.*

Sami sat in one of the velvety chairs, her bottom barely touching down before a servant with silver hair and a girlish face began piling something green onto Sami's plate.

Deciding they might as well all take the same plunge, Tate sat and was assisted just as quickly.

She pondered everything Faidhia claimed while she filled her belly with the succulent bird meat, yeasty rolls in the shape of flowers, a salad—of sorts—and finally white cake topped with silver berries. She couldn't resist the peculiar dessert, and was rewarded when the taste of kiwi, yet sweeter and lighter, exploded in her mouth.

Perhaps it was true, and the Fae could not lie. But they were master manipulators, so she would be wise to pay attention to every word that fell from the queen's berry-hued lips.

After all, they were well known for their ability to glamour unsuspecting individuals, to create entire realities for a weaker, more human mind. And wasn't that a type of deceit?

Once they'd eaten their fill, the queen, having sat with them to enjoy a small slice of cake and a deep blue substance that smelled like chicory, announced it was time for the Daughters of Nadia to meet the oracle.

"Oracle?" Brit asked, wiping his mouth. He'd tried the "coffee," so his ivory napkin came away with a bit of a blue stain.

"Why yes." Faidhia steepled her fingers and leaned back in her chair. "She is the only one who possesses knowledge of the *dychymyg*."

"The what now?" Sami asked, a bright red tart halfway to her mouth.

"*Dychymyg*." The queen snapped her fingers, looking upward, as if searching her mind. "What is the name in your language? A . . . a puzzle. Words that form a puzzle?"

"A crossword?" Fiona asked.

Sami snorted in response. "Yes, Fee. The great unsolvable oracle crossword."

"At least I'm trying to help." Fiona gave Sami a smile that would have sliced the cake on her plate. Then she sent out, *Why don't you do us all a favor and stuff that tart in your mouth?*

Faidhia watched them with eyes wide and lips turned up in amusement. "You must someday tell me of these crossed words. But what I meant to say is words that are spoken to create a puzzle for the listener."

"A riddle," Jack said, and all eyes turned to him.

"Precisely." Faidhia beamed. "That is the word the oracle used. She is sworn to reveal the riddle only to the Daughters of Nadia."

"You haven't heard it?" Tate asked. "But you've been expecting us."

"Oh, for many years now. But I've been allowed only the knowledge of your impending arrival and the role you were to play. The rest, I'm afraid, is solely for you."

The queen rose with fluid grace. "Now, let us go. I will guide you to the oracle's lair."

Lair, Fiona thought. *That sounds pleasant.*

"And the males," Faidhia continued, "are welcome to amuse themselves in the armory."

"Where will you take them?" Tate asked, stopping at the doors as they were pulled open by two footmen.

Faidhia waved her fingers to Brit and Jack. "I assure you, your men will be safe. And remember," she lifted a brow, "I cannot speak an untruth."

Tate was still uncertain of how much she could truly trust the queen. But so far, she didn't notice any ill-effects from lunch and hadn't sensed anything unusual about the food.

Besides that, the queen was under no obligation to treat them so graciously. Not long ago, she'd been about to judge them—harshly. Tate could think of no other reason for her kindness, except that their arrival had indeed been predicted.

For once, being the famous Daughters of Nadia was an advantage.

"While you are in the armory," Faidhia said to the men, "you should decide which weapons you will take with you on your journey." Then she spoke to Tate, Sami, and Fiona. "Your own blades are there as well, though I'm afraid they won't be thawed until the morn."

The queen grew serious. "And I would have your word that you will not use your blades against any of my Winter Fae. Iron." She shuddered. "Ghastly substance."

Tate carefully arranged her response in her mind, replying before anyone else could. "We will swear not to use our weapons against any of the Winter Fae . . . *unless* we are put in a position to defend ourselves against them."

For the first time since having learned she was dealing with the sisters three, the queen seemed displeased. But she nodded. "Well enough."

The others agreed to the oath, and they left the luxurious dining room.

"Your Majesty," Fiona said, "you mentioned a journey?"

"Yes, though I do not know how far or to where you will travel. I can only tell you that the Jeweled Ceffyl is not within my realm." Faidhia tapped a finger to her chin. "You must travel for a full day before winter will begin to fade, but I own properties beyond my borders, residences to make voyages more comfortable."

She linked her arm with Fiona's. "I will open all of them to you, of course."

Still hooked to Fee, she led them around several turns, and still more passages, until Tate questioned how large the castle could possibly be. Finally they went down wide, carpeted steps that brought them to a single white door.

There they stopped.

"Enter here the oracle's lair." The queen turned and gently grasped Tate's fingers with her own. "Daughters of Nadia, I must depart. But please know you are welcome here and safe. Never question that."

Her violet eyes softened. "And I look so forward to entrusting the Jeweled Ceffyl to hands that will yield it more wisely than . . . others have previously."

Before Tate could respond, Faidhia shifted her attention to Brit and Jack. "Oimen will take you to the armory," she said, gesturing to a servant who appeared beside her like smoke.

Regal posture resumed and all playful smiles vanished, the queen inclined her head to the group. "I'm sure I will enjoy the pleasure of your company at the evening meal." With a whirl of her soft gray mantle, she swept down the lavish hallway. Two guards fell in to follow her at a discreet and unobtrusive distance.

"This way, Sirs," the servant, Oimen, said to Brit and Jack.

But first, Jack moved to Tate. He glowered at the door that would soon swallow her and her sisters. "You be careful down there." His visage was heavy with what looked like concern.

Then he stepped back, as if he felt he was too close to her. And—if it were possible—his brow furrowed even more. "We have a conversation to finish."

"All right," she said quietly, unwilling to share the details with anyone else. Sami, especially.

Glancing over, he winked at Sami and Fiona, then left to catch up with Brit and the speed-walking Oimen.

Before he got too far, Tate called to him, "Jack. Be sure to choose a weapon for yourself."

He looked back over his shoulder. "I don't have to choose." His eyes gleamed. "Don't you know?"

A sly smiled spread over Tate's lips, and a warm spot tingled just behind her sternum. Yes, she did know. Because she knew Jack.

And the man was hell with an axe in his hands.

12

The door opened to reveal a white stairwell spiraling downward, the entire shaft glittering top to bottom.

While Tate and Sami stood gawking, Fiona braved the first step, running her hand over the sparkling material. "Beautiful," she whispered. "Like diamonds frozen in ice."

"It's pretty," Sami agreed. "And yet still creepy." She cast a glance over to Tate. "Makes me feel like we're climbing down into an iceberg."

Tate was inclined to agree and rubbed her arms until her shivers subsided. The prickles over her skin weren't due to cold, but from the thought of being entombed in ice.

She couldn't help wondering what sort of oracle awaited them at the bottom. And why this place was called her lair.

Descending into a frozen chamber beneath a castle was not something that appealed to Tate, yet here she was. Then again, she'd grown accustomed to having little to no control over her actions, or her life.

But she would do what had to be done to keep herself, her family, and Jack safe from harm. To keep them all alive.

The goal was simple. Locate the Ceffyl, get out of Faerie, and appease Emuirdane by giving him his prize.

And if she hoped to succeed at any of those tasks, her first step—an extremely cold and slippery one at that—was making her way down these steps, so she could listen to a riddle. From a

Fae oracle. In a frigid underground lair.

Tate blew out a breath. How she missed the days when the most terrifying thing in her life was a deadline.

"It's changing," Fiona called from a few steps below and around a bend.

"Then wait on us." Tate didn't want them to get separated down here, especially since there was no light in the shaft, save the lone blue torch at the entrance up top.

Rounding the curve to catch up, she saw what Fiona meant. The pure white of the walls was being overtaken by swirls of indigo, like blue ink stirred through milk. The pattern actually reminded Tate of the dining room carpet, lovely and whimsical.

Until they descended even farther, and the impenetrable blue surrounded them, absorbing what little light filtered down from the single torch so high above.

A few more steps, and they were in the dark.

"I can't see anything," Tate said. "Can either of you?"

"No," Sami said, just before she shuffled in the shadows and— "Ow!" A moment of soft curses, then, "Well, that way's a dead end."

"Oh, what are we doing?" Fiona's voice sounded embarrassed. She laughed and released a witchlight into the air.

"Good idea." In the soft illumination, Tate shared a sheepish look with Sami. "Glad *one* of us is thinking."

"I still don't reach for my magick as quickly as I should." Fiona's lips were pressed into a tight line. "Even for simple things like seeing in the dark. I have to do better."

"We all do, Fee," Tate said. "I've used witchlight but, obviously, I still forget about it. We haven't had our powers that long, and Mom told us it would take time before it became second nature."

"I know. But we're in Faerie, and we need it to be second nature *now*."

"One thing at a time, Fee." Sami was sucking on her knuckle

and glaring at the plain wooden door she'd run into. "All this ice, and I get a splinter."

"Who's out there?" a melodic voice called from the other side. The voice was light and airy, certainly not the sound of the wizened old crone Tate had been expecting.

Fiona tucked her arms to her chest and made a we've-been-busted face.

Sami shrugged. "No more stalling. We might as well see what this is about."

The voice rang out again. "Come in, sisters. I hear you." She gave a cackle that was more in line with the hag in Tate's imagination.

With a deep inhale, as if accepting a duty that frightened her, Fiona pushed the door open. She eased inside with Tate and Sami close on her heels.

Together they entered a large, round room—the floor, walls, and ceiling all of the same dark indigo, and still imbued with the diamond-like chips. They sparkled fiercely against the midnight blue, and Tate felt as if she'd stepped into the nighttime sky.

All around, shelves had been carved into the walls, each filled with a menagerie of books, candles, and brightly-hued bottles. Here, at last, every color of the rainbow existed. Even poppy-pink and sunflower-yellow, warmer tones that Tate hadn't spotted anywhere else in the castle.

Because they were the colors of summer.

After a quick perusal of the room, she turned her gaze to the woman who stood at a circular fire-pit in the center of the room. She held a long stick, stirring a cauldron that seemed to be overflowing with bright green storm clouds.

They even threw off the occasional lightning bolt.

With her back to them, the oracle resembled the queen, of similar height with straight black hair falling to her waist. Then she released her stirring stick and turned around.

Tate's body clenched. Sami whistled. And Fiona stifled a gasp.

Barely.

But the oracle only grinned. "Shocking, isn't it?" She leaned forward. "And I don't mean what's brewing in my pot." Another cackle echoed off the frozen walls, the sound incongruous with her youthful face.

A heart-shaped face that should have been beautiful—with high cheekbones, candy-pink lips, and a small, straight nose. Even the winged arch of her brows would have been enviable.

If not for the two gaping holes beneath.

"I'm sorry," Fiona said.

"For the loss of my eyes? Or for your reaction?"

Fiona wrung her hands. "Um . . . both."

"Don't waste your sympathy on me, girl." The oracle pointed a long fingernail, as dark as her sockets. "No one took my eyes. No one, that is, but me."

"You did that to yourself?" Sami asked.

"I did." Shoulders back, the oracle stood proudly. "The loss of one sight improves another. Only the most dedicated of my kind are willing to make the sacrifice."

Tate was split between amazement and repulsion. The woman had carved out her own eyes to improve her vision. Her *psychic* vision.

Putting a hand to her stomach where it pitched, she addressed the oracle. "The queen directed us to come here. She said you have a riddle for us."

"I do, indeed." She curled two fingers, a signal for them to move closer. "But first, gather around the pit. You should know the story of what it is you seek."

Despite her hollowed-out eyes and dark lair, the oracle didn't give off a menacing vibe. In fact, she seemed quite pleased Tate and her sisters had come.

Tate eased closer, as did Sammy and Fiona, encircling the pit at equal distances as the Fae woman directed. Soon they stood at four points, like cardinal directions on a compass.

The oracle waved her hand over the cauldron and the contents flared brighter. Their faces were shadowed, cast in green light from the churning storm inside the pot.

The oracle pointed one gruesome fingernail toward the sparkling ceiling. "You have come to learn of the Jeweled Ceffyl, a mystical artifact created long ago." She let the words fade away and cocked her head. "But I am sensing you already know this part of the story."

"Yes. Our grandfather told us." Sami gave a skeptical look to the swirling cauldron. When electricity crackled from it again, she pulled an elastic band from her pocket and used it to tie back her long, auburn curls, as if afraid a stray spark would set them afire.

Unperturbed, the oracle nodded. "Then I will move ahead through the years." She cleared her throat and resumed her story in a low, throaty voice. "It began with the child who'd been granted a wish from the gods themselves. And for many years thereafter, the child's family maintained possession of the Ceffyl, passing it down—along with its good fortune—through the generations."

A question burned in Tate's mind. "How did the Ceffyl end up here, in your world?"

"Lust. How ever does anything terrible occur?" The oracle maintained a bland expression for a long, quiet moment. But then she burst out in the cackle that, oddly enough, was beginning to grow on Tate.

"I jest," the oracle said. "No. Not really."

Sami and Fiona looked at each other and grinned. An eyeless beauty who laughed like a shrew and was inclined toward stand-up comedy.

But her expression fell into staid lines when she resumed her tale. "The Ceffyl was stolen from your mortal world and brought to Faerie ten years after the turn of your human millennium." She pointed at them one by one. "Not the one you've seen. The one before."

"The year one thousand and ten?" Tate asked, leaning forward, eager to hear more.

A nod from the oracle. "A foolish Shellycoat crossed into the mortal lands, intent only on seducing a lovely young woman with whom he had become enamored. But once inside her family home, he spied the Jeweled Ceffyl, and his Fae eyes could see it for the magical object it was."

"So he took it," Sami guessed.

"He did. He brought it here, to his homeland. He had his wish and became a wealthy Fae." The oracle's eyebrows lifted, stretching the empty sockets upward. "But the Shellycoat wasn't only a greedy trickster. He was also vainglorious, telling all who would listen his fantastic tale of how he'd become wealthy overnight."

Now Tate added her own conclusion. "And someone else used the Ceffyl."

"And another and another until the Ceffyl's gifts were abused by many." The Oracle lifted her arms in a dramatic fashion. "A Summer Court king wished for a bigger army and almost decimated the Winter Fae. A century later, the Ceffyl changed hands, and a horrid plague was set upon the Summer Court, a return of the deadly favor."

Disgust rose inside Tate, and something more. Something like . . . trepidation. She hadn't considered such horrible misuse of the Ceffyl and couldn't understand anyone wasting the precious gift on murder or revenge. Not simply murder, but attempted genocide.

She and her family had wondered why Emuirdane, an Iele of such power and status, would desire the Ceffyl. Now a slew of possibilities unfolded before Tate. None of them good.

And certainly none she wanted to be responsible for.

The oracle continued, her voice pulling Tate from her morbid speculations. "Too many years of devastation passed before a council was convened, created with members of both Seelie and

Unseelie courts. They decided the Jeweled Ceffyl was too hazardous in any of their hands, and they called upon the mortal world for an army of sworn protectors. Ferocious warriors, they are, human in form, yet blessed with magick."

The oracle hissed a breath in through her teeth. "They are known as the Legion, and you must beware. For wherever you find the Ceffyl, they will also be."

"So, wait." Sami moved her hand in a circle in front of her, the universal motion for "back up a minute." "This Legion. They still protect the Ceffyl?"

"Of course. As I said, they are sworn."

Fiona's emerald eyes blinked rapidly. "Do they know we're here? That we're coming?"

The oracle tilted her head to the side. "You would fare better if they do not. However, they are aware of the prophecy, just as all who live in Faerie are aware."

Again, she drew up with pride. "My very grandmother served the Winter King so long past, and she was the one who foretold of your coming. Three hundred human years ago."

Tate did some quick calculations. "I'm sorry, but I have to ask. How old are you?"

The oracle winked, or . . . something like that, and Tate tried not to cringe.

"The women of my family have faithfully served the Winter Court," the eyeless woman said. "Our sight is keen, and for my loyalty, *I* was gifted with the riddle."

Oh, yes. The riddle. The reason they'd come to find the oracle in the first place. Tate had almost forgotten, too absorbed with the notion of the Legion, the ferocious army of warriors she and her sisters would have to battle their way through to get to the Ceffyl.

As if reading her thoughts, the oracle smiled and put her hands palm to palm in a gesture of calm. "Be at ease, Daughters of Nadia, for the fates have chosen you for a reason. You hold within yourselves all that is needed to succeed. And never question, never fear, for your cause is worthy."

Her head drifted slightly, as if she were seeing something far away. "And remember," she whispered, "not all things secure are at peace."

"What does that mean?" Sami asked, apparently as confused by the cryptic words as Tate was.

"And now, for the riddle." The oracle raised her hands again, blatantly ignoring Sami's question. "Close your eyes and listen well."

Fiona jumped as if she'd been startled. "Do we have to memorize it? Can we write it down?"

"Listen well," the Oracle said.

Do as she says and close your eyes, Tate sent to her sisters, quickly shutting her own. Maybe this message would stay in their minds like the one from the heolig had for her. Preferably without the painful, pounding brightness.

The oracle's voice was full and smooth, and the scent of wintergreen flowed along with the tingling magick Tate sensed. Sami's sharp intake of breath and Fiona's hum of pleasure told her they felt it too.

And as the oracle spoke, the words appeared in Tate's mind. She watched them script to life, like a fiery gold pen writing on a black canvas.

Look toward the setting sun
Far to Mount Aeylwon
Dare its warren dark and deep
Survive and find a boon to keep

As serpents strike the sisters three
And flame is upon the flesh
Prism and light lead to the fight

For one's greatest wish

As soon as the last line was complete, the golden verses fizzled away like fireworks falling across the sky. But Tate knew the riddle was safe, locked inside her for whenever she needed it.

When Tate opened her eyes, she found the oracle beaming, her face lit up and tears on her cheeks. "Thank you." Though she could not physically see, she seemed to hold Fiona's gaze, then Sami's, and finally Tate's. "I have been waiting for this moment."

She sighed. "Though I fear my honor, yet my burden, now belongs to you."

Tate didn't ask her to explain, for she could sense the importance of the task she and her sisters had been assigned. She could feel the weight.

The oracle wiped her cheeks and seemed to perk up, as if she, in contrast, truly felt lighter. "You'll find a map, created by me and magickally sealed so that only the Daughters of Nadia may reveal its contents. I'm certain the ink is dry by now." Again, she cackled. "Since I drew it eighty-seven years ago."

With that, she clapped her hands together and beelined straight to a small wooden chest on one of the carved-in-ice shelves. She opened the strongbox, for it had a lock, and pulled out a scroll.

She held it out to Fiona, who was nearest, then snatched it back. "The men who came with you through the *dryys*. Do you trust them?"

"Yes," Sami and Fiona answered as Tate nodded. She was thinking of Brit, the uncle who'd helped raise her and her sisters. Her faith in him was unshakable.

And Jack? That answer came just as swiftly.

Yes. She trusted him. With her life.

As soon as she acknowledged her faith in him, guilt crushed down on her like a rockslide. Because Jack probably couldn't say the same of her.

"Good," the Oracle said, snapping Tate back to the present conversation. "Share this map with no one but those closest to you. Nor the riddle."

Fiona bobbed her head.

"Now," the oracle opened her arms, "share an embrace with me to commemorate the day."

Surprisingly, Tate was happy to hug the peculiar woman, and she slid into her arms with Fiona and Sami. Though they'd never met, or even heard of, this Fae woman before today, the connection they shared was almost palpable.

And very emotional.

She'd waited a long time for them to arrive and, Tate believed in her heart, wished only the best for the Daughters of Nadia.

She sniffled when they all broke apart. "Be safe. Watch the skies." She folded her hands across her stomach. "Now I can say no more."

"Thank you . . ." Tate trailed off, because she did not know her name.

"Rhosyn," the blind yet sighted woman replied with a small smile, and turned away from them again, moving to the cauldron.

Only at that moment did Tate realize the cauldron no longer crackled with the green clouds. Rhosyn lifted the large black pot and carried it to a grate in the floor where she poured out a thick, gelatinous substance.

She continued with her work, cleaning the cauldron as if Tate and her sisters had already gone.

And so they did, slipping silently out the wooden door, closing it with a small *snick*.

Tate couldn't say why she suddenly felt melancholy, but her sisters seemed to share the sentiment. The three of them climbed the winding stairs back up to the blue torch that marked the exit from the oracle's lair.

A female servant was waiting outside in the corridor. "My

ladies." She tipped her head at them. "My name is Laen, and I am to show you to your guest quarters or anyplace within the castle you might wish to visit."

"The armory," Tate blurted. The need to see Jack and to finish her long-overdue explanation—her apology—throbbed desperately within. Like a wound that had been stitched shut, yet still contained infection.

She'd been right before. He didn't have any reason to put his faith in her. But now, with the foreboding riddle—containing words like survive, and serpents, and fight—it was imperative that he did.

So she needed to start repairing that gap. The chasm of her own making.

"As you wish." Laen pivoted with a quick turn and started off in the direction Jack and Brit had followed Oimen earlier. But unlike the stoic manservant, this Fae woman was vibrant and talkative.

"I understand you'll only be with us for a night, but you should be sure to visit the guest showers and the baths." Laen glanced back. "Though I am of Winter and would never use the warmer facilities myself, they are truly something to behold."

"I could stand a long, hot bath," Fiona said, stretching her arms out in front of her and craning her neck.

"I'm for the showers," Sami said, untying her hair again.

They followed the servant down the hall and around to what seemed to be the opposite side of the castle. But the place was huge, and Tate didn't have her bearings.

"It's just a short walk on the outside, but you'll be protected by the cloister."

Sami leaned over to Tate. "What's a cloister?"

Tate chuckled. "A covered walkway," she said, knowing that hardly described what they were about to experience.

When Laen pushed through one side of another set of huge doors, Sami's and Fiona's *oohs* and *ahhs* confirmed it. The cloister was indeed a walkway, but one with smooth tiles lining the path, enclosed by the exterior castle wall on one side and pillars on the other. The pillars provided support for the arched covering above and allowed a view of the courtyard as they passed.

Laen led them through the cloister with Sami and Fiona right behind her, Tate falling back a few steps to enjoy the gardens gracing this particular courtyard. A fountain sprayed high in the center, shooting up from the mouth of a creature that looked like a cross between a fish and an eel. Shrubbery with glossy green leaves and holly-like berries enclosed the perimeter, and short evergreen trees stood in curving lines, creating borders for the white-graveled paths.

But the flowers—blossoms in full bloom as snow trickled down—they were what caused Tate to slow down and take a deep breath of floral-scented yet crisp, clean air. Red and white seemed to be the theme, displayed in a variety of blooms.

She paused, moving to stand between two pillars that opened to the courtyard. She let the pristine snow and floral scent soothe her.

Female laughter floated from inside, the sound like silver wind chimes caught in a mild breeze. Curious, Tate walked several more steps, angling for a view of whomever owned such a sweet, infectious laugh.

Another two steps, and the mystery woman came into view.

Tate went still. The cold of the snowy ground seemed to seep into her body and condense around her heart, so all she could do was stare.

The Fae woman stood near a red-flowered shrub, rosy lips smiling as her laugh chimed out again. With an angel's face and silver-white hair, her beauty was incomparable. A perfect winter princess with pale, dainty hands.

Hands that were roaming all over Jack.

13

Jack ran his hand down the formal dinner jacket he wore that the steward, Oimen, had delivered to his room. A slate-gray material with a bit of a sheen, the suit was like nothing he would have ever chosen for himself.

But, judging by the many sparkly ensembles they passed in the hallway—and not just on the females—he reconsidered the unadorned fabric and decided he'd gotten off easy. At least he hadn't been bedazzled.

As he and Brit followed Oimen to the dining hall, he sent a sidelong glance to Tate's uncle. He'd fared even better in the clothing department, decked out in a suit of plain bark-brown. Though it did still have that special faerie luster.

Jack laughed out loud at his own thoughts, drawing a slow smile from Brit who asked, "What's so funny?"

"I was just thinking," Jack let the last of his chuckle fade away, "that you and I look like a couple of disco-era pimps."

Brit crinkled his mouth in distaste. "Don't remind me. Let's just hope the travel clothes they're making for us have a little more durability." He frowned down at his jacket. "And a lot less *shimmer*."

"Agreed." Earlier, Oimen had informed Jack and Brit that the castle clothier was creating an appropriate wardrobe for the two of them, as well as the three sisters. Supposedly, the styles would be more along the lines of human fashion.

He wished for a good old-fashioned tux as he tugged on his

cuffs and prepared to face a grand dining experience with the Fae aristocracy. Nobles had traveled from all over the Winter realm, thrilled with the chance to set eyes on the famed Daughters of Nadia.

Oimen stopped beside an open set of double doors and bowed. "Sirs," he said to Jack and Brit, "enjoy your evening."

The tinkle of glassware and soft rumble of conversation filtered through the doorway. Jack had a moment to wonder how tonight's feast would compare to the extravagant luncheon they'd been served earlier. That would be hard to beat.

Then he took one look inside the dining hall and had to shut his gaping mouth, realizing today had been little more than a picnic.

In the center of the hall stood another of the pure white trees, directly underneath an opening in the ceiling that allowed the snow to fall inside. The flakes cascaded gently, dusting across the lacework of ivory-hued limbs and leaves.

The table itself was a large ring that encircled the tree, covered by silver fabric and surrounded by high-backed chairs. White and silver dinnerware completed the theme and created a setting that sparkled like gemstones.

If not for the garishly-dressed attendees, the entire scene would have been without color.

Clearing his throat, Brit asked, "What do we do now?"

Jack shook his head. He couldn't fade into the white walls if he tried, and he had no interest in mingling with the strange, babbling creatures clustered in different groups around the room.

"Stand here and try not to be noticed?" he said, receiving a low laugh from Brit in response.

And wait for the girls, he added silently to himself.

More specifically—he couldn't wait to see Tate.

He hadn't laid eyes on her since he and Brit had left the three women outside the oracle's lair. So not only was he more than ready to be assured of their wellbeing, he also wanted to see Tate in the kind of dresses the Fae women were wearing.

Dazzling in all manner of winter colors, the gowns hugged their figures and made the most of each female form. Maybe it was wrong, considering the dire situation, to be thinking of Tate that way.

But honestly—Jack snagged a snifter with green liquid off a passing tray and downed it—he'd never really stopped.

She was and always had been his ideal. No woman he'd ever dated had come close to what he called the "Tate standard." Even after all she'd done. Even after she'd crushed his heart.

Tate was still the woman he pictured himself with. The one he dreamed of having and holding. Forever.

"Damn it," he said, reaching for another drink.

Brit hiked a black brow. "Do I need to try one of those?" Then he added, "Before you drink them all?"

Jack was saved from answering by a tap on his shoulder. But when he turned around, he was facing the Fae woman who'd all but accosted him today in the courtyard.

"Brigidelle," he said with a slight bow, remembering her name. And her status. She was the Winter Queen's niece and—unless the queen married and had a child—her only heir.

The gorgeous female, next in line for the throne, did little to hide her interest in Jack. "We will all be seated shortly," she said, notching her chin slightly to indicate the table. "We only await the guests of honor, and then, if you'll allow me," she nodded to Brit as well, "I'll show you to your seats."

Jack smiled and tipped his head.

"It would be an honor," Brit said. He too had met Brigidelle and knew exactly who she was.

Unfortunately, he and Jack had parted ways when the queen's niece had offered them a tour of the courtyard. Looking back, Jack wished he'd refused like Brit had, because she seemed to have read much more into his acceptance than he'd ever intended.

Jack was about to drag Brit deeper into conversation as a type of buffer between himself and Brigidelle, when a servant near the doors rang a crystal bell. Everyone in the room turned in unison, emitting gasps and murmurs of awe as they gazed upon the guests of honor.

The Daughters of Nadia.

The three sisters stood there, practically walled-in by excited onlookers. Sami was dressed in cobalt-blue while Fiona wore a deep green to match her eyes. Both were beautiful and regal in their own way.

But Jack couldn't take his eyes off of Tate.

She too wore an elaborate gown, though hers was a deep scarlet, the color of a good Cabernet. The lustrous red fabric complemented her fair skin and deep brown eyes, and her glossy black hair was pinned up in what he thought might be called a chignon.

But Jack wasn't complaining. He'd always loved Tate in a ponytail. With her hair pulled back, he could appreciate the elegant line of her neck, the grace of her shoulders, her high, sharp cheekbones. And, of course, the stubborn angle of her chin.

She caught his eye then, and Jack inclined his head.

She nodded stiffly and averted her eyes. She gave her full attention to the queen who greeted Tate and her sisters before beginning introductions.

All of these powerful, magickal, and noble beings couldn't get close enough. They clambered and competed for the attention of the three mortals.

Tate looked a bit nervous as the royals pressed closer, and Jack wanted nothing more than to go to her, to be by her side, to offer support.

To tell her she took his breath away.

But Brigidelle tugged on his arm insistently. Unwilling to offend the second most powerful person in the realm, he forced his eyes from Tate and met the icy-blue gaze of the queen's niece.

He fanned his arm outward and said, "After you."

Releasing a soft giggle, she pivoted around him to take Brit's arm as well, guiding both men toward the circular table. When they neared two Fae women who were already seated—one a silver-blonde, the other a stunning brunette—Brigidelle paused.

She motioned to the empty seat between the ladies and told Brit with a sly grin, "I believe you'll find your company this evening most entertaining."

With a What-can-I-do? glance to Jack, Brit shrugged. "Guess I can at least do my part to keep the peace." He eased into the chair, falling instantly into conversation with the two faerie beauties.

Left with no other option, Jack let Brigidelle walk him a quarter turn around the table to another two chairs. She sat in one and indicated he should join her.

Telling himself he could make it through one dinner, he plastered a smile on his face, tamped down on his need to speak with Tate, and did his best to play the part of the charming companion.

An excruciating fifteen minutes later, he almost breathed a sigh of relief when Tate and her sisters were finally seated alongside the queen. And in his line of sight. He'd been afraid she might end up opposite him and blocked by the huge white tree trunk.

Those seated nearest the sisters still demanded their notice. They bombarded them with questions, barely giving them time to eat the first course after a tidal wave of servers set plates all around the table at the exact same time.

Meanwhile, Jack was getting his own share of unwanted attention from Brigidelle. He tried to keep his expression even and his mind distracted, focusing instead on the quality meal before him.

A façade he had to maintain throughout all seven courses.

The evening was tolerable—barely—until dessert was served, and the queen's niece insisted on helping him eat the mousse-like substance from a frosted bowl.

He might have enjoyed the light taste of toffee, if he weren't being spoon-fed by his overzealous dining partner. And every time, she leaned against him, giving him an unobstructed view of her porcelain-white cleavage.

Ignoring the blatant offering, Jack looked over to see how Brit was faring. He too was being fondled, but unlike Jack, Brit didn't seem to mind his adoring audience. He was obviously enjoying himself, despite being fed like a baby, just like Jack.

Maybe it was a Fae thing.

Knowing he'd find no sympathy in that corner, Jack looked instead to Tate. He jolted to see the glare on her face. Then, after a moment of puzzlement, he followed her stare to the woman beside him.

The lovely woman who was still pressed against him, vying for his notice and simpering like a coquette.

When Tate's eyes shifted to Jack, she seemed to catch herself and pasted on a brittle smile. But her attempt to hide her true feelings failed.

To Jack, she was completely transparent.

Lifting her chin, Tate resumed conversation with the queen.

And Jack had to cough to cover his laugh.

"Are you all right?" Brigidelle asked, rubbing his back.

"I'm fine." Jack finished the faux-cough, and this time the smile he gave the queen's niece was dazzling. "I'm just fine."

There'd been no mistaking the antipathy darting from Tate's eyes straight to the pale-haired Fae beside him. And he would have kissed Brigidelle in gratitude, if he weren't sure it would spark even more arduous advances.

He did, however, owe her thanks.

For making Tate jealous.

Yes, he was being petty, but after seven years of wondering how Tate felt and if he'd ever see her again, he deserved a moment of triumph.

He happily took the last bite of dessert from Brigidelle and wiped his mouth. Then he hailed a waiter and snagged another of the green drinks, truly enjoying himself for the first time all evening.

He should have been angry with Tate. He should have been supremely pissed off that she would show any sign of resentment.

After all, wasn't she the one who'd ended it all? The one who'd severed their relationship? The one who'd left him alone, to ache and wonder what he'd done wrong?

Yes. Tate had done all of that.

But being away from her today had come with one bright advantage. Jack had had time to himself. Time to consider everything she'd told him in the pavilion last night.

And one thing had stuck with him, needling his mind throughout the day. "Home," she'd told him. That was where the pain had been.

He recalled the story of her mother being trapped underground, right beneath the Whiteburn house. So close that Tate had been able to *feel* her.

Jack glanced across the table, observing the woman she had become.

And he remembered the girl she'd been.

What kind of torture must she have endured? Never healing but always suffering, caught in a constant state of raw, fresh grief. A mourning period that never ended.

It was no wonder Tate had fled the island. And him.

Hell, it was a wonder she hadn't lost her mind.

Jack had always thought her motivations selfish. He'd credited her as being thoughtless and cruel.

But now, as he glanced around at the leering Fae and their sparkling world, her behavior came into sharp, clear focus.

Tate hadn't acted out of selfishness. But self-preservation.

Brigidelle was still chattering in his ear, content to fill him in on all the latest gossip of the Winter Court. She pointed out various aristocrats, providing names, titles, and more information than Jack really needed.

But he was content to nod and murmur, as if fascinated by every detail. Until he noticed a dark-haired Fae. A male seated several chairs down from the queen, on the opposite side from Tate.

What caught Jack's notice was the man's rapt gaze. His calculating eyes, that were locked on Tate and her sisters.

In truth, all of those gathered here tonight were intrigued, spellbound even, by the Daughters of Nadia. But there was a certain speculation in this man's demeanor that made the hairs on the back of Jack's neck stand upright in a primal warning.

Head bent slightly down, the faerie focused on Tate, his irises so pale they might have bled into the whites of his eyes, if not for the stark, black rims. He was no enchanted gawker, no fawning admirer of the three human women.

His stare was—predatory.

Jack couldn't be certain of the man's intentions, or if he was a legitimate threat.

But he intended to find out.

With perfect timing, the queen stood and thanked everyone for their attendance. She offered a few more words of praise for Tate, Sami, and Fiona, before leaving the table and effectively dismissing everyone else.

Jack took the opportunity to excuse himself. He lifted Brigidelle's hand and kissed her fingers, no longer concerned with keeping her mollified. "Thank you for your company." Then, pretending he didn't hear her speak, Jack pushed away from the table and into the swarming crowd.

He wanted to find the man he'd been watching, maybe even strike up a light conversation. Just a polite tête-à-tête. With some very pointed questions.

Supposedly, the Fae couldn't speak a lie. Well, if that was true,

Jack was about to put it to very good use.

He was edging through the talkative mob, trying to keep the dark-haired man in sight. But he growled his frustration when his quarry exited the dining room too far ahead of him.

By the time he made it to the doors himself, he saw no sign of the man in the hallway.

Jack ground his teeth and slammed the heels of his hands together. Should he pick a direction and just go? Leave his friends behind to pursue the strange man?

"Jack." He heard Sami's voice and turned to find her fidgeting with her dress, an irritated scowl on her face. Beside her, Fiona looked weary, with barely enough energy to stifle a yawn.

"We're escaping to the guest wing," Sami said. Then she added in a lower voice, "We're hoping the summer colors there will keep these Winter Fae away."

"Walk with us?" Fiona asked. "Brit's still inside, and so is Tate."

Jack glanced back into the dining hall. "Do you think we should leave them?"

"They'll be fine." Sami ran a finger down his shiny arm and grimaced. "Nice suit. Besides," she added, "we also came to rescue you."

"Me?" Jack pulled his head back, confused.

"Oh." Sami feigned surprise. "Did you *want* to wait around for the white-haired lady you had dinner with? Because when I saw her, she was headed this way."

Jack glanced down the corridor again, telling himself that Tate would be fine. The pale-eyed male was nowhere in sight, Brit was still inside with Tate, and there were plenty of guards around. Guards who were under strict orders to guard the Daughters of Nadia with their lives.

"All right," he relented. Because he did not want to get snared by Brigidelle again. Two times in one day was more than enough. "Let's go."

He comforted himself with the idea that Tate and Brit wouldn't be far behind. They were all staying in the same area of the castle and, to his knowledge, there were no rules on visiting hours.

So maybe he'd get lucky and see Tate later tonight.

And just maybe, after an entire day in Faerie, they'd finally get a chance to be alone.

Tate made her excuses to the older couple who'd cornered her in the dining hall and made her way to the exit before anyone else could intercept her. Then she dashed out into the hallway when she spotted Laen waiting.

Gasping slightly from a combination of tight corset and hurried steps, she rushed over. "Laen, I hope you're not busy."

"No, Ms. Tate." Laen gave a sweet smile. "I am at your disposal."

"Thank goodness. Can you take me back to the guest wing?" She still didn't know her way around the castle.

"I'd be happy to."

"There's no need for that, Laen."

Tate and Laen both glanced to the woman who'd spoken.

Tate stiffened her face into a mask. She might not be able to work up a smile, but she could at least avoid a scowl.

Since the woman who'd joined them was the queen's niece.

"I'll show Tate back to the guest rooms." She beamed at them and gestured, inviting Tate to walk with her.

Her amiability seemed genuine, and a stream of guilt started to trickle over Tate's conscience.

Then she recalled how the woman's hands—and other body parts—had pressed against Jack all evening.

To save face, she diverted her gaze as they eased away from the crowd. She remained silent.

"I'm so glad to have a moment with you," the woman said. "My name is Brigidelle."

"Yes," Tate said. "I understand you're the queen's niece?"

"I am." Brigidelle nodded. "I must say," she fingered the rich red lace on the shoulder of Tate's dress, "you and your sisters are all so lovely, so dark-eyed and exotic. And your uncle." She put a hand to her chest. "What a handsome man. I can certainly see the family resemblance."

"Thank you." Tate wasn't sure what else to say, and she didn't feel quite friendly enough to return the compliment. So she added, "That's very kind of you."

"Not at all. It's the pure truth. As you know—"

"You cannot tell a lie." Tate looked at her now and forced a smile, hoping her underlying annoyance didn't show.

She didn't know what to make of this gorgeous creature. And why now did she feel the urge to speak with her?

Tate was glad she and the others were leaving in the morning. For such a sprawling castle, the place was beginning to feel way too crowded.

"And your friend, Jack," Brigidelle said.

And now, Tate realized, they were getting to the heart of the matter.

The queen's niece fluttered her fingers at the base of her throat and sighed. "He is strikingly handsome."

Yes. I know. But Tate didn't say it out loud.

"And," Brigidelle continued, "he was telling me at dinner about his work in the human world. How he wields such heavy, dangerous tools to gather the dead, useless trees in your world. And then," she sighed, "uses those strong hands to transform the wood into art."

Tate often shared this exact same sentiment in regard to Jack, but something in the way this woman said it made her want to gag.

"Such a man to have both brawn and sensitivity." Brigidelle leaned close and said in a conspiratorial whisper, "They are rare in any land, no? And often make the most exquisite of lovers." Her laughter tinkled like tiny bells.

Tate kept her face forward, giving away nothing.

She happened to know from first-hand experience that Jack's lovemaking skills were, in fact, . . . *exquisite*. At least, they had been in his younger days.

But there was no way she was divulging that little tidbit.

"I must ask you, Tate." The hand she placed on Tate's arm was gentle. But the command to stop walking and face her was there nonetheless. "Do you claim Jack?"

Something in Tate's chest gave one hard *thunk*. "Excuse me?"

"Do you claim him?" The woman's blue eyes seemed to frost over. "Is he *yours*?"

A slow-building ache began to form inside Tate, right where she'd just felt the kick of her heart.

She wasn't barred from dishonesty, not like the Fae, but after all she'd done to Jack, she couldn't bring herself to lie about him now. She felt compelled to tell the truth.

And the truth was that she couldn't claim him. She'd thrown away her right to do so.

So she answered honestly, even as a tiny piece of her fractured. "No." Her nails bit into her palms. "He isn't mine."

"Oh, good!" Brigidelle gave a small clap, then she spun in a circle and motioned to the first servant she saw. "Well, I must be off," she said, before asking the servant to guide Tate back to the guest wing.

"But it was so lovely to talk to you." She took Tate's hands in hers and laughed gaily. "So very nice." Then she pranced away on light feet without giving Tate a second glance.

Part of Tate wanted to call her back and renounce her own words, the admission that had made Brigidelle so very happy.

Because as the white-haired beauty whisked away—likely in search of the man in question—Tate couldn't help feeling she'd just made a terrible mistake.

Her second terrible mistake . . . when it came to Jack.

14

Tate immersed herself in the luxurious water and tried to think of nothing other than the warm aqua-blue liquid as it caressed and soothed her bare skin. After the celebratory dinner, she and her sisters had decided to explore the bathing facilities, the ones the castle servants insisted they must try.

And she was so happy they had.

When she'd walked in with Sami and Fiona, all three of them had come to an abrupt halt, their stunned gazes taking in the splendor before them. A brilliant blue pool spanned the length of the room, its water the color of the purest turquoise, replete with a waterfall streaming down in the far end.

Ivory tiles covered the entire space, punctuated by intricate designs of gold and teal. The exotic pattern adorned both floors and walls, all the way up to the arched ceiling.

Braziers burned in corners, their low golden flames adding yet another layer of warmth. And for those who desired a little more privacy, each corner offered a covered alcove.

As she lowered herself into the liquid bliss, Tate knew the words "long, hot bath" would never conjure quite the same images again. The opaque waters concealed her required nudity—since it was technically a bath—and she was grateful for the experience.

Because more than ever, she needed to relax. Before she set out on the dangerous trek, she needed to unspool. Both her muscles and her mind.

Her conversation with the queen's niece had left her reeling, particularly the questions the woman had posed.

Do you claim Jack? Is he yours?

Innocent enough questions, Tate supposed, though they'd stabbed into her chest like tiny frozen darts.

Jack was a single man who had every right to pursue the woman—or faerie—of his choice. And misleading the queen's niece would have been underhanded, unfair, and deceitful.

But oh, how Tate had wanted to lie. Her instinct had been to clutch the truth inside herself, where it couldn't be used as a weapon against her.

Because that's exactly what it felt like. Like she'd handed Brigidelle a sharp icy spike, one that had pierced all the way to Tate's heart.

"What's going on with you?" Fiona shoved her hand through the water, sending light ripples in Tate's direction. "This whole time, Sami and I have been raving about the pool and its magickally-cleansing water, and you've been staring a hole into the wall."

Tate lifted a bare shoulder. Energy and optimism depleted, she was unable to drum up more than the slightest gesture. "I'm just tired." An easy excuse to cover myriad symptoms—confusion, frustration, depression.

Contrition.

The last one was the biggie. She regretted so much, so many mistakes, and though her body floated languidly, she felt swamped by repercussions.

During her period of seclusion, her separation from home, family, and friends, she hadn't spoken to Jack—hadn't shared so much as a single glance with him—for seven full years. And all that time, she'd thought she was being smart. That she'd been protecting herself.

But now that she'd seen him, talked to him, looked into those deep blue eyes that saw her so well, she realized—there'd been no protection. No defense. Avoiding him hadn't brought her safety at all.

Only loneliness.

And despite the time and separation, she still cared for Jack. Enough so that watching Brigidelle flirt and fawn all over him had spiked her blood pressure.

There was no denying that she'd been jealous. The emotion had invaded her system like a plague, coating her vision until the white dining hall turned red.

Tate let loose a heavy sigh. She had to let it go, because Jack's love life was no longer tied to hers.

She exhaled again, slowly, and refocused on the soothing, calming, relaxing water. She concentrated on the vivid blue and how lovely it was. And especially soft, like swimming in warm silk.

Jack looked so handsome tonight, even in that awful, shiny suit.

No! She needed to think about her gorgeous surroundings and unique experience instead. The bath was similar to the ones in Turkey, and she'd always wanted to visit those luxurious spas.

Despite the circumstances that had brought her to Faerie, she should enjoy the luxury of this environment, focus on the positive. The pool was so nice, the liquid soft but not oily, running off her skin to leave it clean, smooth, and fragrant.

I wonder where Jack is right now. Is he with Brigidelle? Are they off somewhere—

"Hey, Tate." Sami snapped her fingers.

Tate jerked her eyes to her sister, grateful for the interruption. For the disruption of the torturous images playing in her head. A flashy reel of horror-slash-porno starring Jack and the beautiful princess.

Hair piled into a messy knot of reddish-brown curls, Sami rested against the decorative tiles. "Why are you making the face that I make when I'm doing taxes?"

Tate mustered a lazy smile. She hummed in her throat as if

she were too drowsy to respond, hoping the act convinced her sisters. "Sorry. What were you saying?" She added a yawn for good measure. "I may fall asleep right here."

"Don't worry. We'll save you if you start to drown," Fiona said with a laugh. Then she added, "Although Sami's the one I'm worried about."

"For the tenth time, I am not drunk." Sami shook her head and finger-thumped the water, sending a few sprinkles in Fiona's direction. "I just got a little overwhelmed by the chaos at dinner tonight. There was too much sparkle and too much chatter. It all went straight to my head."

"Along with those little green drinks," Fiona said.

"Okay," Sami allowed with a cheeky grin. "Those too."

The mention of drinks reminded Tate of her own cocktail. The tall flute sat on the edge of the pool. The thick liquid resembled ice-blue milk but bubbled in her mouth like champagne. Glacierberry wine, Laen had called the beverage. It was light, sweet, and decadent.

And exactly what Tate needed.

Fiona rolled her head around and stretched before settling deeper into the water. "I'm just glad we finally have some time alone, just the three of us. We can catch up on girl talk. No mention of morbid riddles, fighting, or anything that has to do with whatever happens next. Just for the rest of the night, let's all pretend to be perfectly *normal*."

Sami glanced around at the lavish room and then stared down into her own cocktail, a thick black drink that looked like oil. "Normal." She sipped it and smiled. "Right."

Fiona bared her teeth but kept her smile intact. "Just give it a try."

"Okay," Sami said, tossing back the rest of her sluggish drink. "I can do girl talk." She set the glass aside and cut her eyes to Tate.

Tate flinched under the scrutiny, certain her sister was going to bring up Jack, a subject she did *not* want to discuss.

But after a thoughtful expression passed over her face, Sami turned to Fiona instead. "Did you ever hear back from the realtor about that building for rent?"

Fiona's face and shoulders slumped. "No. And I've left her two messages. She must be busy. Or maybe she's upset that I missed the last appointment." She laughed, but the sound held no mirth. "But if she decides to call anytime soon, I won't be able to answer, will I? Because I'm stuck in Faerie."

Fiona had always dreamed of opening her own sweet shop, and on the night of her birthday Sami had told her about a building for rent in town. The perfect location, perfect layout, and exactly what Fiona wanted.

But before she could act, their "normal" lives had been shattered by magick.

"You can tell the realtor an emergency took you out of town," Sami said. "Technically, that's the truth."

"It doesn't matter." Fiona dragged her hand back and forth over the top of the water. "I'm probably out of the running now. I didn't show up to meet her when—"

"Because you'd just discovered you had three days to find a supernatural key." Tate sat up, her voice firm. "It's not as if you didn't have a good reason."

"I know, but I can't explain any of that to her." Fiona cleared her throat. "It's fine, really. I was being too ambitious, dreaming too big. What do I know about running a business, anyway?"

Tate would have interjected, but Sami got there first.

"Stop that." Sami's voice was gentle but held a snap. She waggled a finger at Fiona. "You know I hate it when you talk that way."

Tate kept quiet, but she hated to see the dejection on Fiona's face. Despite her skills as a pastry chef, her self-confidence was tender and fragile, crushed as easily as the pretty fondant flowers she put on her cakes.

Fiona's delicate self-assurance was a remnant side effect from growing up without a mother. No one was really to blame, since their father had died and their mother had been taken against her will.

But the absence of parents often caused feelings of desertion in a child, a reality Tate and her sisters had each struggled with in their own way.

Tate sipped her wine and remained silent. She wouldn't judge, and she probably couldn't help, since she was clearly still her own work-in-progress.

The three of them had suffered a loss, and their personalities had developed in different ways. When it came to life's obstacles, their reactions were practically hard-wired. Fiona faltered, Sami shrugged, and Tate barreled through any problem she faced.

But when she couldn't? Well, then she just ran away.

"Ladies."

Tate opened her eyes to find Laen standing near the edge of the pool, smiling. She was such a jovial person, and Tate would miss her after they departed tomorrow.

"The kitchen has sent several trays of confections up to your rooms," Laen said.

"Confections?" Fiona perked up, instantly cheered. "I'd love to see more of what the chefs here do with their sweets." She reached for the robe she'd discarded, wrapping it around her as she rose from the water. "The decorations they come up with are so inventive."

Sami nodded. "And they taste good too. I'm in." With less modesty than Fiona had displayed, Sami hopped out of the water and then grabbed her robe.

With a chuckle, Tate shook her head. She glanced to Laen, but the Fae woman seemed unaffected by Sami's nudity.

"You coming, Tate?" Fiona asked.

In answer, Tate lifted her glass of sky-blue wine. "I think I'm good." She wasn't in the mood for dessert and could use a little more time to herself.

To mope over bad decisions and lost chances.

"Okay." Sami unbundled her hair. "We'll save you some for later."

"Thanks." Tate watched the trio exit the baths, then let her eyes drift closed again.

But after a moment of imagining Jack in another's arms, she sat up, looked down the length of the pool, and opted for a light swim.

A few easy laps worked out some tension, and then she spent time under the waterfall, enchanted by the flood of blue and stray drops that sparkled like topaz.

Several minutes more, and she returned to where she'd left her wine. She picked up the flute and swam into one of the shadowy alcoves.

An underwater shelf lined the sides of the niche, so she sat and studied the tiles, watching the gold pattern shimmer in the glow of a brazier. She wasn't ready to go back to her bedroom, where she'd likely just end up in bed, unable to fall asleep.

Because she couldn't stop thinking about Jack.

For so long, she'd shut him out of her life, blocking any feelings that might cause her pain. Now, after only one day in his company, she was already wounded.

And she doubted there would ever be enough time, or enough distance, to make her forget how much she cared.

A huge splash interrupted the constant drum of the waterfall, and Tate's entire body jolted. Her head flew up as she strained to listen. Was someone else here? Had her sisters come back?

A heaviness in the silence told her no. Her chatty siblings—with their confections and drinks—hadn't returned and splashed into the pool. But someone else had.

Tate eased over to peer around the corner. Her chest suddenly seemed to shrink in on itself, becoming too small to contain all the air in her lungs. So she breathed out with a *whoosh*.

She was definitely no longer alone, because Jack was breaststroking through the water.

And he was headed her way.

Pressing herself into the farthest corner, Tate submerged her body down to her chin and sat absolutely still. Maybe he would pass right by, so caught up in swimming he wouldn't notice he had company.

As his splashing strokes grew louder, Tate curled her arms over her bare chest. She wanted nothing more than to sink into the water and disappear.

Because part of her expected him to call out to another person. Part of her expected to hear that tinkling bell of a laugh, the one she was learning to detest.

Jack sliced through the unnaturally bright water, sailing past the alcove. He glided to a halt and touched the side, then pivoted in the water to gaze up at the ceiling. He stood with a surge, so the aqua-blue water came to just below his waist.

Not revealing, but low enough for Tate to conclude that, like her, he was completely naked.

A gasp escaped her, and she clamped her lips together.

But Jack had heard. His head whipped in her direction, surprise lighting up his face. He stared into the darker recess, as if his eyes were adjusting.

Then his mouth turned up, and the corners of his eyes crinkled with amusement. "Tate?" He cocked his head. "What are you doing in there?"

The pool water wasn't clear, so body parts beneath its surface remained concealed. But Tate still shivered inside.

Considering her current emotional upheaval, she was in no condition to have a naked heart-to-heart with Jack.

"I'm hiding," she all but whispered, and then felt ridiculous. She cleared her throat and spoke more firmly. "I didn't know who you were."

"Well, now you do. It's just me."

A sensation that was very close to relief washed through her. "Just you? You mean you're alone?"

"Yeah. Brit's in the room." He moved a few feet closer. "They brought a bunch of little cakes and tarts up and he was done for."

"Oh." She nodded and tried to smile.

But the tone of her voice or the half-hearted grin must have given something away, because he stopped advancing.

As the waves he created rolled over to buffet her shoulders, he studied her. "You weren't talking about Brit, were you?"

Tate tucked her wet hair behind her ears. She didn't reply.

Jack's laughter was unexpected, and Tate hiked a brow.

But then the deep rumble—so rich and so utterly *male*—crashed into her like the waves before. The sound hit a tripwire in her belly, releasing hundreds of pleasant flutters.

Now he did come closer. A lot closer.

Mindless of his nudity, he plowed through the pool, blue water sluicing over his chiseled torso and muscular arms, like an ancient god arisen from the sea.

The flutters in her stomach coiled together into one tight rope. The tension twisted, and ached, and *yearned*.

Jack didn't stop until he was but an arm's length away. His golden hair was dark with dampness, and his deep-ocean eyes locked on hers.

That low voice stroked into her again when he said, "Tate. I'm not interested in Brigidelle."

Mortified, she managed a nod. "Okay. It's none of my business."

"How could you ever think I would be?"

Tate made a scoffing sound and looked over to the glowing brass brazier. "Oh, I don't know. Maybe because she's amazingly gorgeous. Not to mention wealthy and royal. And," she pursed her lips, "she was glued to you at dinner tonight."

"Yes, she was." Jack crossed his arms—such powerful arms—over his chest. "But you know me better than that, don't you?"

Tate had to admit, she did. And the falsely sweet, clingy, eyelash-batting girls had never been Jack's type.

"You should know she doesn't matter." The light from the low-burning flames burnished his skin as he edged even farther into the alcove. "No other woman does."

He closed in on her, so Tate put out her arm, her hand splaying over his chest to hold him back. She licked her lips. "What are you saying?"

"I'm saying that despite my best efforts, and hers," he lowered his head, holding her in place with his stare, "I still find myself drawn to one woman in particular."

"Jack." Tate locked her elbow, suddenly terrified of letting him past her flimsy barricade.

He didn't budge, just pressed into her palm. "I shouldn't ever trust you again."

She shook her head, fully aware that she deserved the harsh words. "I understand."

"Quiet." His tone was soft but held the strength of steel. "I want you to hear me. I want you to know how badly you hurt me, Tate. How angry I've been with you."

She gulped and remained mute. What could she say? Her behavior had been inexcusable.

"God knows," he continued, "I've tried to hate you. But I could never quite get there." He wrapped his fingers around hers where they pressed against his skin. "I never came close."

Tate's heart pounded, knocking behind her ribs, thrumming through her body, pulsing inside her head.

His eyes shuttered. "I can't hate you, Tate."

Her throat seemed to be frozen, her mind a jumble. She wanted to know why but couldn't form a single word. She couldn't even nod.

Then the dam inside her crumbled, letting the words pour from her lips. "I'm sorry, Jack. I'm so sorry. I shouldn't have left the way I did, sneaking away like a coward and never calling you, not once. Never a letter of explanation."

"Or apology," he interjected.

"No, you're right. I was terrible. Selfish. And you never did anything to deserve it. I need you to know that. It was all me. All my fault." Her babbling subsided, forced by the need to drag air into her lungs.

She thought he might speak again, that he might take advantage of the silence. When he didn't, Tate knew she'd left out the important part. One crucial piece was still missing.

He still didn't know *why*.

"I was scared," she blurted.

Jack nodded, as if she'd confirmed something he already suspected.

"When we both went away to college, away from each other for the first time, I was devastated."

"Me too," he said.

"But months passed, and I got used to being alone. I embraced it. The isolation felt . . . safe."

She put her other hand on top of his, sandwiching his fingers between hers. "I was young, Jack. And I know that's no excuse, but I was confused by things I didn't understand."

"Like why you never stopped mourning your mother." Jack held his gaze steady on hers. Then he heaved a great sigh and reached out to push a stray lock of hair from her face. "And in your youthful experience, you only knew that the loss of a loved one brought never-ending pain. A hurt that just went on forever."

His knuckles brushed her cheek. "So you decided love wasn't worth the risk."

Tate's lip trembled, but she bore down on the rising emotion. "Pretty much."

Jack still got her, better than anyone else ever had. In one sentence, he'd summed up her greatest fear.

But it had taken her a lot longer to understand why she was so messed up.

"Tate." His eyes grew soft, and he kept brushing at that same piece of hair. So she leaned her face into his hand. "You've got a lot of crazy stuff going on in your life. And a lot of people to worry about."

Sadness was a shadow over his face. "I think you always have." He stared at her for another moment.

Then he eased back and let her hands drop into the water. "So I'm going to give you one less thing to worry about."

"What?" Had she said something wrong? Was he leaving?

"Everything in the past is done." He waved a hand, skimming over the water. "I think I finally understand."

"Do you mean—"

"I forgive you, Tate."

The frozen spike that had pierced her heart before now melted into a warm liquid pool. "Jack." Her lip started trembling again, and this time she couldn't stop it. "Are you sure?"

"You were right about being young, Tate. We both were." He brushed his thumb over her cheek. "No, don't cry. Your tears always undid me."

Again, he wiped her face, but instead of retracting his hand, he cupped her cheek, using his thumb to catch another tear.

Then he slid that thumb to her lips, gently stroking. "Please, don't cry."

Tate put her palm against his chest again, allowing his heat to soak into her skin. They stared at each other, energy sparking between them. Their mutual attraction was an undeniable force, contracting and tightening, pulling them closer together.

Jack clenched his jaw and went rigid, releasing a groan. He eased away from her but a hiss rushed from his mouth, as if the retreat cost him dearly.

"I shouldn't be here," he said at last.

Tate snapped to awareness, realizing he looked pained. "I know. I know. But I told you I'd get you home, and I *will*."

Again, he surprised her with laughter. "Not in Faerie, Tate." He shook his head, splashing some water in her direction. "I mean I shouldn't be in this pool. Not with you looking at me that way and nothing between us but blue water that smells like . . ." He put his palm to his face. "What does it smell like?"

A wave of comfort and bliss rolled through Tate. This felt just like old times.

"I don't know." She lifted a shoulder. "Faerie flower?"

"Sure. That'll work." With another aggrieved look, Jack sunk into the water and floated backward. "I'm going back to the room now. Maybe I'll even hunt up some of those cakes." His gaze smoldered for a moment, but then he shook his head. "The sugar will help me think straight again."

Stomach jittery, like a teenager after a first date, Tate just sighed. "Good night, then. I'll see you in the morning."

"Good night." He rolled over to swim away, the lean lines of his muscular back disappearing into the blue. He was doing an abbreviated version of the breaststroke, making sure certain body parts stayed hidden from view.

Mischief rose up in Tate, and she couldn't keep herself from calling out, "Hey, Jack."

He paused and turned to look back.

"Did you only forgive me because I'm naked?"

With one side of his mouth kicked up in a sinful grin, he dropped his eyes to where the water met her collarbones. Then he looked up at her and winked. "It didn't hurt."

15

After rising with the sun and enjoying the final meal they would have at the Winter Castle, Jack and the others followed Oimen and Laen outside to an open area Tate described as a barbican. On the front side of the castle, completely opposite of the labyrinth, they stood in front of a monstrous set of white metal gates.

Through the bars, Jack could see dense forest with a lone road winding into its depths. Falling snowflakes were bright against the darkness beyond.

The Winter Queen waited near the gates, the light gray mantle draped over her shoulders. Her niece, the lovely and persistent Brigidelle, stood at her side. Both Fae women were smiling.

"Ah, the Daughters of Nadia, preparing to set out on their quest for the Jeweled Ceffyl." The queen clasped her hands together at her chest. "You, and your friends," she indicated Jack and Brit, "have honored us with your presence." She tipped her head.

Two guards stood nearby, a chest of ice between them on the ground. The queen gestured to the box. "Your weapons are here for you, as promised. And," she made a snapping motion with her fingers that produced no sound, "the additional weapons chosen by your companions."

The two guards opened the ice chest and quickly stepped away, as if they'd released a plague. Brit's crossbow and the three daggers belonging to Tate and her sisters rested inside.

"Thank you, Your Majesty," Tate said. She eyed the open box for a moment. "We will gather them as we leave."

The queen beamed even more brightly, recognizing the gesture of good will. After all, it would be rude to wave iron blades around a group of Fae who were considered allies.

"And for Jack." Brigidelle spoke up, just as another guard walked up to hand him the axe and knife he'd chosen in the armory. Neither contained iron. Instead, they'd been fashioned out of a metal known as vellinium. Created in Faerie, the substance wasn't toxic to the creatures of this world, but deadly just the same.

He accepted the gifts, and the guard moved on to hand Brit a large knife as well.

"Thank you." Jack bowed to the queen and her niece.

"Use them to protect the sisters, the Daughters of Nadia." The queen's pale purple eyes gleamed as she looked to Tate, Sami, and Fiona again. "We have horses to help you on your way, though I'm afraid they will take you only to the the border of my lands."

The queen pulled a scroll from the folds of her cloak. "Here is a map of the realm to aid you on your journey." She handed the parchment to Tate. "Many dangerous creatures inhabit the lands of Faerie, and I'm sorry I cannot prepare you better, since I am unaware of your route."

She spread her hands. "Yet I have every faith that you will succeed. After all, the sisters three were chosen for this quest."

Brigidelle nodded to the scroll Tate held. "You will find the Winter Court properties marked on the map. Please, avail yourselves of the shelter and amenities. They are all well-stocked."

"You are always welcome here, so please return whenever you wish." The queen lifted her arm, and the huge white gates slowly opened. "I hope we meet again, after your triumph. Once the Ceffyl has been secured, I would enjoy hearing all about your adventure."

"It would be our pleasure." Tate bowed to the queen. "We appreciate all you've done for us, Your Majesty." Jack and the others bowed as well and offered their gratitude.

With a clap of her hands, the queen dismissed the onlookers, then she and Brigidelle made a swift exit, heading back into the castle. With the faeries cleared from the immediate vicinity, Tate, her sisters, and Brit all retrieved their iron weapons from the ice chest.

"I've never ridden a horse," Fiona said, biting her lip and eyeing the animals that were already packed with travel clothes and portable food and drink.

"I haven't either." Sami looked excited, in contrast to Fiona's frown.

"Don't worry," Jack assured her. "We'll go slowly."

"Not too slow." Tate studied the unrolled paper the queen had given her. "I can't be positive, because I don't know the area."

"Obviously," Sami quipped.

"But," Tate continued, unperturbed, "judging by the scale, it might take us until nightfall to reach the first house."

"Oh. I don't want to get stuck sleeping outside. Not in this place." Fiona moved to one of the horses and patted its hindquarters as if she'd decided to get to know her ride. "You heard what the queen said about dangerous creatures."

"Which way are we headed, Tate?" Brit joined her and perused the map in her hands.

"It looks like there's only one road leading away from the castle."

"And after that?" Brit pointed to the map. "Which way do we—"

"Let's talk about it when we get to the bottom." Tate rolled the map back up and shoved it in her pocket. She held her uncle's gaze for several seconds. Finally, he gave her a slow nod and went to choose a horse for himself.

The idea of camping in a faerie forest instantly cured Fiona's fear of horses, but Jack still helped her mount. Once she was settled, he saddled up on the remaining steed, in back of the convoy and next to Tate.

The road beyond the gate was wide and smooth, so Brit led them into a canter. Sami whooped and, despite her earlier concerns, Fiona laughed as the wind kicked up her short black hair.

The road felt more like a tunnel, enclosed on both sides by tall trees with deep green needles. The gentle snow continued to fall but didn't accumulate on the path ahead.

They kept up the moderate pace for what seemed like a couple of miles, but once the road began to twist and turn, they slowed their speed for caution's sake.

Now that it was easier to talk, Jack wanted to question Tate about her strange behavior before. He pointed to the pocket where she'd stored the map. "Why didn't you want to say where we were headed when Brit asked?"

She glanced over her shoulder, as if making sure no one was behind them. "I may have been a little paranoid, but the oracle warned us not to share the riddle or the map with anyone but you and Brit. *Her* map, I mean."

Tate reached into a different pocket, one on the inside of her coat. "Here's the one the oracle made for us. I guess we'll need both maps, though. This one for the specific landmarks, and the queen's for directions to her properties."

Tate gave him the second map, and Jack took in the details, noting the landmarks she'd mentioned. "Do these places have anything to do with the riddle?" he asked, another thing about which he and Brit were still uninformed.

The sisters hadn't wanted to talk about their visit with the oracle while still at the castle. Now he understood why.

"Only one, as far as I can tell. Mount Aeylwon is specifically mentioned, but the other places marked . . ." Tate trailed off, her hands clenching on the reins. "They seem to be included as warnings. As places to avoid or to be prepared for."

Jack's gut clutched. Numerous markings inked the page.

What would they find as they made their way into the foreign lands? What were these creatures they needed to watch out for?

Were they the typical claw-and-fang variety?

Or did they possess magick, like the "people" of Faerie?

He returned the map to Tate, more than willing to defer conversation about the direction they'd be taking. They remained silent for a while, but as the sun rose higher above, the sky grew brighter and the forest less menacing.

Snow still covered the curved limbs of cedar-like trees, and the lower they traveled down the mountainside, the more plentiful the white and silver trees, some dotted with bright crimson berries. Sunlight glistened on frost-covered rocks, and light, airy birdsong carried through the woods.

Jack glanced to Tate, and they shared a smile. Though still deep in Winter's realm, the serenity and beauty made the ride enjoyable.

Jack took another, more furtive glance at Tate. When she caught him staring, and smirking, she narrowed her velvety brown eyes at him. "What?" she said, the one word heavy with meaning.

He opted not to tell her that he was imagining how she'd looked in the pool last night—eyes glistening and black hair sleek from the water. Instead, he quirked his mouth and remained silent.

After another moment passed, Tate spoke. "I have to say, Jack. You have adjusted really well to all of this." She indicated the strange land they rode through. "Faeries, farworlds," she cut her eyes to him, "and magick."

Staring at the winding road ahead, he only shrugged. "Brit said the same thing, and yes, I sometimes have to stop and take a moment, because it's all just too surreal. It's hard to explain how I feel, but the closest thing is that it's like waking up one day and finding yourself in Germany."

"Germany?" Tate laughed. "The land of faerie tales?"

Jack looked around at the tall, dark wintergreens. He saw the similarities. "Maybe so." He smiled at his own comparison. "So, I wake up to find myself here, in a strange land. And on top of that, there are no flights home."

Beside him, her expression grew somber.

"But I'm not worried," he said in a rush, so she wouldn't be either. "Because I know the flights will start up again soon. I'm just not sure when."

Tate tilted her head. "Interesting perspective."

"What I'm telling you, Tate," he waited until she turned to him, "is that I know you and your sisters will get us home."

She stroked her horse's neck. "Because of our magick?"

"No." Jack's voice dropped, low and serious. "Because you promised."

The breath she drew was ragged, as if his willingness to trust her again caught her off guard. She didn't offer any other assurance. She didn't ask him if he was sure. She only nodded and kept her eyes on his.

"Now," Jack said, "about that bath last night."

With a pretty pink blush on her cheeks, she shook her head. "Oh, no. I'd rather talk about you." She gave him a cheeky grin. "Tell me what you've been doing for seven years."

And so they talked. He took her through the evolution of his artwork, and she told him about landing her dream job. They swapped tales of the adventures they'd had and admitted the dreams they still had on hold.

He told her stories of Bar Harbor and some of the people they'd known in school. And she regaled him with stories of the Boston highlife.

In a softer voice, she told him, "But I'm glad to be back home." She opened her mouth as if to say more, but then seemed to think better of it.

"When we get back," he said, "you should go by and visit my parents. They would really love to see you."

"I will." She suddenly looked sad. "I should have gone by before."

But she'd been afraid to run into him. She didn't have to say it, but Jack knew it was the reason she'd stayed away.

"Does your mom still make those gingerbread men at Christmas?" she asked. "The ones with the elaborate outfits?"

"She does." Jack chuckled. He'd gotten his artistic talent from his mother, but what she could do with icing was far beyond his scope. "She's branched off into gingerbread families."

"Now that, I would love to see." Tate shook her head. "I really have missed them." She locked eyes with Jack, her voice wistful. "I've missed you too. And these talks."

Everything inside Jack seemed to go soft. "So have I. I never thought it would be this easy, being with you again."

He watched the tiny snowflakes land on her hair. "It's almost as if . . ."

"No time has passed." She voiced his very thoughts.

If the two of them hadn't been on horseback and surrounded by her family, Jack would have crushed her to him. And made up for some of that lost time.

His lascivious imaginings must have been clear in his eyes, because Tate flushed a little deeper and dropped her bottom lip to release a long, slow breath.

Brit called Tate's name, and she and Jack turned their attention forward.

"The road splits up ahead," Brit said.

The route had been a slow wind down the mountain but had finally begun to level off. Tate and Jack eased their horses up beside the others and dismounted before she retrieved the two maps again.

This time, she told Brit about the warning from the oracle and why she'd kept quiet before. Then she, Sami, and Fiona filled both men in on the riddle.

Jack didn't like the sound of it, especially the part about the three sisters having to "survive" the warren of Mount Aeylwon. He bit down on the argument that sprang to mind, reminding himself that Tate and her sisters were prepared. That they possessed magick.

Though he'd be more at ease if he'd seen some sort of demonstration. He still had no idea what they could actually do. Besides communicate with their minds and conjure white flames in their palms.

Until he knew more, it felt good to have the axe on his back.

Tate looked back up the mountain road. "I don't have any reason to mistrust the people of the Winter Court," she said, "but the oracle must have had good reason to guard this information."

Reins in hand, Brit nodded. "From what we've been told about the Jeweled Ceffyl, there must be Fae who want to get their hands on it. And its location has been kept secret for all these years. No one has ever had the information needed to find it."

"Until us," Sami said. "That means we're walking targets."

Jack mulled over her meaning, then said, "Not yet. You won't be in danger until you've actually located the Ceffyl. But then . . ." He looked again to Tate, took a step closer.

"Then we get the hell out of Faerie." Sami punctuated the declaration with a sharp bob of her head.

"Agreed," Tate said. "Here." She handed one of the maps to Brit. "If I'm reading this right, we have to go," she pointed down the left fork in the road, "that way. It leads toward Mount Acylwon."

"And there's a house on the way." Brit trailed a finger across the paper. "Just past these ruins."

Tate glanced down at her own map, the one created by the oracle. Then she frowned. "Right. We'll have to cross Mist River."

At her words, the horses neighed in unison, and two of them reared.

"Whoa, whoa." Jack sweet-talked his own steed as it tramped its feet in agitation.

"Uh. Did that just happen?" Fiona asked. "Did the horses just react to what Tate said?"

Sami whispered, "You mean when she said Mist River?"

Again, the horses snorted and danced in place.

"Holy hell." Sami shifted her eyes to Tate and Brit. "Are you sure that's the only way we can go? Because the animals sure don't seem to like the idea."

With their eyes still fixed on the maps, Tate and Brit nodded. "It's the only way," Tate confirmed. "And Rhosyn has written some words beside the river. Wind and fire."

Jack assumed Rhosyn was the oracle. "What do you think that means?" he asked. "It's called Mist River, so why would she write wind and fire?"

The horses reacted to the name again, and he almost lost his hold on the reins.

Tate raised her eyes. They were dark with apprehension when she said, "I think we'll know soon enough."

❈❈❈

After three attempts to lead the horses, it was clear the animals would go no farther. They'd apparently understood the words "Mist River" and, if the dug-in hooves were any indication, were having none of it.

"We may as well get our stuff and hike from here." Brit opened the saddlebags on his horse and removed the packs inside. Jack and the others followed suit.

The moment they were relieved of cargo, the horses trotted off together to make their way back to the Winter Castle. Jack didn't want to think too hard about why the animals had seemed so afraid. What could make them refuse to cross the river?

"Is there a bridge?" he asked when the notion occurred to him.

"I assume so. There was one drawn on the map." Tate hiked her pack onto her shoulders and fell in beside him.

The snow along the side of the road was thinner now, creating a patchwork of white over the earth beneath. Despite the milder temperature and the mid-morning hour, the light grew dimmer the farther they traveled.

The trees were still thick, blocking out most of the sun's rays, but the dense canopy wasn't the only reason for the increasing shadows. "Tate." Jack chin-notched toward an upcoming bend in the road. "Look."

Her jaw tensed. "I guess that isn't a low cloud bank."

"No. I don't think so."

In the front of the pack, Brit slowed to let them all catch up. "We should stick closer together." He too had noticed the thick mists, gray tendrils crawling through the green and silver trees.

"We must be close to the river." Sami shook both of her hands like a swimmer preparing for a match. "And my palms are tingling."

"Mine too," Fiona said.

When Jack looked to Tate, she nodded. "I feel it too. Sometimes our magick is like an internal radar system." She focused on the swirling haze. "Someone out there has power."

"Or some*thing*," Sami said.

An eerie sense of expectancy washed through Jack. He didn't know if it was the heavy fog they'd encountered or the ominous way Sami had spoken, but his back tingled as if a thousand tiny needles had struck him from behind.

He spun around, his hand automatically reaching for the axe on his back. Eyes darting from road to trees to sky, he scanned the surrounding area.

Tate was beside him in an instant. "Did you see something?"

Jack shook his head but stayed focused on the woods. Had he heard something? Had his subconscious registered a threat? "I'm not sure."

Together they stood in silence, their breaths mere whispers as they waited. Watching. Listening.

Eventually, the panic clenched around Jack like talons began to loosen its grasp. "It felt like we were being watched. Followed."

He exhaled. Jack relaxed his muscles and slid the axe back into its scabbard. "Just jumpy, I guess."

"No." Tate lowered her hands.

And only then did Jack see the white flames she held in her palms. She snuffed them by curling her fingers.

"You're not jumpy," she said. "I've been feeling it all day, ever since we left the castle."

"Everything okay?" Brit was standing between Sami and Fiona. All three appeared ready to do battle.

"So far," Jack replied, taking Tate's hand in his and giving her a reassuring squeeze. He thought there might be some residual heat on her skin, but her hand felt normal in his.

It felt right.

"But let's keep moving," he said. Just in case they *were* being followed.

Or stalked.

In unanimous agreement, they pushed on, making their way into the gray haze. Streams of mist curled and undulated, slipping forward as if seeking warmth from the human bodies, then abruptly jerking back, just shy of contact.

When one rose up and brushed Brit's face, he tensed as if expecting an attack, but the pale fog only dissipated and floated away. Brit wiped at his cheek but seemed unharmed.

Soon, a distant roaring reached their ears, the distinctive sound of rushing water. Along one side of the road, the trees became fewer and fewer.

Jack strained to see through the mists, but he could make out the serpentine shape of a flowing river.

"I see the bridge." Fiona extended her arm to point.

So far, the mists had done little more than darken their passage and obstruct their vision, but Jack was relieved they'd finally made it to the crossing. The cumbersome haze emanated from the water, so once they made it across the bridge, every step they took would carry them farther from the mist and back into the light.

But first, they would have to cross. He slowed, looking at the bridge in dismay. The posts on either side and the sign designating the structure as "Mist River Bridge" were visible. But just a few feet beyond, the bridge itself was lost in fog.

Here, along the water, the mists were a deeper gray and more thickly meshed together, like steel wool.

"It's a barrier," Tate said beside him. "Why do I feel like the horses did?" She sent him a sidelong look of hesitation. "Skittish and like I'd rather bolt the other way?"

"Because that is not natural." Sami jabbed a finger toward the churning haze. "Even for a faerie land."

"Fire and wind. Wind and fire." Fiona chanted the words.

"Okay. You're going to have to stop that." Sami lifted a hand and turned to her sister. "You're starting to freak me out."

"Sorry," Fiona said, grabbing Sami's hand and spinning around to Tate. "What if the words weren't a warning but the way through?" She dropped Sami's hand and held out her palms. "What if wind and fire aren't sources of danger, but what we're supposed to use?"

Tate stepped forward. "We have the fire." She wrinkled her brow. "But what about the wind? We would have to call the elements."

Brit crossed his arms. "Try."

"But—" Fiona started.

"Just try." Brit looked to Jack. "They never got that far in their training." He returned his gaze to his nieces. "But the three of you came into your magick faster than anyone I've ever known. And the power comes from inside you. You don't even need the regular tools and implements of the craft."

He stepped forward, his dark eyes fastened on Tate. "You, Sami, and Fiona. You *are* the tools." He threw a hand toward the seething wall of fog. "So just try. See what you can do."

Tate drew a deep breath, nodded, and moved to stand with her sisters. The three women faced the bridge. As one, they raised their arms.

Jack felt a surge from above, and then a strange sensation prickled the back of his neck.

Something stirred in the air around him, and a primal instinct told him what it was.

Magick.

He curled his hands into fists and locked his eyes on Tate. Earlier he'd wished for a demonstration of her power.

And now, he thought, as three voices rose in unison, now he was going to get one.

16

"Hail the mighty spirit of the East, power of air and intuition." Tate let the words flow from her lips, arms raised and face to the sky. Sami and Fiona stood beside her, all three of them testing their gift of magick, the strength of joined bloodlines that was theirs by right.

"We call upon the might of wind. We summon the breath of life." The first tickle of breeze brushed Tate's face, and she smiled. The next gust lifted her hair, causing her to laugh boldly, the sound carrying an echo of both joy and gratitude.

Three voices rang out, strong and clear, issuing the final command. "Hear us now!"

The wind whipped as their power rose, and suddenly Tate's body felt light, almost weightless. The new ability she'd awoken roared from deep inside, but she maintained control and held it in check.

Another strong blast of air and the dark mists began to shift. She and her sisters had invoked the spirit and stirred the air. The resulting gales made her eyes sting and water, while stray leaves tumbled helplessly across the ground.

Behind her, she heard Brit's shout of amazement. "Look at that! Would you look at what they can do?"

Tate's pride shimmered and swelled, but she quickly tamped it down. Overconfidence could doom her before she truly grasped the reach of her magick, so she kept her focus. She held the balance.

The energy zinging through her body was stronger and faster

than any she'd ever created. What she and her sisters could do . . . was almost scary.

Now she understood why her mother had urged patience, why she'd encouraged Tate and her sisters to wait. Calling any of the four corners was no small matter, and the spirits here, even in Faerie, had swiftly answered their summons.

And they'd answered with a shout.

Beside her, Sami laughed. "What a rush!" She waved her hands to direct the breeze, forcing the gray haze to whirl and thin.

"Keep going," Tate told her. Then to Fiona, "Fee, you ready?"

"Ready?" Fiona's tone practically danced with excitement. "I can barely hold it in!"

Tate broke into a smile. "Then let it go!"

Together they shoved the ugly mass back another ten feet. Deciding to test her new skill, Tate spread her hands. The breeze obeyed, spiraling in two directions to part the fog.

Tate allowed herself a moment of pure satisfaction, then she pushed with everything she had. Sami and Fiona thrust their powers as well, sending the thick mists up into the air and away from the bridge.

Euphoria buzzed in her head, and a sense of accomplishment rippled through her body. Together, they had not only called the wind—they'd created their own personal tempest.

She watched the heavy mist rise away from the bridge, clearing the way for them to safely pass, and was staggered by the sheer immensity of her magick.

Drawing several deep breaths, she shared another moment of victory with her sisters. She turned to face Brit and Jack, and found both men wearing huge grins.

Her uncle clapped. "Now that was impressive."

"I can't believe I did it." Fiona did a small jump in place. "That we did it."

Jack was shaking his head as he crossed to Tate. He didn't say a word, but his blue eyes shone, filled with an emotion that seemed like awe. Like wonder.

As if he were seeing her clearly for the very first time.

Something in Tate's chest clutched and then released with a soft sigh. Tenderness filled her up, almost overriding her magick. Unable to tear her gaze from his, she forgot all about the fading wind.

Until Brit cleared his throat. "I hate to break up the celebration," he said, "but maybe we should cross before the mists settle again."

Tate blinked a few times and finally broke the connection between her and Jack.

She studied the dilapidated bridge. Wooden planks had faded with time but still looked sturdy enough.

Sami walked out, taking tentative steps to test their strength. She seemed to find them worthy and strode farther out. "Why did we have to clear the mist at all? I don't see any holes in the wood, so what was the risk of crossing in the fog?"

Tate followed Sami but paused to look over the railing. Beneath the structure, the rapids flashed by, but the railing prevented any chance of falling. "I don't know," she said, considering the words written on the map.

Then somewhere in the mist, a creature roared.

Jack and Brit hurried up with the packs the women had left on the ground slung over their shoulders. "Time to go," Jack said.

A surge of water struck the underside of the bridge, as if a huge shape were advancing through the depths.

No one needed further convincing. They broke into a sprint and raced over the planks, pounding steps vibrating the entire length of the bridge. Their feet hit solid ground again, but they kept running.

They didn't slow until the bridge, river, and whatever lived within the deep, were all far, *far* behind.

By the time they stopped to catch their breaths, Tate's pulse pounded and her lungs heaved, in desperate need of oxygen.

Jack caught Tate's gaze. "Whatever was back there, I have no doubt that you three could have handled it." His mouth quirked to one side with an appreciative grin.

Then he zeroed in on her with an intensity that made her knees weak. "You," he said with a shake of his head, "were *amazing*."

Despite being tired and winded from the run, Tate answered with her own beaming smile. With magick humming through her veins, she believed she and her sisters could handle anything, that they were destined to succeed.

And with Jack at her side, looking at her the way he was now, she thought maybe, just maybe, she could deserve him again.

And that possibility? That slim chance?

Made her feel . . . amazing.

Tate's contented mood had sustained her well beyond their triumph at the bridge. Unfortunately, the same could not be said of the breakfast they'd eaten that morning, so they'd followed the road until the sun reached its zenith, then taken a break to rest their feet and shovel down a quick meal.

Now, Tate estimated that a few hours had passed since they'd stolen the short reprieve for lunch. She squinted up, peering through the trees in search of the shining orb. She caught a glimmer in the distance, and despaired to see the sun much lower in the sky than she'd expected.

Without a phone or watch—neither of which would function in this world—it was difficult to keep track of time. The sun's position was the only indication of how long they'd been on the road, and how much daylight they had left.

Like Fiona, Tate didn't relish the idea of sleeping outside, especially after they'd heard the bellow from the river. The beast in the water had sounded gigantic, and she had to wonder what other monsters might be lurking in the forest.

Or what might wake up when the sun went down.

But her legs ached and her throat begged for water, and despite the dwindling day, she needed another break. "Hey, guys." She paused and slid the pack off of her shoulders. "I need to rest."

She pulled out her map and motioned to Brit. He carried the other scroll, a precaution in case either of them got wet or damaged in any way. Then at least they'd still have one map to follow. "Let's take a look and see where we are."

They'd breached the Winter realm's boundary a short time ago. The temperature change had been impossible to miss, rippling through them as if they'd stepped from a cold night and into a spring day.

The terrain had softened shortly thereafter, changing from wintergreens and snow-frosted fields to yellow grasses and verdant boughs with lush leaves.

Since she'd removed her coat, Tate now stashed her map in the pocket of her new pants, a remarkable imitation of cargos she could have bought back home. The castle's clothier had indeed been talented.

Jack sat next to her on an overturned log and drank from his water pouch. He gestured at the map. "According to this, we're in the wyldwood, territory that belongs to neither the Winter nor the Summer Court." His finger brushed over a line of ink. "I'm fairly certain that's the creek we just passed, back on the north side of the road."

Brit nodded his head and bent over, hands on knees. "Nix Creek. I'd say that's right, because there's the edge of the Winter realm."

Tate eyed the map, glanced up at the sun. "It's hard to tell through the trees, but I'm guessing we only have a couple hours of light left." She tapped the paper and a crude drawing of a destroyed building. "We have to pass through another block of forest and then these ruins before we get to the Winter Queen's house."

"I can't wait to see it, and I'm so glad her royal highness maintains properties for when she travels." Sami sat on a boulder. Her hair was pulled back in a tail, long curls shining auburn in the late-day sunlight. And, per her norm, she was eating. "I can't imagine the queen would own anything smaller than a mansion."

Tate stretched. "At this point, I'll be happy with a shower and a bed."

"At least the weather is nice." Fiona leaned against Sami, shoulder to shoulder. "In case we don't quite make it by dark." She cast a nervous look to the shadowy woods. "Though I still really hope we do."

"Aw, no worries, Fee." Sami patted Fiona's leg. "If it gets too dark, we'll just send up a few witchlights."

"You're right." Fiona looked upward and shut her eyes briefly. "I'm just being a chicken."

"No, you're not." Jack shot a killer half-smile at Tate before he stood and walked over to Sami and Fiona. "I, for one, want to be inside with the doors locked long before the moon rises."

Fiona gave him a doubtful look. "You're just trying to make me feel better."

"No, I'm not." Jack held up both hands in a gesture of innocence. "Who was the first person off that bridge?"

"Sami," Fiona dead-panned, her green eyes sliding to her sister.

Sami only nodded and kept eating her faerie trail mix.

"Okay. Who was second?"

"You were," Fiona relented. "But only because you were half dragging, half carrying Tate with you." Her gentle laughter was familiar music in the foreign land.

Jack shook his head, adding his own deep chuckle to the comforting sound.

Brit was still standing next to Tate. He lifted his chin, indicating the map. "You're right, though. The sun won't be up much longer.

If we're going to make the house in time, we'd better keep pushing on."

"I'm ready." Fiona bounded up. She turned to tug Sami with her.

"I'm coming." Sami kicked up her foot and studied the sole of her boot. "They do really good work at the castle. I wish I'd asked for two pairs of these."

Tate had to agree. Her own boots were holding up quite well and were surprisingly comfortable. And a good thing, since they would have to pick up their pace to make the safety of the house by sundown.

The marked road continued, cutting through another open field of golden grass resembling wheat. Tiny motes drifted in the air, floating on the gentle breeze and adding a layer of softness to the scene.

The road they'd followed from the castle had been flat and clear, eventually changing to a rougher path. Now even that trail terminated at the edge of a vibrant green forest.

Brit checked his map. "This should be the forest of *Gean-canach*, named after a solitary faerie known as the love-talker." He rolled up the paper and stuck it in his satchel. "I know this tale, so if you happen to see a lazy guy with a pipe in his mouth, that's him."

Sami peered into the trees. "It's pretty in there. Sort of . . . glowy."

Tate stepped up to take in the new scenery. Though they were trying to beat the clock—or in this case, the sun—she had to agree. The fading light did wondrous things to the faerie forest.

Sunbeams cut down at sharp angles, highlighting large fronds that littered the ground. The leaves had a lace-like pattern with intricate detail, and they shimmered wherever they caught the light.

More shining particles drifted in the air, as if the mystical plants had shed their spores. The effect was one of lustrous beauty, of a fantasy come true.

Finding a trail, they entered the woods in single-file. The

silence of the magickal and radiant woodland lent the place an air of reverence, so they all stepped lightly, keeping to the path and respecting the plant life.

Tate came upon a sizable yellow flower, the breadth of its bloom the size of a dinner plate, with whisper-thin petals springing slowly open and closed again.

She had to stop and watch in wonder.

The blossom seemed to be sighing, so Tate stood, enraptured, and sighed along with it.

Something touched her shoulder, but she ignored it. A hand closed over her arm and pulled her around.

"Are you feeling sick?" Jack was giving her a hard stare. He was up close to her face, then far away. Then close again. Why was he jumping all over?

"No," she replied, but the single word echoed again and again in her head. She lifted her hand and waved her fingers back and forth. The blurred digits followed themselves, creating one long wave the color of her flesh.

"Whoooo," she heard herself say. Then she yawned. "Jack, I think I'm high. How did I get high?" She tried to frown, but her mouth refused to cooperate, lifting into a happy smile instead. Laughter bubbled inside of her and trickled from her useless lips.

Abruptly, the world tilted, and she found herself staring at the yellow flower again. Only this time it was upside down and swiftly retreating from sight.

"Hurry up. We have to get out of this forest." Jack's voice from somewhere up high. Way, way, way up high.

"Damn it." Another male voice.

Tate had no idea where she was or who was talking. Or why she was bouncing like she was on the backside of a pack mule.

But since the jostling showed no signs of stopping, and she was so very tired, she let her head fall. She closed her eyes to sleep.

Cold water hit her in the face. She yelped and sat up with a start. Four faces stared down at her.

It took her a minute to recognize them as Sami and Fiona, Brit and Jack.

"What happened?" She looked around and saw the shiny woodland far behind her. They'd exited into another field of tall yellow grass, as if the strange forest they'd passed through were an island unto itself.

"Now we know why Gean-canach was so lazy." Sami held out a hand and helped Tate up.

"We do?" Tate groggily accepted a water pouch from her sister and drank deeply.

"He was enchanted by the forest," Jack said. "And so were you." He gripped her chin with a light touch. "How do you feel?"

"Better. I think." Tate had a vague recollection of feeling drunk, but the more she breathed in the clean, non-shimmery air, the better she felt. She rubbed her eyes. "Why was I the only one affected?"

"Maybe because you were practically making out with that flower." Sami clapped Tate on the shoulder, but her attempt at levity didn't hide her worry.

"I'm feeling much better now," Tate assured them. "My head's clearing." She registered the sunset and jerked her head. "Oh, no. How much time did I cost us?"

"Not much." Brit held her gaze. "Maybe fifteen minutes," he added when she gave him a disbelieving look. "But we can make it up."

"Then let's start doing that right now." Tate took her pack from him and slipped it over her shoulders.

Brit, Sami, and Fiona took the lead, but Jack stayed back with her. As they hiked, she curled and flexed her fingers. "I think that scared me more than the river monster." She swallowed, her throat rough as sandpaper. "I don't like being drugged, unable to control my own actions."

When she shivered visibly, Jack wrapped his arm around her shoulders. "You're okay now, and it could have happened to any of us."

She looked up into his kind face, leaned into the strength he so willingly offered. "You saved me, Jack."

"I hauled your ass out of there like a sack of potatoes."

"Whatever works," she said, resting her head against him for a moment. "But still, thank you." She straightened and moved away so they could walk faster. "And now we know how deceptive this place can be. Just like the Fae, using beauty to disguise tricks and traps."

As if on cue, Fiona halted in her tracks. "Oh! Do you smell that?" She lifted her nose and sniffed like a dog scenting a steak. "It's cinnamon."

"Maybe it's just your baker's imagination," Sami said.

"I'm not imagining anything." Fiona brushed past Sami and Brit and barreled ahead. "It's coming from up here."

"Fiona, wait," Tate called after her, recalling her own intoxicated stupor. She could barely smell the cinnamon herself but was wary of any strange enticements this land had to offer.

Fiona didn't stop, so Tate and the others jogged after her. But the wheat-like field grew high, and they quickly lost sight of her.

Alarm raged through Tate like wildfire. "We can't lose her."

Jack and Brit streaked ahead, and then she heard Brit yell, "Fiona, stop!"

Running now, Tate and Sami flew through the grass, the golden rushes whipping at their arms and legs. They burst from the field and into a meadow.

Brit and Jack stood with Fiona across the clearing, on the edge of another forest. There the trees towered like redwoods, but instead of rich brown bark, these were ashen gray.

"Holy . . ." Sami didn't finish the expression, but she gaped at the forest. "I could park my car in one of those trunks."

Tate eyed the enormous trees, tall and widely spaced, leaving room enough between them for giants to roam. She and Sami slowed to a trot until they caught up with the others.

"Fiona," Tate said when they drew near, "are you okay?"

"I feel fine," she turned to Tate and Sami. "I'm just really drawn to the scent. Maybe it *does* remind me of baking."

"Or maybe it's just a type of lure," Jack said, his blue eyes shifting to Tate. "We don't know what we'll find if we follow that smell."

"Are we still heading in the right direction?" Sami asked Brit.

He nodded in response and pointed. "We have to travel through the woods, and then the ruins. After that, it should be a short walk to the queen's property."

Tate gazed into the eerily quiet forest looming before them. "Let's go." According to the map, this forest stretched for miles in both directions. They had no choice but to enter.

This time, Tate and Jack went first, Fiona close behind flanked by Brit and Sami. Everyone kept a close watch on her, because she was still sniffing, eyes glazed over in a dreamy expression.

There was no evading the strong scent of cinnamon though, and the deeper they marched into the great woods, the more intense the smell. Soon, the overpowering aroma was all around.

Fiona halted and clapped her hands together. She gasped, staring at a great swatch of purplish-blue on the forest floor. "That's it."

Tate studied the large patch. Hundreds of flowers lay in a pile, their color and shape both similar to periwinkle.

"They do smell just like cinnamon," Sami said, but she didn't seem pleased.

Not like Fiona who, once again, walked straight toward the smell. Just as Brit moved to haul her back, she stopped and leaned forward. "But what are those?"

In the center of the mound, several round objects were piled together, glinting like a trove of jewels. Intrigued but still cautious, Tate edged closer.

Shining and sparkling, covered in gemstones, the oval-shaped objects sat clustered among the blooms. One was jasmine-yellow with a pattern of ruby-hued stones, while another was pure black, bedecked with what looked like emeralds and diamonds.

Their exquisite beauty reminded Tate of Fabergé eggs, the stunning color combinations totaling seven, the same number as the eggs in the—

"Wait." Tate jolted. "Is that a nest?"

Fiona either hadn't heard or didn't care to answer. She edged closer, eyes bright and eager. She reached out an arm.

"Don't touch those," a voice croaked from somewhere over their heads.

Fiona snatched her hand back as if she'd been burned.

Sami raised a palm glowing white, but she kept her flames at bay. Brit and Jack, however, both went for their weapons.

Tate didn't draw her fire either, but she hunched down as she scanned the trees. After two frenzied passes, she finally spotted a bird, perched on a limb. Calm and poised, it gazed at the five humans with mild curiosity.

And was it smiling? *Could* a bird smile?

Tate remembered the ravens from her vision, how they'd tried to intimidate her, all jabbing beaks and screeching cries. But this animal didn't seem aggressive, only interested.

"Hello?" Tate said, drawing its bright eyes. At first she thought it black, like the ravens, but when it fluffed its wings, a shimmer of aubergine rippled over its feathers.

"Hello," it returned.

Just when she thought she'd seen it all. A talking purple bird.

As if she couldn't help herself, Fiona turned her gaze on the lovely eggs again and inched closer.

"Don't. Touch. Those." The creature enunciated its warning. It scooted along the branch and pointed its beak at Fiona. "Don't you know better than to poke around in a vipera nest?"

Appearing dumbfounded, Fiona slowly shook her head.

Brit eased closer to his niece, near enough to grab her if she went for the eggs again. "What's a vipera?"

"A vipera. *Vipera*." The bird said the name twice, as if sheer repetition would make them comprehend.

Tate and the others simply stared.

And the bird rolled its eyes. "A vipera is a great, winged beast, with a raptor's claws and a serpent's teeth." It huffed and flapped its wings.

Tate's mind raced, but the description refused to gel. Even after all she'd witnessed with her own eyes and experienced for herself, the notion was too incredible.

But then she recalled the shape she and Jack had seen flying over the labyrinth their first night in Faerie. She glanced frantically around the huge, shadowy forest.

Definitely room enough for giants to wander. Or . . . She gulped. "Are you talking about a dragon?"

The bird bobbed its head. "Dragon, hmm. I've heard the word."

"Dragon?" Jack echoed. He grew tense and performed his own inspection of the surrounding woods.

The bird twisted its head backward as if surveying the forest one more time. "You can still make an escape, but if you were to touch those eggs, your scent would remain." The animal's purple body shuddered. "And the mother vipera would hunt you to the ends of Faerie."

Brit's words were like hammered nails. "Fiona. Step away."

She whirled and rushed to stand with Tate, crossing both hands over her heart. "I'm sorry. I'm sorry. The flowers just smelled so good."

"It's okay," Tate told her, rubbing her back. She understood the obscure power of this world, the danger cloaked in temptation. She looked back up to the bird. "Thank you for helping us."

The bird spread its wings and bowed its head. "I am Reon. At your service."

"Rayon?" Sami asked. "Like the fabric?"

The animal cocked its head in a good imitation of human bafflement. "No, Reon. Like the bird."

"Reon," Tate said, stepping closer, "we're on our way to the Ruins of Morogost," Tate explained. "Is it safe to continue this way?"

"The Ruins of Morogost." Reon started pacing—up the branch, down the branch—all the while making a low clucking sound. "You've put yourself in a bad spot. A very bad spot."

"What do you mean?"

The bird stilled and spoke in a rush. "You can't stay in the forest with a vipera nest nearby. Yet the sun sets far too soon."

"Too soon for what?"

Twisting his head backward again, Reon whispered, "You can make it through the ruins if you go now. If you rush." He snapped back to face them. "But you mustn't get caught after dark."

A chill began a slow spider-walk up Tate's spine. "Why not?"

"You have no time." Reon fluttered his wings. "Go now." He leapt off of the branch and flew up to a higher perch. "Better hurry."

"Come on, Tate." Jack was by her side, tugging on her arm again.

The others were moving as well, walking quickly but careful to dodge the nest of blue flowers. Even Fiona gave it a wide berth as she jogged after Brit.

"Better hurry," Reon called from up above. "Better rush."

Something in the bird's frantic tone gave Tate the shove she needed. She began to run.

Though she felt the need to thank him one more time, fear was a whip snapping at her back. She dared not stop, for they'd lost too much time already.

As she ran with Jack through the gigantic trees, she looked for the glimmer on the horizon. But the bird's croaking voice carried on the air, and her fear was made real.

"The sun sets too soon!"

17

We aren't going to make it. Jack stared down from a small rise above the Ruins of Morogost, but he kept his pessimism to himself. As he surveyed the ruined city, he realized they'd made a terrible assumption.

"Which way do we go?" Tate asked on a breath. The crack in her voice matched the one in Jack's fortitude. He'd pictured the ruins as a few broken-down skeletons, mere remnants of ancient buildings.

But Morogost had been no lone castle or keep they could easily skirt around. Before them stretched the wreckage of a metropolis, a virtual maze of half-toppled towers and slabs of pale rock.

But the difficult passage they faced wasn't the worst of their problems. Twilight now washed the land in a pale lavender glow. The sun's light was fading fast.

Jack put his hand on Tate's back, reassuring them both. She pushed her hair behind her ears while her eyes darted back and forth over the treacherous landscape.

"We'll find a way," Jack said with more conviction than he felt. "We may encounter trouble, but we knew to expect danger." He lifted her hand and stroked his fingers over her palm. "We came prepared."

A small wrinkle sat between her brows, but it relaxed as she studied his face. "Yes. We're prepared. Unfortunately," she added, turning back to study the ruins, "this is the path we must take."

"And daylight is fading." Sami headed down the slope toward the cracked remnants of what had once been a majestic archway. The structure tilted to one side, fractured through-and-through, a sad reminder of grandeur gone to waste.

Intent on getting them through the ruins as quickly as possible, Jack sought out a marker on the far side, a navigation point they could keep in sight. "There." He pointed. "See that tower? The one that's still intact with the domed top?"

"Yes." Brit focused on the lofty column, tall enough for them to see from any point inside the city. "Good landmark. We can use it as a guide."

"I wonder what happened here." Jack glanced around as they followed Sami down. "Why did the Fae abandon the city?"

Jack didn't want to voice his other questions, the ones that concerned him most. Like why had the bird insisted they were running out of time? What threat would they face once the sun went down?

Tate's posture was rigid, her arms and shoulders tense, as if she were ready to summon flame and strike out at the first sign of trouble. Jack knew the load she carried on her shoulders, that she felt responsible for everyone else.

But despite the powers she and her sisters possessed, Jack's hand itched to hold a weapon of his own. He might be limited to the axe he carried on his back, but he would rise to Tate's defense, just as she would rise to his.

He glanced over again, taking in the tension in her lips and the strain around her eyes. She was so worried, so filled with doubt and fear.

So was he. Bigger issues needed to be dealt with, and he would do all he could to help her find this Jeweled Ceffyl, to fulfill her family's contract with Emuirdane.

But Jack would stay and fight for his own reasons too. He'd just gotten Tate back in his life, and though he didn't know where their relationship would lead, he was certain of one thing.

He didn't want to lose her again.

Rocks and dry branches littered the entrance to the city, but the wide road was easily navigated. Once inside the city walls, however, the level of destruction became more apparent.

Again Jack wondered what could have happened here. Had the Fae who'd lived in Morogost been attacked? Had war raged? Or had the devastation been caused by some kind of natural occurrence?

Whatever the circumstances, most of the structures had been demolished, leaving the main thoroughfare entirely blocked by rubble and the air tinged with the smell of chalk and ash. The five of them fanned out, trying to decide upon an alternate route.

Finally, Sami lifted her hand and dropped it again, her face a mask of frustration. "Might as well toss a coin, because we won't know how far any of these streets stay passable unless we go down them. We might get stuck and have to backtrack."

"All the more reason to get started." Tate gazed at the distant mountains and the sliver of sunset. She curled her fingers into her palms and gestured to the left. "Let's try this way."

For the sake of time, they set off at a jog and soon discovered they'd made a good choice. They came across another wide street, one that was relatively clear of debris and led straight to a central intersection before an impressive building.

The huge edifice consisted of front-facing columns that supported an entablature and pediment, much like the Greek structures Jack had studied in art class. Even more remarkable was the fact the building stood largely unscathed.

With the road clear, he and the others moved quickly, all but running across aged white cobblestones and leaping over the occasional pile of rock. But when they passed through the intersection and got a better look around, they found all the perimeter streets barricaded again.

"We'll have to cut through the building." Jack took the wide steps two at a time, easing past the sizeable columns and into the dark interior. It was open inside with a high ceiling supported by more huge pillars.

"It's some sort of basilica." Tate crept up beside him, the others close behind. "Perhaps where the city held public meetings or forums."

"Well, it's empty now," Fiona said. "But let's make sure before we go any farther." With a flick of her wrist, she tossed a ball of white fire into the air. The witchlight hovered above, illuminating the immediate area.

Tate and Sami followed suit, casting enough light to show the way through. The floors were dirty but clear of debris. Each back corner contained an exit, but they veered to the right, keeping the location of the domed tower in mind.

A round, waterless fountain sat out back with nine statues forming a circle at its center. Like the basilica, the female figures holding various instruments were largely intact. Each smiled happily, their joyous expression in sharp contrast to the surrounding wreckage.

Jack strained to make out what one of the statues was holding, and he realized how much darker it had become in the time they'd spent working their way through the fallen city.

"Keep those lights burning," Brit told his nieces as he met Jack's stare. He too realized the daylight was lost. All around them, broken white stone reflected the dying twilight.

"Humans!" A croaky yet familiar voice cried out in the sky above, just before the strange bird settled atop one of the statues, balancing on a violinist's bow. "Your lights shine so bright."

Jack couldn't tell if Reon was impressed with what the women could do, or panicked they might draw attention. "Should we douse the lights?"

"No, you will need them to see the way." Reon bobbed on the

statue. "It is not unheard of for humans to make their home in Faerie, but very few have magick." He eyed the three women.

Jack shared a wary look with Brit. Where was this heading?

"When I saw you in the forest, I suspected." The bird lowered his head. "But now I am sure. You are the Daughters of Nadia."

"We are," Tate replied without hesitation.

"You have come to free the Ceffyl."

The sisters nodded.

Jack considered the creature's choice of words. Reon hadn't said they'd come to find, locate, steal, or repossess the Ceffyl. But to *free* it.

Was there an underlying meaning? Or was it simply a language gap?

Whatever the case, he didn't have time to ponder the faerie bird's speech patterns, since the animal fluffed his wings erratically and lifted into the air calling, "This way, humans! Follow me!"

In the dark of night, Jack could barely see the bird. Nor could he locate the tower they'd decided to use as a landmark. "We don't know which way to go," he said to the others. "But should we follow him?"

"We don't have any other choice," Tate said. "And I think Reon only wants to help us." She tracked the animal's progress with her eyes. "We'd better go before we lose sight of him."

For the sake of speed, they sheathed their weapons and rushed after their airborne guide. They followed his flight path across the area with the fountain and then down a narrow side street they might never have found if left on their own.

Tate and her sisters kept the witchlights close above, lighting shadowy channels between crumbled buildings and perilous fissures in the shattered streets. When Sami tripped in a wide crack, Jack reached out to help keep her on her feet. "Thanks," she said, and resumed running.

Jack cursed under his breath and kept a close watch on Tate.

This place was nothing but one huge deathtrap, and they were taking its jags and turns at top speed.

Suddenly, the moon came out from behind the clouds, shedding its pallid light across the ruins.

"There's the tower." Fiona thrust an arm toward the marker they'd chosen. "We're almost through."

"Almost." Tate spit out the reply between hard breaths. She was huffing. Along with Jack and everyone else. They were essentially racing through an obstacle course, one that offered real danger if they made the wrong turn or slipped through the wrong hole in the wall.

The tower was in plain sight now, its white dome brilliant in the moonlight. Brit led them through the streets and tossed over his shoulder, "Just past this next wall."

But as soon as he spoke, he skidded to a halt, his hands slapping against a dark slab of stone. The gray wall had blended with the shadows, materializing only when they were right on top of it.

Brit cursed soundly and scoured the high wall in both directions. "I don't see any openings." With a sound of outrage, he glanced to the sky. "Which way?"

They all looked up, but Reon was nowhere in sight.

Gasping for air and turning in circles, all five of them scanned the area for an exit. They'd come to a place of haphazard passageways, a jumble of toppled walls and pillars.

Only one structure stood strong and intact—the long expanse of solid stone that blocked their way.

"Did he trick us?" Sami asked. "Did Reon lead us to a dead end on purpose?"

"No." Fiona shook her head, her breaths slowing again as they stood with nowhere to go. Nowhere to run. "He wouldn't."

"We don't know that." Brit's fists were clenched. "Damn it." He hit the wall that had ended their escape. "We're so close."

Just then, Reon arrowed down from the sky, landing atop the

impassable wall.

"Quiet," the bird said, his voice a low hiss. "Quiet, humans. No more noise."

"Where do we go?" Brit's voice was tight, thrumming with pent-up frustration.

Reon fluttered down from the wall, alighting on an overturned column. "This way. Quickly. You must make your way through."

"Through what?" Jack walked over to look behind the fallen pillar. "Through there?" He scoffed when he saw the tight, dark crevice. The network of rubble created a small tunnel.

No, the passage didn't even qualify as a tunnel, and he had serious doubts whether he and Brit could squeeze inside.

"A city square waits just beyond. The way is clear." Reon was still whispering. "But you must go now."

The small opening was dirty and devoid of light, and based on everyone else's unhappy expressions, Jack wasn't the only one hesitant to crawl into the dark space. Brit crossed his arms and shook his head, the look on his face confirming his skepticism.

Something scraped in the darkness behind them. Jack jerked around, scanning the backstreet from which they'd just emerged.

Two silver orbs flashed in the black corridor.

Muscles frozen and breath burning in his chest, Jack fixed his gaze on the two points of light. Were those eyes? Were they being watched? Or followed?

At last he blinked, and the silver spots disappeared.

"I'll go first," Fiona said, pulling Jack's attention back to the group. She took her pack off her back and slipped it around her front. She'd have to push it ahead of her to fit through.

"Are you sure?" Sami stepped forward, removing her pack as well.

"Yes." Fiona's tone was definite. "I'm the smallest, and we need to know if I'm going to make it. Because if I can't . . ."

"None of us will." Brit heaved a breath and eyed the wall.

Jack scanned it as well, looking for any way they might scale the high structure or pass around. Or hell, even break their way through.

He glanced back to the alley. No sign of movement or any other sound. Maybe his eyes had been deceiving him.

Either way, he was more than ready to be gone from these ruins. He'd had enough of the ancient city and the remains of its doom.

Fiona made her way over the pillar, dropped to her knees, and sent her witchlight into the hole. Then she disappeared.

Tate sucked in a breath and hurried over. She crouched down, staring after her little sister.

It wasn't long before Fiona's voice carried from over the wall. "I'm out. I think you all can make it."

"Sami, you're next." Tate waved her over.

"Nope. You're the next smallest and you're already there." Sami tramped over and gave Tate a push on the shoulder. "Stop holding up the line."

Grumbling to herself but doing as instructed, Tate crawled into the darkness, leaving her witchlight behind. Sami mimicked her actions, and Jack soon realized why.

The women could call fire to their hands if needed, but Jack and Brit would be blind. So they'd left their lights behind for the men.

Brit joined Jack, so they could frown down at the crevice together. Brit hiked a sardonic brow. "You want to argue about who's skinniest?"

With a gruff laugh, Jack answered by throwing his legs over the pillar and crouching. He peered into the constrictive space, sucked in a breath, and crawled into the opening after one of the witchlights. Historically, he didn't consider himself claustrophobic.

But this tight, jagged shaft might make him rethink the classification.

Sharp stone points jutted out from different directions. Gravel bit into his elbows and knees. Thankfully though, the channel was short, and after a few more grunts, scrapes, and shoves, he was out and up on his feet again.

Tate and her sisters were waiting for him and their uncle, standing on the boundary of a large empty space that did indeed resemble a city square. A looming statue of a man holding a sword and shield stood in the center of the open area, collapsed buildings on all sides.

Glancing up and to his right, Jack found the domed tower spearing into the night sky. They'd managed to navigate the city and had finally made it to the opposite side.

Tate must have read his mind, a tired smile playing about her lips. Putting the back of one hand to her forehead, she exhaled long and slow. "We have to be near the edge of the ruins. It shouldn't be much farther to the queen's residence."

"But the whole place is walled in." Sami gestured as she turned in a slow circle.

Brit studied the square, designed to be an open common area but now strewn with rubble and broken columns. "This should be an easy crossing, and then, one way or another, we're getting out of this place." He jutted his chin toward a pillar leaning against one wall. "We'll climb out if we have to."

"Where's the bird?" Sami asked, performing another full turn with her face lifted.

The croaky voice came from atop a broken-down wall of a nearby structure. Reon huddled against the stone. "I told you to be quiet." He swiveled his head all the way around in that disturbing way of his. "I'm sorry. So sorry."

He gave what might have been a sad look to the three women. "You can try to run."

With a small squawk that sounded like distress, the bird thrust from his perch and winged into the sky. His sleek body was a streak across the moon, and then he was gone.

A chill skittered down Jack's nape. "What did he mean by that?"

he asked quietly, afraid he was heeding the animal's warning too late.

Sami gulped. "Try to run?" Her eyes skimmed the square, searching every dark nook and shadowed corner. "Run from what?"

The others all stayed still and silent for a moment, performing the same inspection. Finally, Brit motioned with his hand. "We have to move."

The group began to trek across the square, trying to advance without sound. But dead leaves mingled with scattered shards of rock and, despite their caution, their steps crunched and rustled on the paved ground.

They drew near the statue, and Fiona pulled up short, freezing in motion. "Did you hear that?"

Unmoving, barely breathing, Jack stopped and listened.

Then he heard it. A soft clicking sound.

Tate cocked her head. "Where's it coming from?"

"What is it?" Sami whispered.

Jack did a slow revolution but saw nothing. Then he heard the noise again, coming from a building in Fiona's direction.

Shtick-shtick-shtick-shtick.

This time the raspy clicking came from behind him. He met Tate's eyes. "Whatever it is, there's more than one."

Brit turned to edge around the statue, still intent on leading them out.

Jack made a move to follow, but he stopped when Tate's brown eyes locked on a spot behind him. And widened.

The witchlights still drifted over their heads, but now a soft white light came from below. From Tate's hands. "Draw your weapons," she said. "And move very slowly."

18

"What is it?" Sami asked, still looking around. But she and Fiona both summoned their fire and held it at the ready.

The sound filled the air again—*shtick-shtick-shtick*—from so many locations Jack couldn't pin them down. *Shtick-shtick-shtick-shtick.* The scuttling noise grew louder, closer, echoing throughout the ruins.

Jack stared hard into the darkness searching for the source.

He caught movement along the base of a building and focused there. A dark shape crawled up the outer wall.

Jack eased the axe from its scabbard. "Keep your heads up." He looked at Tate. "They can climb."

Fiona sent her ball of light higher, allowing it to shine down on a broader area. She doused the flames in her right hand and extracted her dagger from its sheath. "Where? What do you see?"

Jack kept his back to the statue, as did the others, forming a circle. "We should make a stand here, out in the open." They still had to get out of the ruins, but whatever had just scaled that wall—he did not want dropping on his head.

A wolf cried on the other side of the barrier, from the dead end where they'd been trapped. Jack pictured the silver spots again. The creature baying at the moon had also been watching them from the shadows.

The mournful cry echoed again, and hackles rose on Jack's neck. Why was the animal howling now? Because it had lost its prey?

But if that were the case, why hadn't the beast attacked when Jack and the others had been stuck on that side of the wall?

"Oh my God." The flames in Tate's palm flared.

Jack forgot about the howling and turned his mind to the threat at hand. With his stomach clenching into knots, he watched the other creatures scuttle out from their hiding places.

The monsters crawling toward them had far too many legs. At least eight, but it was hard to count with them all moving at once. Their black bodies were divided into sections like an ant, complete with two mandibles clicking together in front.

"What the hell are those?" Sami's voice was a terrified rasp.

Jack couldn't fault her for being afraid, because every inch of his skin seemed to ripple and itch. He couldn't tell if the noises they'd heard were caused by the spidery legs skittering over stone, or from the non-stop snapping of the pincers on their heads.

The legs were unnerving, and the size of the bugs intimidating, but the long, segmented tails worried Jack the most. The appendages curved up and over the creatures' bodies, just like scorpions. And the tips of their tails were pointed and sharp.

Stingers.

Fiona rethought the dagger and slid it back into her belt. She fired up both hands instead.

Tate must have come to the same conclusion as Jack. "Watch their tails. Don't let them get close enough to sting."

More of the crawlers emerged from the shadows, some creeping up from a wide crevasse in the middle of an alley. A huge fallen column had lodged in an upper-floor window, and two bugs used it to slink to the ground.

The monsters moved at a leisurely pace, closing in from all sides and ensuring their prey had no means of escape.

Something sharp jabbed Jack in the back, and he spun, ready to slice with his axe. But he'd only bumped into the pointed toe of the statue's foot. "Dammit." He swore at his own jumpiness and turned back to face the encroaching beasts.

His hands tingled where they gripped the axe handle, and his stomach felt full of cement. He couldn't keep his eyes on all of the dark things scurrying in the shadows, not with his vision tunneling the way it was.

Fear had him in its cruel grasp and was making it difficult for him to function. And if he didn't calm down, he couldn't fight. Not the way he needed to.

The way he needed to . . . if he was going to keep Tate safe.

As soon as the thought flashed in his head, Jack realized the core of his fear. He wasn't terrified for himself, but for her. And he was letting that terror control him.

Which was counterproductive to what he had to do. So he zeroed in on the crawling beasts. He drew deep breaths and channeled composure. He'd be damned before he let Tate get hurt.

She might be the one with magick, but he was protecting the woman he loved.

His fingers relaxed on the grip of his weapon, and the blackness at the edge of his vision faded. With his faculties once again intact, he glared at the advancing horde and made a plan.

The tails were the biggest threat, but he couldn't do anything about them unless he let the monsters get close. If he threw his axe, he'd have to chase the weapon down before he could use it again.

So he'd just have to make sure he held onto his blade. And didn't get stung.

Shtick-shtick-shtick-shtick. One of the huge insects rushed at Tate, but Jack was ready. Swinging his axe, he arced up and over the creature's body from one side, slicing the blade down to cut off the stinger.

The huge black body shuddered, and the thing emitted a horrific screech. It scuttled backward before turning to dash into the dark.

Another three beasts rushed in to take its place.

But this time, they came for Jack.

The middle bug ran straight at him, jabbing its stinger at Jack's chest, but he crouched and lunged aside, swinging up and around as he'd done before. He slashed through the tail, amputating another deadly stinger. Just as a blast of white roared past him.

With pinpoint control, Tate streamlined the flames to sear the tails of the other two bugs converging on him. More high-pitched squeals rang out, then the monsters reared and rolled over onto their backs. All those revolting legs kicked in the air as they tried to put out the fire.

Jack glanced over to Tate, and they exchanged nods. He readied himself for the next assault and grinned.

Apparently, he wasn't the only one ready to defend.

Tate, Sami, and Fiona instantly began targeting the tails, which seemed to be the most sensitive part. Still, they scorched a few faces, legs, and pincers as well, anything to keep the swarm at bay.

But for every creature they drove away, two more materialized.

"How many can there be?" Brit yelled. He notched a bolt in his crossbow and took aim, but the beasts were dodging and evading, a countermove to the defensive blasts of fire coming from the women.

"Fiona," Tate called over her shoulder, "can you start clearing us a way toward that house?"

Fiona struck out at another giant creeper and glanced back. "The one near the outer wall?"

Jack sought out the building and saw that the bottom floor was intact.

Tate took a moment to scorch a brave creature that rushed her straight on. "Yes. Maybe we can fend them off better from inside." She called out in question, "Brit?"

"Let's do it. It may be our only chance." Brit swung his bow around and started firing at the insects between him and the dilapidated structure. Fiona joined in with her flames, and as they made headway, Jack, Tate, and Sami eased along behind them.

Maintaining a tight circle, back-to-back, the group made slow progress toward the building.

And still more creatures came.

A howl pierced the air again, but this time the sound was louder, closer. A massive wolf stood near the wall, right outside the tunnel Jack and the others had crawled through.

Had the animal followed? Was he so desperate to make a kill?

The wolf was huge, easily twice the size of those found back in the human world. So how had it fit through the crevice at all?

"Tate, we've got another problem." Jack gestured with his axe to the wolf, its coat gleaming silvery-white beneath the light of the moon.

"This place is crawling with predators." She took down another bug. "No wonder Reon warned us to get through before dark."

The insect-like beasts were getting bolder and more creative. They'd switched tactics and were trying to outnumber the humans, crowding closer in larger groups.

A pack advanced on Jack, the middle insect stabbing out with its tail.

Jack evaded, sweeping around to the outside. With a well-placed swing, he cleaved the stinger from the tip of its tail.

But even as the injured monster screamed and ran, the other two turned on Jack. One of them speared its tail toward him, so he jumped farther out.

Too late, he realized his mistake. They'd purposely corralled him to one side.

They'd separated him from Tate and the others.

"Jack!" Tate screamed, sending a stream of white toward his attackers. But she was being assaulted as well, three more crawling monsters coming at her from the opposite direction.

Two of the creatures coming for Jack ran from the fire, so he raised his axe, ready to slice off the remaining bug's stinger. But the creatures were adept at battle, quickly learning the moves of their adversaries. The beast reared up on its back legs and swept out with those in front.

Jack tried to move, but the bug was too fast. His feet flew out from under him, and he crashed to his back.

"No!" Tate shot fire from both palms in successive blasts, but she couldn't fend off the bugs rushing her and protect Jack at the same time. Sami turned to help Tate defend against the onslaught.

But neither of them would get to Jack in time.

He swung out with his axe, but the insect maneuvered the back segment of its body, easily avoiding the blade. The awful sound of its legs surrounded Jack now. The revolting *shtick-shtick-shtick-shtick* blocked out everything else. Even Tate's cries.

The huge black body thrust forward, legs coming at Jack from everywhere. The insect used two of its limbs—there were so many—to wrench the axe from his hands and send it flying.

Multiple appendages held him down, so he could only stare as the sharp-ended tail curled up and over its head.

Jack tensed, as if he could already feel the pain.

The stinger descended.

A blur of silver came out of nowhere and leaped onto the bug's back. The insect lifted, screeching in rage, and instantly released Jack.

He rolled from underneath the monster and scrambled toward his axe. Latching on to the weapon, he made it to his feet and spun. Blade raised, he prepared to strike.

But the huge wolf had already taken care of its quarry. Massive jaws were clamped around the long tail, just below the stinger. The animal growled and snarled, whipping its head back and forth.

Then, with one great jerk, it ripped off the tip of the tail. Stinger and all.

Stunned, Jack watched the wolf bound from the injured bug to attack another. The animal could have torn into Jack, but it hadn't.

Instead, the wolf was battling the huge monsters.

It was fighting *with* the humans.

With no time to question the unexpected assistance, Jack rushed to stand beside Tate.

"Are you okay?" she asked, eyes tense and terrified, her flaming hands shaking.

He nodded. "The wolf . . ."

"I saw." Tate choked back a sob. "Jack." Her mouth trembled as she gazed at him.

But in an instant, she regained control. Invisible armor seemed to slip back into place and she straightened, facing the advancing line of beasts. "We have to make it out of here."

"We will." The creatures continued to push forward, as if driven by an all-consuming need to kill their prey. To destroy them all.

"No matter what we do, they just keep coming." Tate burned the tail of another, concentrating on the stinger.

Jack took in the number of creatures still crawling from the shadows. The Ruins of Morogast were vast, and apparently, they were infested. If the entire place was overrun by these monsters, he didn't want to imagine how many there actually were.

Even the wolf was backing away, swinging its head back and forth as if unsure which bug to take out next.

Somehow Brit and Fiona had been driven off-track, and the group was nearing the overturned pillar propped in the window. The building it leaned against was half-demolished with one whole side missing. It would provide no protection from the vicious swarm.

Brit aimed his bow at the house they'd been trying to make it to. "What is that?"

Jack and Tate both swung their heads to see what he was talking about.

A dull golden glow filled the interior, bobbing up and down as if someone were carrying a candle inside.

Fiona aimed her hands toward the building, ready to fight yet another foe. "What else could possibly be out here?"

Jack glanced to the wolf as it edged back toward the wall from where it had come. "I have no idea, but I hope it's friendly."

As if understanding Jack's words, the wolf met his stare, its pale silver eyes gleaming. The mutual gaze held briefly, before the animal ducked down and was lost among the debris.

With their mysterious ally gone, Jack turned his attention to the house and the odd illumination. The glow brightened, exposed by the open doorway.

A man stood there, holding the light in his hand. Not just a light, Jack realized, but a globe of some sort, swirling with sparkling energy.

Stepping from the house, the stranger reared back his arm and flung the globe into the square.

"Look out!" Brit yelled, throwing himself in front of Fiona.

The round object landed on the stony ground and shattered, releasing the golden light in a flood.

Jack shielded Tate with his body, unsure what risk they now faced. But the tide of sparkling light washed over them harmlessly.

The crawling beasts, however, screamed and shook as the bright waves hit. Each one dove for the nearest crack or crevice they could find, some scrabbling for dark corners or alleys.

In an instant, the square cleared of the loathsome insects. As if the newcomer had sprayed the whole place with glittery insecticide.

Still, he was unknown to them, so Brit and Fiona faced him, his bow still drawn and her fire still flaming. Jack flanked Brit while Sami and Tate did the same for their sister.

The stranger lifted a hand in greeting. "I mean you no harm." His deep voice carried through the now-silent square as he pushed back the hood covering his head.

Dark-haired and broad-shouldered, he had the look of an outdoorsman—efficient satchel on his back, a single blade, and dressed in plain brown practical clothing. His expression was grim, eyes serious.

"Who are you?" Tate asked. "What are you doing here?"

He studied her briefly. "Passing through."

Jack didn't buy it. "Passing through here?" He waved an arm at the fallen-down city. "At night?"

The stranger focused his stern visage on Jack. "I know this land. I know its dangers." He allowed a smug smirk. "You, clearly, do not."

"How did you get in?" Brit glanced to the house. "And can we get out the same way?"

The stranger inclined his head. "The wall behind the house is down. You can walk out."

"Then that's what we'll do. Right now." Sami closed her hands into fists and snuffed out her fire. "Thanks for the help, but we need to keep moving." Now that the battle was over, she shuddered. "I'm going to have nightmares for weeks."

"Me too," Fiona said and sighed. As if a silent agreement to trust the stranger had passed between them, she extinguished her fire and took a few steps backward and rested against the leaning pillar.

Jack studied the man, but unlike the women, he didn't put away his weapon. Not yet.

Brit was of the same mind and continued to hold his bow. Though he made the concession of pointing it to the ground.

The stranger, however, was uninterested in the men's weapons. His intense gaze shot past Sami. And straight to Fiona.

Tate's youngest sister had her head down, drawing deep breaths as if to calm herself. When she finally lifted her face, she noticed the stranger's interest.

Even from a distance, Jack heard her breath catch. She met the man's gaze and held it.

Something sparked in the air between the two, and Jack wasn't the only one who felt it.

Brit scowled at the newcomer and took a step closer to his niece.

Fiona didn't pay him any mind. She was too focused on the strange man.

So she was still staring at him when a long black tail snaked around the pillar.

And stabbed her in the chest.

19

"What happened?" Emuirdane slammed both hands on his desk and stood. The seer stood before him in his office, cowering, shrinking into herself. "Speak, you old fool! What happened to Fiona?"

She'd come to his office to deliver her latest report, interrupting his work with unsettling news. News that had severed the threads of Emuirdane's self-control in one quick slice.

"I'm sorry, My Lord." The woman wrung her hands, shoulders stooped and head hanging. Tendrils of gray hair escaped a bun on the top of her head, and she listed to one side, favoring a crippled leg. "I forged a psychic link to each of the three sisters, so I could watch them all, even when separated from one another."

She shifted her feet, her rheumy eyes darting to the side as if she feared meeting his gaze for too long. "But the three were still tied together. So when the young one was stung and she fell unconscious, the connection to all of them was broken."

"Unconscious." Ignoring her explanation, Emuirdane fixated on the word. He drew and expelled his breaths through clenched teeth, trying to contain the foreign sense of panic. "So she isn't dead?"

At his question, the seer backed away, stopping only when she bumped into the sentries standing guard behind her. Her voice was a hiss, barely audible when she said, "I can't be certain, My Lord."

Emuirdane tried to rein in his fury, but his palms sparked with green power. He should have never put his faith in this incompetent fool. He should have gouged out her eyes, just as he'd contemplated doing from the beginning. Anything to boost her abilities.

And everyone knew a blind oracle was more powerful than one with two good eyes. "Perhaps I should do so now."

"My Lord?" she asked in confusion, having heard only the last of his thoughts, the one he'd spoken aloud.

Emuirdane shoved his desk with so much force it slid halfway across the room. The sound of wood scraping stone made the seer flinch.

And when he stalked toward her, hands raised to reveal his magick—magick he so desperately ached to unleash—she shrieked and tried to scurry away, only to be waylaid by the sentries.

"I will blind you, old woman," Emuirdane rasped. "Then you'll grow stronger in your vision. And you will give me the information I require!"

"Please!" Panic flashed in her eyes before she slapped her hands over her face. "My Lord, I beg of you. I have watched the sisters as you asked. I've reported their every move!"

Slowly, she pulled her hands apart to peer through her fingers. "But if you take my eyes now, my visions won't return until a full cycle of the moon has passed." She held out her hands, beseeching. "During that time, I won't be able to see the sisters at all."

Emuirdane's roar rattled the chandelier above, but he curled his hands into fists, containing the power that crackled and hissed in sync with his anger. Still, he glowered at the aged psychic. "When. Will. You. Know?"

She shook her head. "I can do nothing but wait."

When he snarled, she lifted a gnarled finger. "But I expect it won't be long. A night, perhaps, for the girl to recover. The connection will return as soon as she wakes. And once she does, I will tell you *everything*."

Crossing his arms over his chest, Emuirdane angled his head and looked down at her. "And if the connection doesn't return?"

The crippled seer gulped so hard the sound carried throughout the room. Her entire body seemed to deflate. "Then, My Lord . . ." She quaked where she stood. "Then we will know she is dead."

20

Fiona fell back against the pillar as her body spasmed. Her eyes were closed, but her mouth had fallen open in a silent scream.

"No!" Tate yelled, but she couldn't move. Sheer horror froze her in place, flashing like a lightning storm inside her head and strobing her vision to turn the whole world white.

Before she could react, before she could even process what had happened, Jack's axe whizzed past her. His blade severed the tail before imbedding in the stone pillar.

The bug's shrill cry ruptured the air, followed by the sound of its spidery legs scrambling for escape.

With the stinger still piercing her flesh, Fiona slid to the ground and slumped forward. Her eyes dimmed and slowly closed.

Jarred from her paralysis, Tate rushed to her sister, kicking away the revolting tail that had finally fallen free and still oozed black venom onto the white stones. "Fee!"

Fiona sagged against her and Tate's chest ached from the fear twisting inside. She took her sister's face in her hands and shook her gently. "Fiona! Please wake up. Wake up!"

Sami kneeled on Fiona's other side, her face strained with misery. She stroked Fiona's cheek. "Come on, Fee. Don't do this."

The stranger fell to one knee before Fiona and ripped the satchel from his back. "Pull back her clothing." With quick hands, he rummaged inside the pack and removed a small leather bundle tied with twine.

"I need you to expose the wound." His tone was harsh with command.

Tate snapped into action and pulled at Fiona's shirt. The fabric wouldn't give, but then Brit was there with his knife, slicing open the front.

The puncture on Fiona's chest was a furious red with pink streaks radiating outward. Her head lolled to one side, but Sami caught her. "It's okay, Fee. We've got you." Her dark eyes brimmed with unshed tears.

Tate clamped her lips together but couldn't stop the moan from slipping out. Still, she held Fiona's shirt with one hand and stroked her hair with the other. "You'll be okay," she murmured. "You'll be okay."

The mantra and consolation were as much for her and Sami as their baby sister, who was passed out and completely unaware.

The man unfolded the bundle, revealing a sticky green substance inside. He slapped the goop to the wound and used both hands to mash the leathery-material against Fiona's skin. Then he smoothed outward from the center to the edges.

With his palms still pressed to her chest, he murmured in a deep voice. The low intonation sounded like the chant of a Tibetan monk as he repeated the same words three times.

Once finished, he sprang to his feet and retrieved another item from his satchel. "We have to get her to shelter."

"We know somewhere close," Jack said, reaching out to take whatever the man had pulled from his bag. "We're headed to a house belonging to the Winter Queen."

The stranger paused and stared at Jack, but then he looked away and quickly unfolded the item he'd retrieved. To Tate, it looked like small sticks wrapped in thin fabric.

But Jack must have recognized it for what it was, because he helped the man fashion the wad of sticks and cloth into a field litter. The two men laid the stretcher on the ground and nudged

Tate and Sami away so they could transfer Fiona's limp body to the contraption.

Tate reached for Sami's hand as the stranger slipped his satchel back on his shoulders. The man was certainly prepared for the crisis, but like he'd said, he knew these lands. And its dangers.

He and Jack lifted the stretcher to carry Fiona. "I know the way," he told Brit before setting off toward the building where he'd emerged earlier.

Tate and Sami exchanged a look of despair and embraced. But then Brit came up behind them and put his hands on their shoulders. "We have to go. We have to take care of Fiona."

With his usual succinctness, their uncle both assured and encouraged them.

Tate was grateful for Brit's strength, because at the moment, she needed a push. She felt like someone had carved her heart out with a dull spoon, and the shock was trickling back in to numb her brain.

They made their way through the half-destroyed house to discover the man had been telling the truth. The wall had apparently fallen long ago, and they exited into open land with nothing above but a starry sky.

They kept a brisk pace as they entered into a forest and followed a winding path. Though the trip was short, it felt like hours to Tate. Her head pounded with relentless questions.

Who was this man? What had he put on Fiona's skin? What kind of toxin had the creature injected into her sister's body?

And then the recriminations began.

Why didn't I move faster? Why didn't I see the tail before it struck?

Clenching her hands into fists, Tate forced herself to stop playing the what-if game. There was no undoing the past, and those kinds of thoughts would only make her crazy.

So she kept her head down and concentrated on putting one foot in front of the other. Until Fiona was safely indoors, there was little else she could do.

At last they broke from the trees and crossed a large, well-tended yard. A two-story manor house rose from the mists. In the dark of night, Tate had the impression of dark blue masonry, and lights burned in the windows as if their arrival had been expected.

Brit rushed ahead, opened the front door, and held it for Jack and the stranger so they could carry Fiona inside. The man glanced around at the foyer and adjacent sitting rooms. "Bedrooms must be upstairs."

He and Jack hurried straight up and through an open door.

Tate followed closely, barely taking in the rich scarlet and deep blue shades of the bedchamber. Once the men eased Fiona from the litter, the stranger pointed to the fireplace. "You'll need to keep a fire burning at all times."

Jack moved straight to the hearth and set a match to the kindling and logs.

Tate and Sami covered Fiona with a plush blanket as the stranger instructed, "You must make sure she stays warm. The cretid's poison has slowed her system." He scowled down at Fiona's pale face. "Her body is very close to shutting down altogether."

Dread stabbed jagged knives in Tate's gut. She put her palm to Fiona's cheek and flinched to feel the cold. "She's freezing. And so still." She pressed a trembling finger to Fiona's neck and almost cried with relief when she felt a pulse.

"As I said." The man looked grim. "She is very close to death."

Sami sobbed and crossed her arms over her stomach. "What can we do?"

"Keep her warm. Keep her breathing."

"What else?" Tate demanded, choking back her raging emotions and trying to keep a clear head. "There must be something we can give her."

The man was solemn when he spoke. "I have done all I can for her. The balm will draw what venom it will." He indicated the leathery patch he'd put on Fiona's chest. "Leave the terra leaf in place. Do not try to check the wound. Do not lift the edges of the leaf."

He turned to Jack and repeated instructions. "Keep her warm and watch her breathing." He clenched his jaw. "And wait."

"But those words you spoke." Brit held out a beseeching hand. "They were a spell, right? Some kind of magick? We have magick too. We can help her if you'll tell us how."

"I'm sorry. The words I spoke only released the healing properties of the leaf and balm, but no other magick can touch the cretid's poison."

"You're not Fae," Jack said, more of a statement than question.

"No, I am human."

"But you used something at the ruins. Some kind of power that drove away the bugs." Brit didn't seem willing to let the idea go.

Neither was Tate. "Can't we can try a healing spell?" She took Fiona's cold hand between her own. "You must have some ability."

"What magick I use is not my own. I live in Faerie because I am in service to another." The man held up his hand when Tate would have pleaded with him. "I'm truly sorry. I can do no more."

He looked at Fiona then, his gaze softening with something that looked like pity. "She is so small."

With that, he turned abruptly on his heel and left the room.

Tate didn't want to leave her sister, but she wouldn't let him go before he answered her questions. She ran out and caught him halfway down the stairs.

She grabbed his arm. "What can we expect? How long until she wakes up?"

The man heaved a sigh and raised his eyes to Jack as he walked down to join them. "You should know something within four days' time. No one has ever taken longer to revive. Or . . ."

"Or to die." Tate curled her fingers into his arm, but he didn't seem to notice. "That's what you're saying, isn't it? That she'll either wake up or die? And we can do nothing." She raised her voice as grief took over. "*Nothing?*"

"If she wakes, then she will live." He stared at Tate for a moment, considering. He exhaled and shook his head before pulling a small glass vial from his satchel. "If she wakes, go outside. Break this. I will return and help you."

Tate accepted the small tube. "What is—" Tate began, but he was already at the bottom of the stairs and opening the door to leave.

This time, she didn't go after him. There was no point.

Instead, she studied the tiny cylinder with green liquid rolling inside. She suspected it was another of his borrowed magick tricks.

She fixated on the tube, stared at it, and willed Fiona to wake up. She wanted to hear her sister's voice more than anything. She wanted a reason to break the glass right now.

But the house remained still and silent.

Jack's hand slid over hers and took the vial from her palm. "Let's put this somewhere safe."

In a stupor, Tate let him lead her to the lower level. "Fiona," she heard herself say. Anxiety and heartache washed over her, dulling her senses. She couldn't focus, couldn't think straight.

Fear pulsed inside her like a huge black heart.

She'd known the risk of coming to Faerie, and she'd foolishly thought herself prepared.

But now she knew, even with her mother's return, she was still fragile inside. She couldn't handle losing anyone else that she loved. She simply couldn't go through it again.

But now Fiona was up there, barely clinging to her precious life.

And Tate's worst nightmare was coming come true.

"Tate." Jack's hand was on her face. "Come here." He pulled her through the lamplit rooms and into a large kitchen.

"Fiona," she whispered, unable to focus on anything else. "I need to help my sister."

"Brit and Sami are with her now." Jack gripped her shoulders, holding her in place. "Take a moment, Tate. Stay with me."

She shook her head, blind to the surroundings, seeing nothing but that tail and its horrible stinger jabbing into Fiona. The sickening scene replayed again and again.

But it was too late. Too late to stop it from happening.

Tate put her hands over her eyes as if she could blind herself to the memory. "I can't just stand here. I have to do something."

"You will. But you can't help Fiona until you take a minute for yourself." Jack pulled her against him and wrapped her in his arms. "Just breathe."

His heat flooded her, and she leaned into his strength. She felt drained, all but hollowed out. So she accepted the comfort and support he offered.

"I failed her." The words burst from her as she clung to Jack. "I shouldn't have let her come. I should have protected her."

"You couldn't have stopped her from coming if you'd tried. You and your sisters are in this together."

She shut her eyes and pressed her face into his shoulder. "But I wish I could do this alone. I never wanted anyone else in danger." Her arms tightened around his waist. "This hurts so much, Jack. I don't think I can stand it."

"Yes, you can. And you will." Jack rested his head against the top of hers. "You'll do whatever you have to do. Because you love Fiona."

"But that's why it hurts so much." Tate's throat choked and burned. She tried to hold the anguish in, but tears forced their way out to roll in hot rivulets down her cheeks. "I don't know how to fix this."

Jack held her tighter, his voice soft. "But you can be here with Fiona and help her through. You'll make her stronger just by being here." His ocean-blue eyes were steady and enduring. "And whatever it takes, we *will* get through this."

She nodded, but her lips trembled so hard she could no longer speak. As her heart fractured completely, as the grief poured out, she fell helplessly back into Jack's strong arms. So he could hold her while she cried.

21

Jack held Tate until her tears ran dry. And when she was finished crying, when she was ready, she went back upstairs to sit by Fiona.

The first night, she kept watch with Sami and Brit, none of them willing to leave Fiona's side.

By dawn of the next morning, all three were glassy-eyed. With no apparent change in Fiona's condition, Jack worried the vigil would go on for days.

At this rate, they would have to take shifts.

"We'll sleep in schedules," he argued when the others wouldn't leave the room. "If we aren't rested, we won't be able to watch Fiona like we should." He stared straight at Brit. "If we're too tired, then we might miss something."

Finally, they accepted that the best way to help Fiona was to be sharp-eyed and alert. And though sleep came easily to no one, the four of them took turns getting what rest they could, napping in short, fitful bouts.

Tate opted to be the last to rest and sat up through the remainder of the day. She'd found a collection of books in the room, including a copy of *Little Women*, and had been reading out loud to her sleeping sister.

Though sleeping wasn't quite the word to describe Fiona's state. She was cold, unmoving, and nearly lifeless.

Tate was utterly distraught over the thought of leaving Fiona, and even as the sun began to set, she insisted she needed to finish the book. It was as if she believed the sound of her voice—and a story of sisters—was somehow anchoring Fiona to this world.

But she'd been awake for more than twenty-four hours, so Jack finally went for reinforcements. He returned with Brit. In the first show of his magick Jack had ever seen, Tate's uncle pressed his fingers to her temples and murmured in a strange language.

Her eyes drifted shut almost immediately.

Brit shot a guilty look to Jack but said, "It had to be done."

Sami took over the next shift, and while she didn't spend her time reading to Fee, she did talk to her. In a sweet, loving voice, reserved for the baby of the family, she spoke of her own art, their mother and grandfather, and the shop Fiona dreamed of opening. She shared nothing but hopeful and happy stories of life back home.

Eventually, Jack pushed Sami out as well, all but forcing her to go downstairs and eat. He sat quietly, always listening for Fiona's raspy breaths, checking her wrist to make sure she had a pulse.

Jack hated to see Fiona so ill, and to see his friends in so much pain. He ached for the people who'd once been like family to him. And had become like family again.

Brit returned along with the twilight. Unlike Tate and Sami, he was stoically silent. He sat in the bedside chair Jack had vacated, gently brushing Fiona's hair away from her face.

A face Jack felt was still far too white.

And deep in the dark of that second night, Fiona stopped breathing.

Jack was in the next room trying to sleep when he heard a commotion. He rushed in to find Tate giving her sister mouth-to-mouth.

"Nothing!" Eyes wide with panic, Tate held out shaking hands. "No breaths, no heartbeat!"

Brit and Sami barreled in after Jack, but he'd already lifted Fiona to place her on the floor for better support. Sami dropped to her knees, and for the next two minutes—the longest two minutes of Jack's life—they performed CPR.

Finally, after their third set of compressions, Fiona sucked in a breath. The sudden gasp sounded like a death rattle, but at least she was breathing on her own.

With no other option, they put her back in bed. To watch. To wait. And if the waiting had been hard before ... Now it was pure hell.

No one could sleep now, including Jack. Not after such a close call.

But there was nothing any of them could do for Fiona, so he did his best to be supportive. He made sure Tate, Sami, and Brit had nothing else to worry about but watching her sleep.

He tried to stay busy with household chores and keeping the others fed. But however much food he prepared, whatever the size of the mess, he always returned to a clean kitchen, washed dishes, and a full pantry.

Something strange was happening in the manor house, but the occurrences posed no obvious threat. And Jack had no time or energy to spare on needless worry.

The next morning, just after daybreak, Jack managed to coax Tate downstairs with the hope she would eat something. Again, he found the kitchen spotless, this time with fresh sandwiches prepared on a platter.

"You didn't have to do all this," Tate said, her brown eyes dim with sorrow.

"Actually—" he began, but cut himself off when he heard a noise. "What was that?"

Tate jerked her head and listened.

This time, they both heard Sami cry out from upstairs.

A terrified breath whooshed from Tate's lips, and it carried a single word. "Fiona."

22

Tate's heart was in her throat by the time she flew into the bedroom. She stuttered to a halt, staring at Sami beside the bed. And Fiona, who was awake, sitting up and smiling.

Happiness welled up in Tate like a bright fountain, and she broke into tearful laughter. Rushing to the bed, she took her sister in her arms. "Fee, oh Fee. I . . . I'm just so—" She broke off when happy crying took over.

Fiona hugged her and patted her consolingly. "I'm okay, Tate. I'm safe."

A sound made Tate look up. Brit and Jack stood behind her, both looking more at ease than she'd seen them in days. She imagined she had the same relaxed shoulders and calm expression now too.

Still holding Fiona's hand, Tate asked her, "How do you feel?"

"Honestly, I feel fine." She made a face and glanced down. "Except for this sticky thing on my chest." She reached for the leaf.

"Wait." Tate stopped her. "Don't touch that." She got up and took a step toward the door, then moved back to kiss Fiona on top of the head, before finally edging through Brit and Jack. "Give me a few minutes," she told Fiona, holding up a finger. "I'll be right back."

Tate swore she floated on air as she ran downstairs to the kitchen and retrieved the stranger's small vial from a drawer. Just as quickly, she rushed back through the house, bumping into Jack as he came down the stairs.

With a smile so big it strained her cheeks, she grabbed his hand. "Come on."

They went out to the front lawn—outside as the man had instructed—where she held up the glass tube with green liquid. "He said to break it," she said with a guess-we'll-see-what-happens glance to Jack.

She bent the tiny glass vial in the center until she heard a snap. The deep green fluid grew lighter in color, to a happy yellow-green that reminded her of a miniature glow stick.

The glass then dissolved in her hands as the vivid green seeped out like a gas. The particles lifted on the breeze and spread out over the forest.

With his eyes on the treetops, Jack asked, "Now what?"

Tate lifted a shoulder. "I don't know." She put a hand to her heart where it pounded with joy. "But Fiona woke up." She leaped into Jack's arms and whispered against his cheek, "She woke up."

His arms enfolded her, making her feel a blend of so many emotions—safety, security, warmth, exhilaration.

Relief over Fiona blended with gratitude. The last days had been excruciating—the horror, the waiting, the not knowing—and through it all Jack had been there. He'd been Tate's strength when she would have faltered. He'd been her logic when she couldn't think straight.

He'd been hope, when she was lost in despair.

Now that Fiona was mending, Tate had countless things she wanted—needed—to say to him, and she was almost dizzy from the rush of so much affection. So much love.

She'd barely dropped to the grass again and was staring adoringly up at Jack when the stranger walked out of the woods. Though his bearing and countenance were still as serious as they had been the other night, his mouth tipped up at the edges.

"Good news," he said when he drew near. "Your loved one has passed through the danger." Then he met Tate's gaze and confirmed her blossoming hope. "She will live."

"Thank you for everything you've done." Caught up in her joy, Tate wrapped him in a quick hug.

The man's brows shot up to his dark hair, and he cleared his throat. "There are many in the wyldwood who are pleased with this outcome," he told her when she stepped back. "You can tell . . . Fiona, that was her name?"

Tate nodded.

"Tell her to expect a gift this evening. Just after dusk."

"A gift?" Wrinkles marred Jack's brow.

"Just a gift. You will see."

"We don't even know your name." Tate beamed at the man who'd saved Fiona's life.

He tipped his head. "I am called Ronan."

"My name is Tate and this is Jack. Sami and Fiona—Fiona was the one who was stung— they are my sisters."

Ronan maintained his smile, but it strained at the edges. "You are very lucky. The cretid's sting is most often lethal." He hedged, his golden-brown eyes shifting between Tate and Jack. "This may not be my place to ask, but I have to wonder why five people, so clearly unfamiliar with Faerie, are traveling across its treacherous lands."

A shadow crossed Tate's mind, and she faltered. "Well. . ." Should she tell him why they were here? It seemed to be no great secret. The bird Reon had known who they were and what their quest entailed.

For some reason, she held back the truth. "We have something we must do."

"Very well." Ronan turned his head and gazed across the lawn. "As for your sister, she may remove the terra leaf and resume normal activity. She may eat and drink, move about. Her strength should return straight away."

Jack held out his hand. "We appreciate all you've done."

Ronan stared at his extended hand as if unfamiliar with the custom, but then he reached out and the two men shook.

"There is something else." Ronan pressed his lips together. "I can help you get home if you wish, to the human world."

"What?" Tate gasped at the unexpected offer.

But you must come with me soon. Within the next few hours. I can take you to a *lana*, but it is only open for a certain time."

Jack edged forward, his expression eager. "Is a lana the same as a portal?"

"No, though they are similar. A lana is something you follow." Ronan looked upward as if thinking. "Like a heolig or as you call it, a—"

"A pathway," Tate said, remembering her grandfather's translation of the word.

A pathway that could lead them home. Today. At first, the idea was like a burst of sunshine. Home. Her mother. Safety.

Then the clouds of reality rolled in. Nowhere was truly safe, not until they found the Ceffyl and delivered it to Emuirdane's vicious hands. The Iele prince couldn't touch Tate and her sisters here in Faerie, but he could still reach out to their mother and grandfather back in Bar Harbor.

If Tate accepted Ronan's offer, and she and the others went home without the Ceffyl . . . then all they'd been through would have been for nothing.

Danger here. Danger at home.

There was no alternative. They had to push on and complete their quest.

Tate glanced back to the house, and her eyes flared with surprise. Fiona had gotten out of bed. She and Sami looked down from a front-facing window, and their eyes fell to Tate in question.

He's offered us a way out, Tate communicated with her sisters from afar. Telepathy did have its advantages.

He says he can help us go home. Tate drew a breath to calm herself, to assure herself. *But I don't think—*

No. The voice that sprang back at her was Fiona's. *We have to do what we came here for. We've come too far to just leave now.*

Tate's thoughts exactly.

I agree, Sami chimed in. *We're almost there. We have to keep going.*

Tate nodded at them and turned back to Ronan. "Thank you for the offer, but I'm afraid we can't accept."

"I urge you to reconsider." He scowled. "The lana will not open again for days, and the longer you stay in Faerie," he also looked up to her sisters, his gaze locked on the window, "the more peril you will face."

A chill bumped over Tate's arms, whether from the cool breeze or his intensity, she couldn't say.

"Again, we are grateful." Tate conveyed her sincere thanks with her eyes, but her tone was unyielding. "We won't be leaving today."

Ronan's glower deepened. "But—"

"Ronan," she said, stopping him from further insistence, "you saved my sister's life, and I can never thank you enough for that. But for now, we will stay in Faerie."

Ronan inclined his head, but it was clear he didn't understand or approve of her decision. "As you would have it." This time his smile seemed forced. "I must go. May you keep yourself safe and . . . make wise choices."

Tate shivered again at his cryptic words.

Jack put his arms around her shoulders and spoke to Ronan. "We will. Thank you."

Ronan's golden-brown eyes flicked up at the house one more time, and he turned to stride away. Once he was deep in the forest, Tate sighed and said, "Well, that was a little weird."

"Just a little." Jack pulled her around to face him. "Now, let's get you back inside, so you can spend some time with Fiona."

"Yes." Tate let the elation from her sister's recovery flood back in. "I think we should have a celebratory feast."

He put his hand on her lower back as they walked to the house. "We certainly have the supplies for one." He shook his head. "A never-ending supply."

Tate caught his wry smile. "What do you mean?"

"Well . . ." He opened the door.

And they almost tripped over a gigantic fruit basket sitting in the foyer. The huge arrangement was flowing with green ribbons and had a folded piece of flowery paper tacked to the front.

"What on earth?" Tate gasped.

"I think what you mean is," Jack reached for the note, "what in Faerie?" He unfolded the paper and read aloud. "Happy blessings on your recovery. Ever in your service, Herb and Havva Brownie."

"Who?" Tate studied Jack, but he only smiled and bobbed his head as if it all made perfect sense.

Before he could answer, Sami bounded down the stairs. She hurried to Tate and grabbed her in a hug. "Fiona's hungry." She squeezed harder and pulled away but kept her hands on Tate's shoulders.

The glisten in Sami's brown eyes summoned tears to Tate's as well. She sniffed. "That's good news."

"That's awesome news." Sami hugged her again, and with arms clamped around each other they jumped up and down. They laughed. They cried.

Then they jumped and laughed some more.

Finally, Sami shook her head. "Whew. What a crazy few days. I'm bushed. And I'm hungry too. Speaking of which . . ." She turned to Jack and rubbed her stomach. "Did I just hear you say 'have a brownie?'"

Fiona was content to munch on one of the sandwiches while they all sat crowded around her bed. When Tate told her about the mysterious Herb and Havva, Fiona angled her head in thought. "Aren't those the small Fae people who like to do housework?"

Jack, standing at the foot of the bed with his arms crossed and a grin on his face, raised a blonde brow. "That would definitely fall in line with what's been going on the last couple of days."

"Brownies." Tate laughed, watching Sami gobble down a real brownie. Just minutes after Sami had voiced her question, a plate of the chocolate treats had magically appeared on the kitchen table.

Tate had eaten two herself, giggling and laughing with her sisters the whole time. It seemed all she did was laugh and smile, now that Fiona was alive and well.

Her sister appeared to be much stronger than anyone had expected so soon after her illness, and Tate was thrilled to see the sparkle in her green eyes.

Sami had one of the green ribbons from the fruit basket holding back her long curls. She'd also tied one around Tate's shoulder-length tresses but, with Fiona's short hair, she'd only been able to drape one over her ear.

"I'm keeping these ribbons forever," Sami said. "To commemorate this special day."

"That sounds nice," Fiona said, taking hers off her ear. "But I think I want a bath or shower before we start playing dress up."

"Spoilsport." But Sami said it with a wink and leaned over to give Fiona a smacking kiss on the cheek.

"And I can take this icky thing off now, right?" Fiona pointed to the leaf on her chest. Thick and green, it had begun to dry and curl up at the edges.

"Yes." Tate helped her stand. "While you're bathing, I'll ... Well, I guess I'll stand in the kitchen and call out for schnitzel, since it's not one of my specialties."

Fiona had woken with a craving for the German food, and Tate was determined to see that she got it. Truthfully, she'd do her best to grow wings and fly right now if that's what Fiona wanted.

But the brownies must have heard Fiona's request, because when Tate went downstairs she found another note in the kitchen. This one read: *Brunch will be served in one hour.*

So after showers, they all enjoyed a festive "brunch" featuring schnitzel, sausage pizza, garlic penne pasta, and cherry cheesecake. Once bellies were full, eyelids began to droop, and everyone unanimously voted for a nap.

Even Fiona yawned and grumbled how she couldn't possibly be sleepy.

"Well, I am," Tate said, hardly able to keep her own eyes open. She dropped her head forward, still sitting in her chair at the kitchen table, and closed them for a few seconds.

And she woke up an undisclosed number of hours later in one of the many bedrooms. Someone had carried her up and tucked her in, all snuggly and warm.

With a secret smile, she imagined it had been Jack.

Crawling from beneath the covers, she changed into some of her new Faerie-wear. After opening the door to peek out, she tiptoed down the stairs, careful not to wake the others.

But the others, it turned out, had done a fine job of not waking *her*.

The light seeping from beneath a door down the hallway gave them away. Tate pushed open the heavy wooden panel to find her sisters and the men circled around a table in what seemed to be a large study.

An especially bright-eyed Fiona spotted Tate first. "Hey there, sleepyhead."

Sami snorted. "You're one to talk."

"Ugh." Fiona feigned insult. "I don't think hovering near death is quite the same thing."

And, Tate thought with a thump of her jubilus heart, things were back to normal.

Spying the papers spread over the table, she edged closer. "What are you guys doing?"

"We were deciding the best route to take tomorrow." Fiona eased one of the maps over and pointed. "There are two ways to Mount Aeylwon, but we think—"

"Hold it. Hold it." Tate waved both hands impatiently. "Fee, you can't possibly be considering a journey this soon. Tomorrow? You just opened your eyes after being catatonic for days."

"Yes." Fiona ground out the reply. "Tomorrow. I feel fine, and I'm ready to move on." She gestured to the others. "Plus, we all have lives to get back to. Mom and Granddad have got to be worried." She pursed her lips. "We can't stay in Faerie forever."

"Yes, but what does one more day in bed—"

"I don't need another day in bed." Fiona jerked the map back to her side of the table. She raised her eyes to Tate, and they flashed like emerald fire. "I'm tired of feeling weak."

Sami touched Tate's arm lightly. "Her mind's made up." The look on Sami's face told Tate she'd already had this argument with Fiona. And had apparently lost.

Tate studied Fiona's healthy flush, her clear eyes—and most of all, the willful set of her jaw.

Today was just too special to let her own stubbornness cause any strife, so she let her usual obstinacy flow out of her body like melted ice. "Okay," she said. "You know best."

Fiona's mouth almost dropped to her feet. She must have expected more of a fight from her oldest and most tenacious sister.

Tate was actually happy to surprise her with the change.

After a moment, Fiona kicked her lips up in a grateful smile. "Okay then."

She pointed to the map again, the one with the marked houses. "Here is one of the Winter Queen's homes." She tapped the paper. "And it seems to be the closest to the Mount Aeylwon entrance."

"Entrance," Tate groused. "That's right. The riddle mentioned a warren, dark and deep." She twisted her lips and glanced to Sami. "I'm getting pretty sick of going underground."

"Yeah, but just think," Sami said with false cheer, "if we survive, then we get a boon to keep."

A boon, Tate mused, remembering the riddle. And for some reason, the old-style word made her think of Ronan.

"Oh." She slapped her hands to her head. "I totally forgot." She hurried to a set of windows and stared out at the darkening sky. "Ronan mentioned a gift when he was here."

"Ronan?" Fiona's brow wrinkled.

"The man from the ruins. That's his name. Guess I forgot to mention that."

"Oh." Fiona nodded. Then her eyes slid to the side. "Ronan," she whispered.

Tate wondered over her sister's odd reaction, similar to when they'd first seen Ronan that awful night. But she quickly dismissed the mild concern.

"He said to tell you to expect a gift." Tate gestured to the setting sun. "Just after dusk."

"What do we really know about this guy?" Brit put his hands on his hips.

"Really?" Sami tilted her head. "We know he saved Fiona's life."

"He saved *all* of our lives," Tate added, jutting out her chin. "He drove the bugs away with his glowing ball."

"With his *borrowed* magick," Brit countered, his stance still aggressive. "I can't put my finger on it, but something about the guy bothers me."

"Look!" Fiona's expression lit up, and she rushed past Tate, her outburst distracting even the suspicious Brit.

Turning around, Tate joined her at the window. And was awed by the spectacle outside. Lights floated and danced in the trees, each tree boasting its own individual color.

"Could that be the gift?" Fiona whirled and dashed across the room.

Curious, the rest of them followed her outside. Where they soon realized they could better appreciate the show.

All the trees surrounding the house flashed and twinkled as if strung with Christmas lights, except this celebration featured every pastel shade imaginable. Not only was the theme different, but the tiny lights were moving.

Cherry-blossom pink, mint-green, robin's egg-blue, and many more. The entire forest seemed lit from within, and a subtle, sweet scent flowed all around, earthy and floral.

Fiona twirled out into the grass, and Sami followed. They clapped their hands and spun in circles like two young girls.

A lone violet spark drifted up and carried through the air to land on Fiona's outstretched finger.

Fiona stared at the light as if enthralled, and Tate watched in fascination. Then, in the pale purple glow, she saw a single tear roll down Fiona's cheek.

The violet dot suddenly flew up and waltzed around Fiona's head before zipping back to its tree.

"Faeries," Fiona called to Tate across the grass. "Real faeries. They're happy we're here."

Tate didn't know she was crying too, until Jack's hand caressed her cheek. She slipped right back into an old habit, holding out her arm to pull him against her.

They stood that way, together, for several minutes more, watching her adult sisters dance and play among the pretty faerie lights.

When Sami and Tate entered the woods, Brit heaved a breath from nearby. "Someone's got to keep an eye on those two." But he winked at Tate as he walked past. "And I thought I was done with Tinker Bell parties a long time ago."

He jogged across the lawn to keep watch over Sami and Fiona, both grown women and talented witches in their own right.

Yet to Brit, they would always be the little girls he had helped raise.

"This is your party too, you know." Jack took Tate by the hand and led her over the soft grass. He pulled her to a tree on the far side of the property. Its long drooping leaves reminded Tate of the weeping willow.

The lights—or the fairies—in this particular tree glittered in a luminous silvery-gold.

Face lifted to take in the lovely vision, Tate felt weightless, mesmerized by the hundreds of sparkles. "Oh, they are so amazing." She closed her eyes and could still sense the glow. "So beautiful."

Jack's hands slipped around her waist and he whispered, "Just like you."

With a smile, she turned into his embrace, fitting naturally and easily, as if she belonged in his arms. "Jack." She gazed up into his eyes. She knew that ocean-blue could turn hard with betrayal, shutter over when he was pain, or blaze with heated fury.

But now they were tender, with an underlying hint of mischief. "I guess I shouldn't take advantage of your emotional state." He ran a knuckle along her jaw and under her chin.

She drew an unsteady breath as the soft touch stirred something deeper inside.

"I'm not emotional," she said, her voice sounding strangely breathy. "I'm rock-steady." Then he trailed his fingers down the side of her neck, and her legs turned to putty.

But Jack held her against him. He held her up, supporting her when she grew even slightly weak. Just as he'd been doing since the moment he'd found her passed out on the rain-drenched sidewalk.

"I'm still sorry you got dragged into this," she told him, reaching up to run her hand through his tawny hair.

"Tate," he started, but she shushed him with a finger to his lips.

"I am sorry," she pressed into his warm chest, channeling strength again and lifting on her toes, "but at the same time, I'm glad you're here with me."

He drew her hand to his mouth and kissed it, and Tate's heart did a double-thump.

"I don't think I could have made it this far without you, Jack." She shook her head when he started to speak. "No, I'm serious. You were there for me, even when you were still angry. You're too good to me, especially after . . ."

"No." Now he was the one to halt her words by gently cupping her jaw. "I told you, the past is behind us. And I meant it."

"I was such a fool, Jack. I stayed away from you because I was scared," Tate said, her hands shaking. She licked her lips, drew a halting breath, and whispered, "But I missed you so much."

"Tate," he shook his head, looked into her eyes. The glow from above cast shadows that only accentuated Jack's handsome face.

He lowered his mouth, hovered teasingly, his breath mingling with hers. Then he kissed her, with a potent combination of longing and heat. His lips, his tongue, glided over hers. Feverish, demanding, yet heartbreakingly gentle.

Love exploded inside Tate, brilliant and hot. And she realized just how cold she'd been before, how much she'd denied herself by running away from Jack, by hiding from all that he offered.

Beneath the silvery-gold tree, she finally let go of the fear that had controlled her for so long. She opened her heart to her first love, her only love, as they clung to each other, caught up in a storm of passion that had been quietly brewing for seven long years.

Finally, Jack pulled away. "I missed you too," he said, cradling the back of her head with one hand, holding her close as his lips brushed against hers. "I never stopped waiting for you, Tate. When others might have called me a fool—hell, when I called myself a fool—I just held the thought of you in the back of my mind. Like a quiet flame, always burning, never going out."

"I'm sorry I made you wait. I didn't know . . . No, that's not right. I did know, deep down, but I wouldn't let myself admit that I wanted to come back to you. So I forced myself into isolation."

"But we're together now." He lifted his head but kept his arms around her, as if he didn't want to let her go for a single second. "And I don't want to waste any more time questioning our actions from before. I'm here with you, Tate, and if you'll let me, I'll stay with you until the end."

Though her heart knew the answer, she still needed to hear it from Jack's lips. "The end of my quest?"

His mouth moved over hers again, teasing as he brushed against her sensitive lips. "To the end," he said, and angled his mouth against hers, tongues tangling, slick and wet. The innocence of the faerie-lights did little to dampen the pure hunger sparking between them.

All too soon, Jack groaned and pulled away. But when he took her hand, he shot her a look that sent a stream of heat spiraling down through her chest to settle wickedly in her belly.

Tate tried to catch her breath from the surge of arousal as she walked hand-in-hand with him toward the house. She'd spent more time with Jack than any other man in her life, yet her face flushed with warmth as she put a hand to her lips and thought of the kiss they'd shared.

Then she licked her lips. And discovered she could still taste him.

She searched the tree line for her sisters and Brit, wondering how they would react if she and Jack slept in the same room tonight. Scratch that, she thought with a silent laugh. She knew exactly how Sami would react. With a huge, whooping cheer.

Fiona would be thrilled as well, and Brit, well . . . he'd be happy too. After all, Jack had passed the family test a long time ago. Not only because he was a wonderful, kind, talented, brilliant man. But because he'd always cherished Tate.

Now, she was determined to earn his love. No matter what he

said, she knew she had a lot to make up for.

And she intended to start making up right now.

She stumbled when Jack stopped short and threw out his arm to hold her back. "Stop." His voice was a harsh whisper. They were close to the manor house, near the front corner.

Jack just stared at the ground. Then he scanned the forest.

"Jack?" Tate asked, her skin tingling with apprehension. "What is it?"

"Tracks." He brought his gaze back to hers, and his fingers tightened around her hand. "Wolf tracks."

23

Jack still hadn't laid eyes on either Herb or Havva by the time he and the others were packed up and ready to depart the following morning. He did, however, write the two brownies a note of thanks for all they'd done during Fiona's illness.

Tate, her sisters, and Brit all signed their names at the bottom, grateful for the help of the tiny Fae creatures who performed such miracles yet preferred to stay hidden.

With the sun a bare glimmer on the horizon, the group left the elegant manor house behind and set out through the woods. The trees were still green and lush, lovely in their own right.

But when Tate cast a wistful glance up into the leaves, then sent him a small smile, he knew she was thinking of their glowing tree from the night before.

As they walked, Jack's eyes also roamed the quiet forest, though his mind flashed to a less pleasant memory. Like prints in the dirt. And the huge wolf who'd left them behind.

The woods were shadowed this early in the day, and he found himself constantly looking over his shoulder. There was no longer any doubt they were being followed. The question was why? What did the wolf want?

Jack had heard of predators tracking their prey for miles, but surely there'd been an opportunity for attack. Why would the beast tail them for so long but still keep its distance?

With the thought a prickle in the back of his mind, he continued to scour the vicinity. He did so until they exited the forest then followed a dirt road along the River Skye.

Even when the sun arced high overhead, he still found himself searching for a threat. By the end of the day, his suspicious mind was as tired as his feet. The ascent up a winding mountain trail was something of a reprieve.

Nothing would sneak over that rocky rise, and the rough terrain allowed him to finally relax.

The narrow path led into what was known as Murandi's Crown. Ten craggy summits gave the area its name, the "jewels" of the crown their ten glistening caps of snow.

"Not much farther," Brit said when they paused for a break. He pointed up to a turn that led back into tall wintergreens. "The queen's property is about an hour more."

Despite Jack's worry over the wolf, the long trek had proved uneventful. Somehow the lack of danger made him more edgy, as if the worst was still waiting around every new corner.

Other than the gentle drift of snow, they encountered no obstacles. They walked right up to the silver gates of the Winter Queen's estate and into a grand courtyard.

Jack stopped to survey the massive palace. Gables and spires lent it a faerie-tale quality, and stacked stones were the color of swans.

"Not bad," Sami said, wiggling her brows. "I can stand to stay here for a night or two."

"Hopefully just the one." Brit walked up the wide steps and lifted a huge metal knocker on a giant set of double doors. They both swung open in invitation.

Jack put his hand on Tate's back and escorted her in. Even the simple touch reminded him of their kiss the night before.

After he'd found the tracks, they'd all gathered in the study to discuss the wolf and its possible motives. And the talk of the animal and its potential threat had cooled Jack's ardor.

He was thrilled that Tate still had feelings for him, and he wanted nothing more than to pursue their relationship again. But did he have any business trying to romance her here? While they were trapped in such a perilous world?

She needed to focus on one thing. The Ceffyl. Then, as soon as they returned home, they could look to each other.

And to the future.

"It appears there are brownies in residence." Fiona made the announcement from somewhere inside the castle.

Lost in his own thoughts, Jack hadn't noticed the women spreading out to investigate, leaving him and Brit standing at the bottom of a sweeping staircase.

Fiona reappeared. "Dinner is waiting for us," she said before grabbing her pack and easing up the stairs. She trailed her hand up the pure white bannister. "But for *that* dining room, I'm going to get cleaned up first."

A touch on Jack's arm brought him around to Tate. "I'm going up too." Her smile held a hint of wickedness. "But I'll see you in a bit."

Once they'd all cleaned up and enjoyed a grand feast, they gathered on a huge stone balcony in the rear of the palace. The circle of snowy peaks spread before them, glowing gold in the setting sun.

Jack saw why the place was called Murandi's Crown. The bright points all around were nothing short of majestic.

Brit unrolled one of the maps and studied it with Sami. He tapped his finger against the paper. "See these two summits?"

Jack leaned in to look. The two crests Brit indicated were of similar height and created a perfect V-shape between them.

"Here's where we are right now." Brit repositioned his finger. "And here's the pass we'll take to the Mount Aeylwon entrance."

"How long will it take us to get there?" Tate squinted at the map.

"A few hours. We're not far from the pass. We'll continue on the road we followed up the mountain today. The entrance is midway up."

"Good," she said with a nod, before easing over to stare out at the sunset. She glanced to Jack.

Then, as if she'd seen enough of the incredible view, she stepped back from the railing and stretched. "I think I'll turn in."

"Me too. We have a big day tomorrow," Sami said. "We leave at daybreak?"

Fiona groaned. "How about two hours after daybreak?" She held out a hand to indicate the pass. "We pick up the trail right outside."

"One hour after sunrise." Brit chucked Fiona's chin and went back inside. He stopped abruptly and stared at the long dining table. "How do they do that?"

Jack eased around him to see the table cleared of all food and dishes. "I didn't see a thing. No movement out of the corner of my eyes or anything." The brownies had been at work again.

"Must be magick." Tate leaned up and kissed him on the cheek. "Early day tomorrow. Better get some sleep." She sauntered across the room, tossing back one last glance.

Her hips swayed gently, and Jack curled his fingers. He imagined gripping his hands in that shiny fall of black hair. Looking down into those warm brown eyes.

He inhaled deeply and reminded himself of his earlier decision. He'd help Tate get through the challenges still facing her here in Faerie. His passion and need would hold for now.

But as soon as they were back in the human world . . .

Beside him, Brit cleared his throat. "Jack."

"Hmm?" Jack dragged his gaze to the other man.

"If you're going to look at my niece like that," he clapped him on the shoulder, "try to do it when I'm not around."

Jack's mouth worked, but no sound came out. But Brit just

laughed and strode away, his amused chuckle trailing in his wake.

Torn between mortification and the lust that still raged inside, Jack waited until all sounds of footsteps faded. He turned back to the glass doors and stood with arms crossed, telling himself to enjoy the view.

But wondering if he should go out and roll in the snow. His blood felt so hot and his pulse so erratic, he didn't know how he'd kept his hands off of Tate for this long.

Since the beginning of this wild ride, she'd come across as independent, resilient, and decisive. The same Tate he'd fallen for so long ago.

But last night her softness had finally shone through. And that combination of strength and fragility was far more potent than Jack had remembered.

Thinking of her face bathed in faerie lights, Jack cursed softly and turned on his heel. The cold outside wouldn't ease his longing or cool his blood. Nothing could appease that ache but a long, languorous night with Tate.

Imagining her curled up under the covers somewhere, he took the curving staircase one slow step at a time. Though the lights still burned below, the second level was dim, and everyone else seemed to have gone to bed.

With a heavy sigh, he decided to do the same, but as he passed Tate's room on the way to his own, he noticed a faint glow shining from beneath his door.

He didn't remember leaving the light on. He pushed open the door and eased inside, surprised to find a fire blazing in the hearth.

And even more surprised to find Tate, lying in his bed.

"Jack." She saw him and sat up. "I was wondering how long you would be down there."

He'd just been thinking about the soft side of Tate. Now here she was. Firelight played over her skin and hair, and her lean form was draped in white silk.

He closed the door behind him with a *snick*. Then he turned the lock.

He walked to the bed, met her dark, shining eyes, and he was done for. "Damn, you're beautiful." Lifting his hand, he stroked his fingers down her bare shoulder. "And I was doing my best to leave you alone."

"Why?" A shadow of uncertainty drifted over her face.

So he caught her hand, kissed her palm. "To give you space." He kissed her fingers. "So you can focus on your quest."

She eased off the bed with a rustle of blankets, taking his hand to lead him to the wide windows. They showcased the same view as the one downstairs, but the sun was now gone, and only starlight shone on the mountains.

"My quest," she told him, "is exactly why I'm here."

Jack soothed his palms down her arms. "Tell me."

She cast her eyes to the menacing peaks outside. "Tomorrow we go to Mount Aeylwon, and none of us truly know what to expect." The breath she drew was jagged. "I might not return."

Cupping her cheek with his hand, he eased her gaze to his. "Don't say that. Don't even think it." His gut dropped at the idea of losing her again.

"You know it's a possibility. It always has been." The corners of her full pink lips turned up. "But not knowing what will happen tomorrow is why I want to be here tonight." She edged closer, trailed a finger along his jaw. "I want to be with you, Jack. But I need to be sure."

He shook his head. "Be sure of what?"

Her expression fell into serious lines. "After all that's happened, and everything you know. . ." Tate drew another short breath and lifted her eyes. "Are you sure you still want me?"

He took her hand, laid it over his heart, and with his eyes locked with hers he whispered, "Tate, I've wanted you my whole life." He framed her face with his hands. "But never more than right now."

"Then it's only fair that you know," she all but melted into his arms, "that I've loved you my whole life."

Jack's heart paused painfully at her words.

"But never more than right now."

When Tate rose up and pressed her mouth to his, Jack's heart began to beat again. And every throb echoed her name.

He was simply overwhelmed, staggered by the pure female power she radiated.

He'd told her that he wanted her, but want wasn't a strong enough word. His body, his heart, every single piece of him *craved* her.

Tate's arms slid around his neck, her breasts pressing through the sheer silk against his chest.

He pulled back to slip his hand between them, whispering his fingers over a nipple. And thrilled to feel her shiver in response.

She'd offered herself to him tonight. So tonight he would take.

But he would give her comfort she hadn't asked for. Just as she had given him tenderness he hadn't expected.

The blood in his veins pounded thick and hot. And just when he was aroused to the point of pain, she trailed her hand down and into his pants. She stroked him with a cruel delicacy.

"Tate," he growled, "if you keep touching me like that . . ."

He didn't say the words, but spoke with the heat in his eyes. Then he let his greedy hands do the rest.

He bent to slip his hands under her gown, and ran his palms up curving calves and tight thighs. He stopped just as he felt her heat and grazed his fingers up and down her leg, teasing, taunting, drawing closer each time to her most sensitive flesh.

Standing straight again, he put his mouth to that special place on her neck, the one he knew drove her crazy. Then he finally slid his fingers inside her wet sheath. He worked both hand and mouth and let the torture commence.

She let out a sweet little moan and her head fell back. When the pulse in her neck fluttered against his lips, he curled one finger into her sensitive spot.

The throb in her neck was rhythmic and wild, just how Tate felt when she came to her pleasure. When he was inside her and she tightened around him.

The imagery had a primal groan ripping from his throat, and in one move he held her in his arms. In two strides he had her on the bed.

Yanking the silk up around her hips, he held himself above her and pushed against her core. Though he was still dressed, his need for her was clear.

When she moaned, he ground against her. "Ask me again if I want you."

❈❈❈

Tate reached for Jack but he lifted away. "Tell me," he said, smiling smugly, his warm hands skimming back to her thighs. Then with his wicked fingers, he was touching her again.

This wasn't the first time she'd been kissed by Jack, and it wouldn't be the first time they'd made love. But the years had taught him patience and skill, and she was sure his thumb had never done *that* before.

"You want me," she said in between gasps, hoping the admission would end her suffering.

But instead of removing his clothes, Jack leaned down and kissed her mouth. Then he put his lips to her cheek, her neck, and the hollow of her collar bone.

Her back arched as she offered herself to him, and when he didn't take fast enough, she guided him to her breast. When his wet, warm mouth closed around her, she cried out.

Then she latched onto his wrists and held him with a stare. "I want you too. And I want you now."

She made quick work of his pants and took him in her hand—hot steel and velvet. She raised up to hook an arm around his neck, and held him in place as she tasted his skin. His flavor made her hunger for more, so earthy, salty, and so utterly male.

The firelight gilded his skin as he quickly undressed, and Tate matched him by slipping out of her gown. Then they came together again, kneeling on the bed.

Tate ran her hands down his chest, all that lovely gold skin quivering beneath her touch. He was so strong, so steady, so sure, and Tate needed to feel it all.

He gripped the back of her thigh and hiked her leg, causing her to sob out his name. The length of his erection rubbed against her, so close but not yet fulfilling.

Jack held her that way as he lowered them back down.

Then his thumb was tormenting her again, as he slid into her with one easy stroke. When he filled her completely, he lifted his head. And her name on his lips was as reverent as a prayer.

The blue of his eyes seemed darker, heavier. She loved that they reminded her of the sea, such beauty, intensity, and like Jack—such constancy.

As they moved together, he linked his fingers with hers, and the sweetness almost brought her to tears. How could she have forsaken this man? How could she have abandoned this love?

But accepting him now, and relinquishing her heart, brought a slow-building ache, the likes of which she'd never known.

The pleasure grew and spread as their bodies twined together. Then the ache tightened into ecstasy, and Jack took her mouth as she shattered.

Here was magick. Here was her prize.

Still joined together—lips, hands, and hearts—they loved until the fire died low.

Jack held her against him and whispered in her ear, "Never fear my love again."

In answer, Tate kissed him and snuggled close. And when she fell asleep, she was at perfect peace.

24

"I don't see anything." Tate shook her head, turning it side to side as she searched for the entrance to Mount Aeylwon. "According to the map, it should here somewhere." She tapped the paper. "Near that crooked tree," she said, pointing to what looked like a spruce bent over at an odd angle.

The pass they'd followed uphill bisected Mount Aeylwon and another huge mountain. The trail had flattened out and widened, and that's where they now stood. Lost, apparently.

Mount Aeylwon was only marked on the oracle's map. Not on the queen's. It was as if the mountain itself had been kept a secret.

"Let's take a closer look." Fiona walked to the tree. She studied the immediate area, and then focused on the side of the mountain. She jutted her head forward and eased closer to the rock wall. She waved at Tate and Sami. "Come over here."

They both joined Fiona, and as soon as they neared the dark, craggy rock, Tate saw the bending waves of an illusion. "It's concealed by magick."

"So how do we get in?" Fiona waved her hand. "Open."

Brit spoke from the road. "You're the Daughters of Nadia, the only ones meant to find the entrance. Try something a little more . . . organized."

Sami put her hands on her hips and Fiona frowned. But Tate felt up to the challenge. This was what they'd come here to do, and they weren't going home without a shiny little horse in their pack.

So far, they'd seen no sign of the infamous Legion sworn to defend the Jeweled Ceffyl. Now they were literally outside the gate, and still no trumpeting horns to announce an attack. No warriors riding on snorting stallions.

Tate had begun to believe they just wouldn't show. Or was that just her wishful thinking?

With Brit's mild reproach still stinging, Tate leaned her head close to Sami's and Fiona's. Together, they came up with a spell.

"For full impact, I think we should hold hands." Fiona stood in the middle, so she linked up with her sisters on either side.

They faced the deep gray wall and its wavering lines of distortion. And as one, their voices rang out. "We've followed the path of the setting sun, far we've traveled to Mount Aeylwon. By the blood of Nadia and the sisters three, let us see. Let us see."

Tate could feel the tingling rush of power, and as she stared the illusion began to dissolve. Two pillars had been carved into the rock and flanked a doorway. Not a simple cave-like hole, but a cleanly-hewn entrance.

"Hmph." Fiona nodded. "That was easy."

"Simple but effective," Sami said with a smug glance to her uncle.

Brit waved a hand in the way of a gentleman and said, "After you." Then he and Jack picked up the packs and followed.

Tate and her sisters neared the pillars, but as soon as they got close enough to step inside, a panel opened above the entrance. Inside was an hourglass.

"Oh. That's not good." Sami licked her lips as she stared up at the timer. "Are you thinking what I am?"

Tate's freezing-cold blood had coagulated in her heart. So, yes, she'd come to the same realization as her sister. She turned back to the men, both with their brows furrowed.

"What the hell?" Jack stepped up and took Tate by the arm. "What is this? You have to get through within a certain amount of time?" He pulled Tate against him. "Or what?"

Brit seemed equally upset. "I don't like this. The stakes just shot up."

Tate didn't pull away from Jack but put her hand on his face instead. She forced him to look at her. "The stakes have always been high. This is just another step we have to take."

"Or a good reason to turn back." He shook his head and looked to Brit for support. "I'm sorry. But I can't let you do this."

"You have to, Jack. This is meant for us. We are the only ones who can complete this task." She kissed him and gently extricated herself.

More than ever, she was grateful they'd found their way back to each other again. That they'd had last night, and he'd always know how much she loved him.

No matter what happened here today.

"And by us," she glanced to her sisters, "I mean just the three of us."

"No." Jack sliced a hand through the air. "If you do this, then I'm going with you."

"You can't." Sami spoke from the doorway. "I see three tunnels inside. Only three. It was prophesied that we would be the ones to find the Ceffyl, and this test or trial or whatever it is, was designed to keep anyone else out."

"If you want us to be safe," Fiona said, "you have to stay back. You'll only be a distraction."

"They're right, Jack." Brit's expression was one of acceptance laced with fear. "I hate it as much as you do, but," he drew a deep breath, "they're the ones. The only ones. And they're ready."

He moved to his nieces then. "You're prepared. And you've got your mother's stubborn blood running through your veins." He hugged them one by one. "Be safe. Be smart."

His eyes were stern when he stepped back. "And use everything you've got."

Tate nodded. "We will."

Jack's arms were around her again, and she let him hold her for a few seconds more. He kissed her again and then spoke against her lips. "Come back to me."

Tate pulled back and met his gaze. "Always."

A loud *click!* startled her and Jack apart.

"Tate," Sami said, pointing to the hourglass, "I think it's time."

And sure enough, the timer slid out of its cubby, a mechanical arm clamped to its middle. The hourglass flipped upside down.

And the first particles of sand began to fall.

Tate looked up at Jack. "I love you." Then she and her sisters dashed inside the entrance to the dreaded Mount Aeylwon.

❄❄❄

The small cavern was dark inside and led to three separate tunnels.

"So do we each take one, three for three?" Fiona asked. "Or do we have to choose just one and go down it together?"

Sami rubbed her forehead. "I guess we each take one, but how can we be sure?" She turned in a circle to investigate the small chamber. "I don't see any clues or anything other than the openings."

Fiona threw a witchlight into the air and looked inside the center tunnel.

Tate and Sami quickly created fireballs of their own. The warren here was supposedly dark and deep, so they would need light.

"So that means we'll be separated?" Fiona asked.

"Then we'll use our telepathy." Sami nodded. "But time is slipping by. We've got to move."

A trickle of cold dread rolled down through Tate's chest, but she'd known to expect a challenge. The riddle had plainly stated that she and her sisters would have to "survive" this part of the quest.

Now it was literally do or die.

She blew out a shaky breath and looked at her sisters. "I love you both."

"Me too," Fiona whispered.

But Sami only shook her head. "I'll tell you I love you when we're back outside, safe and sound." Then with a yell, she rushed into her tunnel.

Tate and Fiona exchanged a glance and ran into theirs as well.

Thank you, witchlight, Tate thought, racing down the winding tunnel. The shaft was narrow and black as night. She hurried to find the end to see what awaited her, and though she'd expected to descend farther into the mountain, she would swear she was actually on a mild incline.

Her heart was thrumming in her chest, as if a hummingbird were trying to flutter its way out. Her elevated heart rate wasn't from exertion but the sheer rush of adrenaline. Adrenaline spiked with fear.

She sped around a sharp turn and almost ran headlong into a door. By the glow of her witchlight, she saw a lever in the center of the stone barrier. With panicked hands, she gripped it and pulled down.

Nothing happened.

She tried again.

Nothing. *Dammit!*

Her frustration must have carried to her sisters through their telepathy, because Fiona's voice came back to her. *What's wrong?*

I'm at a door with a lever, but it won't work.

I'm at a door now too. Sami sent out. *Mine doesn't work either.*

Oh, no. Fiona's voice. *Mine's broken too.* A pause and then, *Wait. This is a test.*

Tate shook her hands though no one was there to see. *What do you mean?*

Our telepathy. We can communicate with each other. There has to be a way we can get through these doors, Fiona said.

Excitement flared inside Tate. *And we can only get through by doing something unique to the abilities of the Daughters of Nadia.*

But how . . . Sami trailed off. *Got it! We have to pull the levers at the same time. I'm going to count to three, and then we all pull. After three, ready?*

Ready, Tate and Fiona called out with their minds in unison.

One, two, three—now!

Tate tugged her lever down, and the heavy stone panel slid to the side. She jumped through the door, more than ready to be out of the tight passageway.

She looked over to see Fiona and Sami standing in the same room with her, their faces filled with the same awe that she was experiencing.

But she was feeling something else as well. "We can do this," she said, her voice strong with determination.

"Damn straight." Sami slammed a fist into her open palm.

"Let's go!" Fiona took the lead and made her way to the single exit in the small room where they'd been reunited.

Tate fell in line behind her and Sami, only to be disappointed. They were in another corridor, though this one was slightly wider.

Then the door closed behind them.

Tate jerked around to see the passage seal shut. Only one way out, she told herself. And that way was forward.

This tunnel was shorter, and when they exited at the other end, they found themselves in a cavernous room. A door sat on the far side, open and waiting. But there was only one way to get there.

A flat bridge stretched across to the other side, spanning a deep, black gorge.

"Oh." Tate breathed out the word, at a loss for anything better to say. There were no handrails of any sort, nothing to keep them from tumbling into the bottomless abyss.

"What's the trick here?" Sami asked. "What do we do?"

The bridge wasn't made of wooden slats but of rocks. Many rocks, smooth and flat, held together by mortar like a cobblestone street.

Fiona stepped forward. She put a tentative foot on one of the stones. It gave way beneath her, and she threw herself back. Sami and Tate caught her and held on.

"I found the trick," Fiona said, her lips trembling.

Tate released her sister and edged closer. She crouched to put her hand to another rock. This one held. "We can only step on certain ones. The others will fall."

"So how do we know which ones are which? Do we just test them one at a time as we go?"

The mention of time struck in Tate's head like a match. "No. That will take too long. Don't forget, the hourglass is draining as we speak."

"Then we have to check them all at once." Sami put her fingers to her lips. She narrowed her eyes and snapped her fingers. "Let's stir the wind."

"Here?" Tate gazed down at the fall that went on forever.

"Yes. I'm sure of it." Sami held up her hands. "We had to learn to call the wind to cross Mist River." Her brown eyes gleamed with certainty. "And I don't believe in coincidence. Not anymore."

"Okay. Okay." Tate raised her hands. "But be careful. No gale-force winds this time."

Not wanting to delay, they went straight for their magick. No words. No chants. Just the fortitude of their witches' hearts and a wave of their powerful hands.

"Easy," Tate said when the first gust hit her face. "Control it."

Fiona grimaced when the bridge began to tremble. "I hope we don't get stuck in here."

Tate swallowed and tried not to think about it. Because if the whole bridge collapsed, that's exactly what would happen.

They'd be trapped inside a mountain, on a single shelf of rock that overlooked an impassible divide.

She called for her magick. She pulled from deep within herself. "This has got to work!"

The first stone dropped without a sound, falling away into the blackness. The chasm was so deep she never heard the rock hit bottom.

All at once, three or four more stones fell away as the winds buffeted the shaking structure.

"Keep going." Fiona shoved her hands forward and released several more stones at the same time. A pattern began to emerge, a lane of stones curving left and right, but they remained connected, creating an unbroken chain across the gorge.

At last it seemed all the loose stones had dropped away, and Tate intercepted Fiona when she stepped up. "I'll go first this time." She smiled at her baby sister. "Humor me."

After almost losing Fiona once and then watching her totter at the edge of the void, Tate decided to take this risk herself.

She inhaled, held her breath, and stepped on the first stone. It didn't shake or quiver but remained stable. "Okay," she called back, advancing cautiously one step at a time. And never taking her eyes off the next stone. One wrong move and she would plummet.

There was no time to let fear hold them back though, and she was relieved that neither of her sisters seemed bothered by the height. The worst part of this ordeal, Tate thought, was not knowing how much sand was left in the hourglass.

Or what would happen once time ran out.

She made it to the other side and her stomach turned over, releasing the terror she'd clutched inside and pretended wasn't there. But now that she was on solid ground again and gazed down into the abyss, she felt faint.

But she shook off the dizziness and held out her hands for Fiona who'd crossed after her. And then Sami as she took her final steps.

"I wonder how many more?" Sami asked, running a hand along her ponytail. "My nerves are in my stomach, and they seem to be stabbing me with pitchforks."

Tate laughed as she turned to the next door. Looked like she wasn't the only one feeling an aftereffect from the death drop they'd just skipped over.

This time the room they entered was round. The floor was plain stone and the ceiling paneled in wood. Across the chamber stood one more doorway. And beyond it, Tate could see clouds passing across another mountain.

"Did we make it?" she asked, perusing the empty room and searching for the next test. "Do we just walk out?"

"I don't see anything." Sami held up her hands and grinned. "But let's not stand here and talk about it. I want *out*."

"Before the hourglass runs empty," Fiona added.

Together they walked across the room. When they made it halfway, they heard a grumble and moan.

"I knew it," Sami said, exasperation tingeing her voice. "What this time?"

"Whatever it is, we can handle it." Fiona nodded firmly. Then she looked up and said, "Oh."

Tate followed her sister's gaze to the ceiling. The wooden panel had split in the middle, revealing a metal disc that spanned the entire room.

"What is it?" Tate asked, just as the door in front of them shut, and three panels opened in the walls, one on each side.

Strange-looking wheels turned within the walls with ropes attached. Not wheels, she realized, but pulleys.

A *clang!* above their heads drew her attention up again. And there was the final test. Sharp metal spikes now covered the disc.

And the disc was descending.

"Okay. Okay." Sami wiggled her fingers and spun in a circle. "How do we get out of this one?"

"Telekinesis?" Fiona shrugged. "It's one of the abilities we haven't used yet."

"We can try." Tate held out her hands and used her mind to shove against the metal disc. The three of them concentrated on the spiked apparatus as it inched down toward their heads.

"I can't feel it moving." Tate sensed no give in the metal. "I don't think it's working." She released the thrust of her magick.

And when she did, the disc dropped another foot.

"Hold it!" Sami shouted.

But Fiona withdrew hers as well. "No, that's not right. It just fell because we let go, but we weren't making enough of a difference."

Sami let go of her magick, and the disc dropped and shimmied again. The spikes seemed a lot larger to Tate, and they were now much closer to driving into their skulls.

She studied everything in the room, looking frantically for the answer. The only other items in the room were the pulleys and ropes.

And the pulleys were made of wood. "Fire," Tate said, flicking open her fingers so her white flames could burn freely. "Those pulleys hold the ropes. The ropes are controlling the disc. We stop their action, the disc stops moving."

"Or it drops on our heads." Sami ran over to one wall and studied the mechanism. "I can't tell for sure." She ducked when a spike grazed her temple. "Shit!"

Sami was the tallest of them all, but not by that much.

"We have to try." Fiona's eyes were fixed on the descending spikes. Still staring up at hundreds of sharp points, she opened her hands, palms burning bright.

Sami mimicked the action. And despite her doubt, she lit up the pulley and ropes with a blast of heat.

Tate and Fiona cut loose on the other two pulleys. It took only seconds for the wood to combust, and the ropes burned quickly through.

"Here we go." Fiona took Tate's hand when the ropes began to snap, hanging on by a few flaming threads.

"Mine's going too!" Sami called from across the room.

Almost in sync, the ropes popped apart on both sides of the room, releasing the tension that had been controlling the disc. The metal ceiling stopped falling and reversed directions.

The door leading outside slid open once again.

The three women wasted no time getting out of the lethal chamber. They exited onto a ledge, several feet wide and rimming the exterior of the mountain.

"We did it!" Sami hugged Tate with one arm and Fiona the other.

Tate held them both for a moment, her eyes stinging as triumph and relief washed through her. Then she looked over Sami's shoulder.

"Yes," Tate said, drawing back and pointing. "I think we did."

Another bridge extended out from the side of Mount Aeylwon. The stone structure was sparkling white, unblemished by time or the elements.

The bridge connected to a round platform that seemed to float in the sky itself. In the center stood a small altar, white as alabaster, like the bridge.

And atop the altar, sat a glistening box of silver and gold.

The three shared a collective gasp before Fiona whispered, "The Jeweled Ceffyl."

25

The bridge was approximately ten feet wide with thick stone railings on each side. Tate grazed her hand over the thick barrier but felt light-headed if she leaned too far over. She and her sisters had traipsed over a bottomless ravine in the mountain trials, but looking down now, she realized the void had been far easier to walk across.

Now, outside in the sun, she could see how far she actually had to fall.

With her skin looking a little wan, Sami kept to the middle of the walkway. "The winds are too strong up here," she said through clenched teeth. "I feel like they'll just pick me up and carry me away."

Tate gave her a smile that was more a grimace, because she agreed wholeheartedly.

Fiona, however, suffered no such anxiety. She walked steadily ahead of them both, her steps light and quick. She reached the altar first and held her hands over the box. Her eyes sparkled, but she didn't touch.

Letting her arms drop to her sides, she gave Tate and Sami a hurry-up look.

Tate finally made it to the round platform, its girth making her feel slightly more secure. She and Sami lined up along one side of the huge altar with Fiona.

The box glistened, as if made of spun silver and gold. Tate didn't know if there even was such a thing, but if so, this is what it would look like.

"This is it." Sami rubbed her hands together. "How should we do this?"

"Like everything else," Tate suggested. "Together."

The three of them touched the box at the same time. Warmth flowed into Tate's fingers and up her arms. She grasped the lid of the box, as did her sisters. And together they lifted.

The lid didn't move.

"What?" Fiona tugged harder. "Is it stuck?"

Sami bent over to examine the container more closely. "I see a seam, so it should open."

Tate's mind filed through everything they'd accomplished thus far. The tunnels, the breakaway bridge, and the spikes. "We may be out of the mountain, but we're still being tested. Think about it," she said when her sisters gave her puzzled looks.

"We used a spell to make the entrance appear to us. Then we called upon our witchlights, our telepathy—"

"Our wind," Fiona cut in.

"And then our fire," Sami said, completing the train of thought. "But what about the other elements? We've never called all four corners. Never used the powers of earth or water."

"I don't think we were meant to." Tate ran her hand over the flashing silver. "We only learned wind when we came to Faerie, as if it were fated."

"Meant to be." Fiona smiled. "A prophecy fulfilled."

Sami concentrated on the box. "The only other power we haven't used is our ability to move things. With our minds," she amended. "So. Together." She stared at the box.

Tate and Fiona followed suit.

Directing her magick to the top of the box, she focused on lifting the lid. There was no slow creaking sound or gentle lift. The shiny cover all but flew backward, clanging against the altar.

The open box revealed its contents.

"No, no, no, no." Sami stammered the denial, her eyes wide with terror and her body clearly petrified.

Fiona whispered, "I forgot about this part of the riddle."

Tate held as still as Sami, falling back on primal instinct when it came to this particular kind of threat. She too had forgotten the riddle. Specifically, the line mentioning serpents.

Three colorful snakes uncoiled from inside the chest—rising up in a menacing display of red, yellow, and blue. Their slit pupils were fixated on Tate and her sisters, tongues flicking and hissing. Their bodies shook as if agitated. And too late, Tate recalled the words, *serpents strike the sisters three.*

With a loud hiss, the snakes struck simultaneously, launching themselves at the ones who'd invaded their sanctuary. Tate threw up her arms and screamed as she stumbled back.

The red serpent slithered around her wrist, and flailing, she tried to shake it off. But the long, twisting body corkscrewed more tightly, and then, as she stared, the snake turned into gold.

Tate's shriek cut off abruptly. The living animal was gone, leaving only a ruby-eyed bracelet in its place. Speechless, Tate looked over to see Sami marveling at her own golden bracelet, though her stones were the bluest of sapphires. Fiona fingered the silver bangle around her wrist, hers glittering with amber eyes of topaz.

Before they could recover from the shock, the chest erupted into silver and gold flames, burning in the center of the altar.

Sami immediately spoke the lines of the riddle. "As serpents strike the sisters three and flame is upon the flesh."

She glanced to Fiona who finished with, "Prism and light lead to the fight for one's greatest wish."

Tate rubbed her new bangle and squared her shoulders. "Let's put some flame on our flesh and get this done." She released a choking laugh. "My heart can't take many more surprises."

"The snakes are over," Sami said, clenching her eyes shut. "Let's get to the fight."

Borrowing one of Sami's expressions, Fiona said, "Damn straight." She curled her hand into a fist and thrust her arm into the fire.

"Fee!" Tate jolted, ready to help douse the flames, but Fiona seemed unfazed. She didn't shout in pain but scowled disapprovingly at the fire. "Come on, do something." Then she stuck her other arm into the fire, this time the one with the snake coiled around her wrist.

And the prisms, the jeweled eyes, shot out two shafts of topaz-yellow light.

"There you go," Sami said, shoving her bracelet into the flames to release another two beams of brilliant blue. "Your turn, Tate."

Amazement made Tate's movements slow and languid, but she eased her bracelet into the fire, adding her two rays of ruby-red. As soon as all three of them had their arms in the fire, the flames began to coalesce, taking on a new shape.

The shape of a horse.

Jewels appeared, dazzling in color, covering the form of the silver statuette, and this time it was Tate who whispered in awe, "The Jeweled Ceffyl."

Once the transformation was complete, the figurine stood with one foreleg in the air, as if the horse had been frozen mid-prance. The silver body kicked back sunlight, and the facets of the gemstones glistened.

"You take it, Tate," Fiona said, placing a gentle hand on her arm. "You began this quest. You finish it."

Hands trembling from the rush of adrenaline and . . . reverence for such mystical beauty, Tate palmed the Ceffyl with both hands and held it close to her body. Her breath whooshed from her lungs and she smiled at her sisters. "Now what do we do with it?"

"Well, before we can put it away for safe storage, we have to find our way back to Jack and Brit." Sami let her hand flop against her side. "They've got the packs."

The aftershock of the flight-or-fight response flooded Tate's head. Drunk on their success in finding the Ceffyl—and the tiny little fact that none of them had died in the process—Tate let her head fall back as she laughed at the absurdity of it all.

Sami and Fiona shared her good humor, until they were all overcome and felt the need for one more sister hug.

Brit's voice carried on the wind, and Tate stopped laughing. Her head snapped around.

Brit and Jack were both in the middle of the bridge.

But they weren't alone.

A crowd of men stood behind them, all wearing similar uniforms of ashen-gray with steel-splint armor covering theirs torsos. Several of the warriors held long swords in their hands, while others stood with staffs.

No ordinary wooden sticks, the staffs were fitted with huge black stones on either end.

Tate didn't have to be told that she was looking at the defenders of the Jeweled Ceffyl. The soldiers trained in warfare, both physical and magickal. The men sworn to protect the Ceffyl with their lives.

The Legion had arrived after all. And they held Jack and Brit prisoner.

She stepped forward, holding the Ceffyl tightly to her side. She wasn't giving it up, not now. She and her sisters were taking the horse home.

And this time—Tate met Jack's grim eyes—she was taking Jack with her.

Jack tried to throw off the arm of the warrior who restrained him, but received a fist to the jaw for his trouble.

Tate almost bolted forward and struck out with her fire, but a stern male voice ordered, "Hold!"

Though he wasn't speaking to her, Tate went rigid. Not because he commanded it, but because she recognized his voice.

The leader pushed through his horde of soldiers, moving to the front where Tate could see him clearly.

And Tate understood why Jack was so pissed off.

"Son of a bitch." Sami shook her head.

Tate breathed slowly in through her nose and handed the Ceffyl to Fiona. She stepped out to stand in front of her sisters, hands loose at her sides, ready for anything. She glared at the man, notched up her chin, and practically growled, "Hello, Ronan."

The dark-haired man was as somber as ever, but at least Tate knew the reason. The man who'd treated Fiona's lethal sting and helped carry her to safety now stood ready to fight them all to the death.

"I tried to give you a way out, Tate." He walked between Jack and Brit who were still being restrained. "I tried to get you out of Faerie safely."

"You must have known we wouldn't take you up on your offer," she called, shifting her eyes to Jack. He seethed with fury, struggling against the men holding him and watching Ronan's every move.

He still had his axe on his back. The Legion hadn't even bothered to disarm him.

And that was a little insulting.

"You aren't leaving here with the Ceffyl." Ronan took three more casual strides in her direction. "Save yourself." He waved a hand to Jack and Brit. "And save them by handing it over."

Tate shook her head. "Not going to happen. We were destined to find and free the Jeweled Ceffyl. You and all your army won't stop us."

He came closer, his mouth sneering. "Oh, I've heard the stories. I know all the legends about the Daughters of Nadia. And my Legion is well-trained for this particular confrontation."

Tate laughed. "How did you get up here, Ronan? Did you pass through the trials of Mount Aeylwon? I don't think so."

Tate held up her palms and let her fires burn. "But we did."

Ronan didn't seem at all intimidated. In fact, he turned around and ordered for Brit and Jack to be released. When the soldiers let them go and shoved them forward with their packs and weapons still intact, Tate felt the first shiver of dread.

Jack and Brit rushed to stand with her, Sami, and Fiona.

Brit voiced Tate's concern. "What's he up to?"

Jack didn't pull Tate into his embrace, though his eyes told her he wanted to. "Something devious." His jaw flexed when he looked at the man who'd pretended to be a friend.

"Hand over the Ceffyl," Ronan called. "I know all about your magick. And I can assure you —none of it will save you." His gaze flicked to Fiona, and for a split-second his confidence seemed to falter.

Then he tore his gaze from her and pulled a glass ball from his pocket. "We've been assigned the task of protecting the Jeweled Ceffyl from those who would abuse it. We have been granted magick of our own to do as we see fit to ensure its safekeeping." He wore a one-sided smile, tight with loathing. "I told you I serve another."

Tate's mind spun with confusion. She exchanged a fearful look with Jack.

"And I serve him." He pointed to Fiona. No, Tate realized, he pointed to the jeweled horse she held in her arms.

"Only the Daughters of Nadia can remove the Ceffyl from this place." He held up the orb in his hand. This one sparkled with silver energy instead of gold.

Tate tucked her hair behind her ears, suddenly worried about what the glass ball could do.

"And if you are dead," Ronan hiked a shoulder, as if their deaths wouldn't trouble him at all, "the Ceffyl will remain." He ordered his men to back off of the bridge and he retreated with them. He stared at Fiona and curled two fingers in a come-here gesture. "Bring it to me, or you will all die."

Fiona shook her head, her eyes like green daggers.

Ronan returned the baleful glare and threw the orb onto the bridge. The resulting explosion rocked the suspended bridge and platform, loud pops filling the air as the stone began to shift and crack.

Jack grabbed onto Tate while her sisters clutched each other, and Brit crouched to keep his balance.

"Two more of these," Ronan held up another ball, "and everything falls."

"But the Ceffyl!" Tate shouted. "You're sworn to protect it!"

"As I said, if the Daughters of Nadia die, the Jeweled Ceffyl remains." He extended his free hand. "Bring it to me!"

"No!" Fiona shouted back.

"Tate, what are we going to do?" Jack's voice whipped away in the wind. "Unless you can fly and didn't mention it?"

"No." Terror banged inside her chest with a brutal fist. "I don't know what to do." She looked wildly around at Brit and her sisters. "Any ideas?"

"He can't have it," Fiona bit out. She looked past Tate and met Ronan's heated stare. She slowly shook her head.

Ronan roared his frustration and lobbed the second orb. The detonation was much closer this time, and the resulting *crack!* from the fracturing bridge was even louder.

Tate and Jack were thrown against the side rail while Fiona toppled and landed on her backside. Still, she kept hold of the precious Ceffyl.

Sami also pitched as the bridge heaved, but she caught Brit's outstretched hand. "He's fucking crazy!" she screamed. "He'll kill us." Her eyes fixed on Tate with true horror. "Tate, we'll fall. We'll die."

"No!" Tate screamed into the buffeting wind. They'd braved so very much to get this far. Now, no matter what choice she made, she would be putting her loved ones in peril.

Her eyes tracked to the Ceffyl in Fiona's arms, but she didn't move to take it. "We are prophesied to be here," she said, steeling her spine with the certainty that she and her sisters, that all of them, would somehow survive.

She jerked her face toward Ronan. "We are meant to be here! We passed the tests, and you," she stabbed a finger at him, "*you* have no right to defy Fate!"

Fury morphed Ronan's face. "Be damned, Tate. Don't make me kill you. Because I will!"

He raised his arm, poised to throw the third orb. The final bomb that would end them all.

Tate sucked in a breath. She leaned into Jack and looked up at him. "I'm so glad I got a chance to tell you I love you."

"So am I." He kissed her hard. "I was hoping to hear it a million more times."

She touched his cheek. She readied herself for the fall.

Because no matter what Ronan threatened or how dire the situation seemed, a little voice of intuition whispered inside of her. It told her not to give up the Ceffyl.

Shouts from the mountain ledge rang out. Tate turned to see a few Legion soldiers pointing up to the sky. Then one voice shouted, "Vipera!"

The warriors raised their weapons and looked up.

And the oracle's parting words came back to Tate. *Be safe. Watch the skies.*

She had her eyes on the sky now. And it was filled with dragons. Huge, winged serpents, five in total, and as bright as the jewels on the silver horse Fiona clutched.

With the bridge tilted beneath them, it was difficult to find their footing. Sami was still holding onto Brit, and Fiona was staying low for the sake of balance. Jack and Tate still huddled together.

And the bridge gave off an ominous moan before more cracks and pops filled the air.

"The bridge is going!" Fiona yelled from where she sat.

Tate caught movement out of the corner of her eye. Ronan stepped out onto the bridge, his eyes wide and fixated on Fiona and the Ceffyl. But his men pulled him back.

Tate felt another shudder as the stone structure began to lose its battle against its own buckling weight.

Then a horrific screech filled the air, and she glanced up to find a monstrous body hurtling toward her. The crimson flesh of a vipera filled her vision, just before the monster scooped her up in its huge talons and ripped her off of the bridge.

26

Jack watched the vipera swoop down and steal away with Tate. His heart lodged in his throat and he tried to hold onto her, but the dragon's huge claws had locked around her body, hauling her up into the air.

"Tate!" His shout was a hoarse echo of the panic inside, but as soon as he threw himself against the railing to reach after her, another huge body blotted out the sky. A pearlescent white beast scooped him up as well, and the next thing he knew, he was racing through the clouds.

He strained and twisted to keep Tate in his sights, drawing a relieved breath to see the red vipera leading the way. Surely the others had been picked up too, but with the massive tail between Jack and the bridge, he couldn't get a visual. He just hoped they'd been saved from the fall.

Head tilted, he cast shocked eyes to the land far below. The axe was still at his back, but the notion of fighting free terrified him more than the beast's curling talons or sporadic burst of fire. The vipera hadn't hurt him yet, but if he dropped Jack it would mean his death.

He caught a glimpse of what might have been the mountain trail, but wispy clouds soon blocked his view and didn't clear again until he was over the river. Another few minutes, and he caught sight of the queen's manor house. The forest where the faeries had put on their brilliant display looked much different from above.

At this altitude, their flight ate up the miles, and it wasn't long before he spied the giant forest, then the golden fields around Gean-canach's enchanted woods. The vipera banked, however, soaring toward lands Jack had never seen.

The midday sun glared in his eyes, but he could feel the vipera's sudden descent. The creature tucked his wings in tight, arrowing straight for the ground.

Jack gripped the dragon's legs, fully prepared for a rough landing, but the creature slowed its speed and released him with a gentle roll. Well, he reconsidered, as gentle as could be expected since he was bumping over rock.

As soon as his momentum halted, Jack was on his feet in search of Tate. She, in turn, was rushing toward him.

"Jack!" They smacked together in a flurry of kisses and roving hands, each wanting to make sure the other was unharmed.

A whoosh of air drew their attention to see Brit's vipera delivering him as well. Soon after came Fiona and Sami.

"What was that?" Sami yelled, thrusting her hand after the dragons. Two had flown away again, but three flocked to the side as if waiting.

Assured that Tate was all right, Jack pulled her close and scanned the area. They seemed to be atop a flat stretch of what looked like lava-rock. Waterfalls flowed white, down gentle slopes from above on one side. Then off a great precipice in the opposite direction.

"What is this place?" Fiona asked, joining them.

Jack was glad to see she still held the Ceffyl, but she and Brit looked just as baffled as he felt.

"Did those vipera just save us?" Fiona asked. She flattened her mouth at the three docile dragons that remained. "What happened to them hunting us to the ends of Faerie?"

"And where are we?" Sami strolled over, favoring her leg. At Jack's frown, she explained, "I pulled a hamstring or something when I fell at the bridge. But I'm fine."

Tate reached for her sisters and pulled them into a hug. Then she did the same for Brit. "Do you remember a place like this on the maps?"

Her uncle shook his head and swung his pack off his shoulder to check.

Jack eased toward the edge to peer over the drop-off and was alarmed to see they were stranded yet again. Verdant landscapes stretched below, the river from the falls snaking through. But the distance was too far to consider jumping.

Tate joined him. "We aren't getting out that way."

"No, we're not." He brushed a smudge of dirt from her cheek and looked back toward the cascades above. The rush of water struck the black stone, churning up misty sprays before rolling across to the steep plunge.

As Jack watched the whitecaps rush, something in the mists moved. He squinted and blinked, and a shape materialized.

The hulking silver wolf padded its way from within the vapors.

"Brit," Jack said in a subdued tone, drawing the other man's attention to the beast. Brit reached for the crossbow still on his back.

But before he could draw a bolt, the wolf began to shimmer and shift. The silver eyes remained the same, but its body lengthened into that of a man.

Not a human, but a Fae. And one still as predatory as the wolf he'd been. The pale-eyed man from the Winter Queen's dinner strolled casually toward Jack and Tate.

Throwing his arm in front of her, Jack eased Tate closer to her sisters and Brit. And put a hand on his axe.

"Be at ease," the man called out, though his leering grin made Jack feel anything but.

"You're the wolf?" Fiona asked. She slid her eyes from the fully-dressed man over to Jack. "You followed us the whole way?"

He spread his hands. "That was my mission, and as you see," he gestured to the vipera, "it's a very good thing I did."

"Hold on." Jack held up his hand, wishing the strange man would stop stalking closer. And despite the fact that he'd saved Jack from the bug in the ruins, he still gave off the beast-of-prey vibe.

"Are you saying you sent those vipera to rescue us?" Jack glanced at the dragons, trying to fit the pieces together.

"Oh, no. Not I." Wolf-Fae put his fingers to his sternum, but then waved a hand to one side. "But her."

This time two forms emerged from the surroundings, apparently disguised by some type of glamour. The ever-regal Winter Queen in a murder-red gown. And her lovely niece, Princess Brigidelle.

Tate drew a sharp breath and took Jack's hand in hers.

"My queen wanted me to ensure you made it to wherever you were meant to go," Wolf-Fae, said. "To ensure you recovered the Jeweled Ceffyl."

"And have you, Daughters of Nadia?" The queen clasped her hands low over her stomach in a formal fashion. "Have you triumphed after all?"

Brigidelle pointed to Fiona, who'd been trying to get the Ceffyl into her pack. "She has it, Aunt Faidhia."

Jack felt Tate tense beside him, so he rubbed his thumb on the inside of her wrist to calm her.

It didn't work. Tate pulled free of him and moved to stand between the queen and her sisters. "So this is your end game? You had us followed and then saved us," Tate glared, "all so you could take the Ceffyl?"

"Oh my dear, dear Tate." The queen tutted. "I cannot take the Ceffyl by force. The laws of the council forbid it."

"The council?" Jack asked.

"Yes. The council who decided centuries ago that the Jeweled Ceffyl must be hidden away and protected from the Fae." She tilted her head, violet eyes glinting. "I have come to help you, just as I promised."

The queen indicated the steep bluff and the waterfall rushing over its edge. "You've been brought to another dryys."

"A portal, Aunt Faidhia," Brigidelle corrected, using the English word for their benefit.

The first gleam of optimism began to grow inside Jack, and as he took in the mixed expressions on his friends' faces, he could see they held the hope as well.

"That waterfall is a portal?" Tate asked, her eyes shrewd as she watched the queen. "Please state that plainly."

Jack couldn't help it when his mouth turned up at the edges. She was trying to corner the queen, using the Fae's inability to lie as a way to be certain of her intent.

Considering the deadly height of the falls, Jack would prefer being sure himself.

"The waterfall is a portal to your home of Bar Harbor." The queen smiled, stretching her red lips as she approached them. "Tate Whiteburn, you and your family are free to leave Faerie." She inclined her head. "Along with the Ceffyl."

Sami let out a breath of joy and turned to Fiona for a happy embrace. Brit still seemed hesitant, as if he, like Tate, wasn't sure they could trust the queen. But her smile, her amity, seemed genuine. She even held out her arm like a game show hostess, inviting them to take a leap into the spray.

And if she were telling the truth—Jack caught Tate's gaze— they'd be taking a leap back to their home. Back to their lives.

"The Fae cannot lie," Brigidelle said, her way of offering assurance.

Sami and Fiona seemed willing to take the plunge, hurrying to stare over the side.

Brit went next, raising his brows to Tate as he passed.

At last, Tate let a smile creep over her face. "I can't believe we're finally going home." She squeezed Jack's hand and tugged him along.

"Ah-ah-ah." The queen wagged a finger at them, and an ominous shadow filled her eyes. "I told you, Tate. You and your *family* may go with the Ceffyl." Her purple gaze settled on Jack. "But not him."

Jack's nape prickled, and the wolf-Fae laughed.

It was Tate's turn to throw her arm in front of Jack. "What trick is this?"

"No trick, dear. Just a simple fact." The queen swished her blood-red skirts and pointed to Tate. "I told you I can't take the Ceffyl by force, but as ruler of this realm, I am within my rights to detain anyone I choose. And I choose Jack."

Brigidelle preened behind her aunt, and Jack feared she'd been a plotter in this scheme.

Tate lunged, but he caught her around the waist. "Don't," he told her, his brain spinning for a way out of this mess. He sure as hell didn't want to stay in Faerie.

And he didn't want to spend another day without Tate by his side.

Though his mind raced, he could see no means of escape.

"Unless, of course," the queen said, holding out her hands, "you'd be willing to make a trade." She wiggled her fingers, as if the deal were already done. "It's all up to you, Tate, so which do you choose? You can take the Ceffyl, or you can take Jack."

The queen lowered her head, and laughed like a devil. "But you can't have both."

❈❈❈

Tate's ears rang, and her head filled with sound. She couldn't believe the choice she'd been given. She could take the Ceffyl and protect her family. Or she could take Jack and save . . . well, *Jack*.

She wasn't happy with either option.

Recalling how devious the Fae could be, Tate held her tongue and replayed the queen's words in her head.

Because words, after all, were Tate's specialty.

She studied the queen's self-satisfied smile. And glanced to the equally proud Brigidelle.

The queen's statement, her promise, rolled like tickertape across Tate's eyes. "You said that my family and I are all free to leave with the Ceffyl. Is that correct?"

Jack shifted on his feet but didn't offer a word of question or argument. He seemed to be placing his faith in her.

"Exactly," the queen said.

Tate computed every factor, every underlying meaning, and every loophole. When she'd filed the data away, she had her answer. "Fine." She nodded to the two Fae women. "I just want to give Jack something, if you don't mind."

"A parting gift," Brigidelle said sweetly. "How thoughtful."

Tate would have loved to show the white-haired beauty just what she thought about her, but for now her priority was getting out of Faerie.

With *all* of them.

She turned back to Sami, suddenly grateful for the cargo-style pants they'd all been given. What Tate needed was in her sister's left pocket.

Tate had seen her shove it in there this morning. For luck, Sami had said.

Now Tate just hoped that luck held out.

She went for the pocket, and Sami asked a question with her mind. *What are you doing?*

I've got an idea. Just make sure you, Fee, and Brit get through that portal with the Ceffyl.

Hand in Sami's pocket, she curled her fingers around the item she needed, tucked it in her palm, and pulled it out.

Holding Jack's gaze, she returned to his side.

"Jack." She smiled at the man she loved. The man she'd once

lost. "Do you trust me?"

"Always," he said, constant as ever.

"Then take my hand." Tate reached across his body, linking her right hand with his.

The queen and Brigidelle still looked on with delight.

Tate drew a breath. She'd have to speak and move fast before the Fae women caught on.

Opening her left hand, she let the green ribbon from the brownies' gift basket unfurl. She swiftly wrapped it around her arm. "Jack Helmsford." Her voice rang true. Then she wound the green strand around his arm as well. "I wish to bind you as my husband. Do you accept?"

Jack's blue eyes flared. But then he smiled and quickly answered, "Yes."

"What?" The queen dropped her hands to her side. "Stop this at once!"

Beside her, Brigidelle's mouth formed a perfect O.

Tate tried to recall the words of the handfasting ritual she'd read in the grimoire, but for the sake of speed, she'd just keep it short.

"Now you, Jack," Fiona said in a rush.

"No!" the queen yelled.

"Tate Whiteburn," Jack said on a laugh, "I wish to bind you as my wife. Do you accept?"

Tate's chest swelled and tightened with emotion. "I absolutely do."

"This is not allowed!" The queen glowered and stomped her foot.

Tate faced the queen, her hand still wrapped with Jack's. "You must abide by your own promise, Faidhia. Because the Fae," Tate reminded her with no small amount of pleasure, "cannot speak an untruth."

She knew she'd won when the queen screeched and Brigidelle's face fell.

Tate stood proudly. "Jack is my husband now." She turned teary eyes to him. "He is a member of *my family*."

"And we're witnesses," Brit the lawyer piped up.

"Vile, trickster humans!" The queen bared clenched teeth.

Brigidelle sighed and rolled her eyes to her aunt.

The queen looked positively apoplectic, her face red as a cherry tomato and lips pressed so tightly they were snow-white.

"Sami," Tate reminded her sister.

"Oh. Right." As agreed, Sami latched onto Fiona and dragged her to the waterfall, the Ceffyl still secure in her arms. They jumped in together, their screams echoing as they made the long fall.

Tate looked back to the queen and saw Brit move forward in her peripheral vision.

He would stay with them. He wouldn't leave her and Jack.

"Aunt Faidhia." Brigidelle touched the queen's arm, trying to calm her down. "We must respect this act of love."

Tate and Jack exchanged a look of surprise. It was no secret Brigidelle had wanted him for her own.

The queen's entire body shook as she emitted a drawn-out, mewling noise. But at least she didn't argue. Instead she threw her arms up and stomped toward the vipera.

Brigidelle walked to Tate and Jack. "You have won this round fairly." She smiled. "Don't worry about my aunt. She is unaccustomed to defeat, but you have acted with honor. You see, we Fae may have our tricks and ploys, but above all else, we value love. Especially," she said, gliding over to Jack, "romantic love."

She beamed up at him and sighed like a school girl with a crush. "Oh, I'm so happy for you, Jack." Then she kissed him on the lips.

Tate's mouth dropped, and she would have intervened, but before she could, Brigidelle shifted over to her.

And kissed Tate full on the mouth too.

Stunned, Tate could only nod when the lovely Fae princess offered her best wishes to them both.

"But with the Ceffyl gone, you'd better leave too." She tossed a worried glance to the queen. "Her behavior can be unseemly when she is riled."

"We're on our way." Brit jerked his head toward the waterfall then strode to the long, harrowing drop with Tate and Jack close behind.

Tate tried to pivot, but laughed when she and Jack got caught up. She loosened the ribbon—which she would now keep forever—and shoved it into her own pocket before racing after her uncle with Jack.

Brit plunged into the cascade.

Tate and Jack paused at the precipice, smiled at each other, and without hesitation, took the leap together.

Her stomach bottomed out, and like her sisters, she screamed. The river below rushed up to greet her, but then she felt herself standing on solid ground.

"We're back," Jack said with a grin. "In Agamont Park."

Tate instantly recognized the city park, and of course, they were back to freezing cold weather. At least it wasn't snowing.

She frowned when she noticed Fiona kneeling on the bricked walk beside the water fountain. Meanwhile, Sami held a hand over her eyes, scoping the park.

What were they were doing? Tate wondered. But she didn't have time to ask.

Because as soon as she took the first step in her own world again, the air across from her started to waver. And Emuirdane stepped out.

His ebony eyes veered straight to Fiona, then darted between Tate and Sami. "Where is it?" he demanded without preamble. "You had the Ceffyl in your hands. I saw it." He lurched forward, shaking a fist at Fiona. "Where is it?"

Fiona gaped up at him and then at Tate, her fingers plucking jewels from the pavement. Eyes wide with shock, she hunched her shoulders and shook her head. "It ran away."

The expression on Emuirdane's face would have been comical if not for the green bolts of lightning sparking from his hands. "It ran *away*?" His voice reeked of incredulity.

"It did," Sami said, rushing to Fiona's defense. "As soon as we entered this world, the statue transformed, its jewels fell off, and it ran out of the park." She glanced over to the harbor. "And that thing was fast."

Emuirdane raised his fists to the sky and bellowed a sound of desperate rage. Hands still glowing green, he sneered at Tate, lifted his palm, and—

"Don't you touch her!" Fiona leaped off the ground and ran at Emuirdane. Only Sami's quick hand saved the Iele from their little sister's tackle.

Fiona was restrained, but she still fumed. "If you hurt any one of us again, or threaten any other person to try and control us, then we are done! You needed us to find the Ceffyl and we did. And we went through hell to get it."

Fiona finally shrugged out of Sami's hold. "So just back off!"

Tate eased closer to her sisters, motioning for Jack to stay back. Though he already had his axe in his hands.

But the Iele didn't retaliate as expected. Instead of punishing Fiona for disobedience, he simply stared at her and the gemstones in her hands.

Fingers curled to his lips, he gazed into the air.

Tate drew near Fiona and Sami, just in time for Emuirdane to shift his black stare to the three of them.

"You must keep those jewels." He raked a hand through his raven-black hair. "No matter what happens, you mustn't lose them. Because if you do, it will be your life."

"I said no more threats." Fiona jabbed her finger at him, but he waved her off.

"You must get the Ceffyl back." Again he thrust his fingers through his mane. "If you fail, your lives will have no value." He flicked his hands and got rid of the lightning.

Fixated on the scattered gemstones, the Iele prince lowered his voice. "I'm afraid he will be very displeased."

The first suspicious wave rolled through Tate. "Who?"

Emuirdane spared her a spiteful glare. But alongside his usual contempt, another emotion flared in his black eyes.

Fear.

"It is not your concern," he said at last, turning to glower again at Fiona. The soft, raspy tone he now used frightened Tate more than his shouts. "Remember, girl," he said to Fee, "lose those jewels, and your life is forfeit."

Tate clenched her fists. "Emuirdane, who won't be pleased?"

He gave her his back in disregard as silver mists erupted behind him. Without deigning to say another word, he turned and glided into nothingness.

Fiona returned to the brick walkway and gathered up the remaining gems. "I've had enough of faeries." She dropped the jewels into the pack Sami held out, stood up, and hugged herself. "I'm cold. I'm angry. I miss Mom and Granddad."

She laughed a little at her own tantrum. "And I really want to cook something sweet."

"And I really want to eat whatever it is you cook." Brit patted the bow on his back. "Plus, I'd like to get home before someone asks why we're all armed."

"Good point," Tate said. With their odd collection of weapons and packs, they resembled a small medieval troop.

Sliding into Jack's extended arms, she released a sigh. One she felt like she'd been holding in for days. His warmth was a welcome comfort in the frigid air, so she rested her cheek on his chest as he rubbed her back.

But it was too cold to stay there for long. "Should we find a phone and call Mom?" she asked.

Jack notched his chin toward the street. "We can walk to my

parents' from here. They can give us a ride to your house."

"Do you think she's got any ginger cookies?" Tate raised on her toes and smacked his lips.

"It's not quite that time." Jack put his knuckles under her chin. "But I want you to come by anyway." He kissed her back. "I think they'd like to meet my wife."

"I'm still baking you a cake," Fiona said. "We'll have a private celebration."

"You can still have the whole wedding," Brit said with a shrug. "I don't think Faerie-land rituals will hold up in county court."

Jack hooked his arm around her waist. "I'd marry you again and again. As often as I have to until it takes."

"Oh, it already took," Tate teased with a smile. "You aren't getting out of this marriage, *husband*."

"I don't intend to try." He held her strong and true through another kiss. Then he whispered, "Tate *Helmsford*."

Tate's heart overflowed, and she no longer felt the cold. She smiled into her first love's blue eyes and said, "I like the sound of that."

Acknowledgement

At the completion of this particular book, I have so many people to thank. After a year of very little writing, I had a hard time finding my way back. I might never have made it if not for the inspiring and encouraging people in my life.

So I first have to thank my husband. He has shown more patience than I probably deserved, and I know without his support, I would not be where I am today. Thank you for all of the emergency green-juice runs and for just being a great guy in general. I love you and will get a new calendar and promise to stick to it!

Next to my editing team, a group I would take to Mt. Everest if I ever went, because I know that I can depend on them, and that they truly have my back. Sharyn Cerniglia, you have such patience, and I appreciate your hanging in there with me on this one. I also solemnly swear never to make you ride the crazy train again. Donna Wood, you're always ready to jump in when needed, even if you're on the road and have to stop to find a hot spot! I can't thank you enough for the guidance you've provided since the very beginning. Alice Yu, a very talented author and friend, you responded with open arms and a willing attitude. You've been a great help, and I look forward to many more Skype sessions where we can compare the books we have by holding them up to the screen. ;) You've all been simply amazing, and to say I couldn't have done it without is truly an understatement. And Mandi Cranson, you just keeping adding new hats. Editor, friend, psychotherapist, and cheerleader. I could be 10, 000 words down with five minutes to go, and you would be there saying, "You can do it!" On this particular project, I needed that. A lot. I will never forget how you sacrificed your own time to get me through, and like I promised Sharyn (and everyone else, actually) that crazy train has seen its last ride.

I want to take time to mention the Boom! class I met in Denver, CO. I had the best time curled on couches and talking about writing. So many times I wish I could pop back to that work-ation and do it all again.

And of course, this leads me to the incomparable Margie Lawson. I learned so much from your class, and I can't wait to sit down and start working again on all you showed me. This book got away from me from the start, but I'm going to keep pushing and hope to make you proud. And thank you for telling I was being too hard on myself. I needed to hear that exactly when you said it.

My street team was born last year, and since then the Advo-Kates have grown and grown. You guys are just so much stinkin' fun, and I look forward to checking in with you daily. Dorothy, Stella, and Marcy, I'm so grateful for the extra time you spend doing things you're not even asked to do. Dorothy, Stella, Susan, and Cynthia, I am so thrilled we got to meet in New York, and I had a blast! Next year? :)

Finally, I have to thank all of my readers. Like I said in the beginning, it's been a strange year, but all of you have stuck it out. My job is to write stories for you and give you new places and characters to enjoy. I plan to do a lot more of that from now on, and I hope you continue to come back for more.

I know I will, and thank you all for making sure of that--Suza

Suza Kates writes both paranormal romance and romantic suspense. She lives in Savannah, Georgia with her family and four ridiculously spoiled cats.

For more on Suza and her books visit

www.suzakates.com